THE WALLS AROUND US

NOVA REN SUMA

AUTHOR OF *IMAGINARY GIRLS* AND *17 & GONE*

Praise for *The Walls Around Us*

"Unputdownable." —*The Boston Globe*

"With evocative language, a shifting timeline, and more than one unreliable narrator, Suma subtly explores the balance of power between the talented and the mediocre, the rich and the poor, the brave and the cowardly . . . To reveal more would be to uncover the bloody heart that beats beneath the floorboards of this urban-legend-tinged tale." —*The New York Times Book Review*

"A suspenseful tour de force, a ghost story of the best sort, the kind that creeps into your soul and haunts you."
—Libba Bray, author of *The Diviners* and *A Great and Terrible Beauty*

"Fearlessly imagined and deliciously sinister, *The Walls Around Us* is hypnotic, luring the reader deeper and deeper into its original, shocking narrative."
—Michelle Hodkin, author of the Mara Dyer Trilogy

"A gorgeously written, spellbinding ghost story."
—*Chicago Tribune*

★"In lyrical, authoritative prose, Suma weaves the disparate lives of [the] three girls into a single, spellbinding narrative that explores guilt, privilege, and complicity with fearless acuity . . . Unsettling and entirely engrossing."
—*The Horn Book Magazine*, starred review

★"Eerie, painful and beautifully spine-chilling."
—*Kirkus Reviews*, starred review

★ "Gripping . . . Just try to put this down."

—*Shelf Awareness for Readers*, starred review

★ "Powerful . . . The compelling narrative, written in scintillating prose and featuring incredibly real characters, brings the two stories together in an explosive finale with a supernatural twist that results in a satisfying resolution."　　　　　—*VOYA*, starred review

★ "Suma excels in creating surreal unsettling stories with vivid language, and this psychological thriller is no exception . . . A fabulous, frightening read."　　　　　—*Booklist*, starred review

★ "Gratifyingly disturbing . . . Suma craftily sets the two stories against one another, moving between Violet's fiercely grounded account and Amber's hauntingly destabilized one, enticing readers to figure out how the pieces go together."

—*Bulletin of the Center for Children's Books*, starred review

★ "Suma's unflinchingly honest depiction of the potentially destructive force of female friendship and skillful blending of gritty realism with supernatural elements is reminiscent of Laurie Halse Anderson's *Wintergirls*, and the eerie mood she evokes is unnervingly potent."

—*SLJ*, starred review

"A tour-de-force packing immense emotional power . . . Suma takes risks here that few authors are capable of, and most readers do not dare hope for."　　　　　—*Locus Magazine*

"Luscious and deliciously creepy prose not easy to forget."

—*Book Riot*

THE WALLS AROUND US

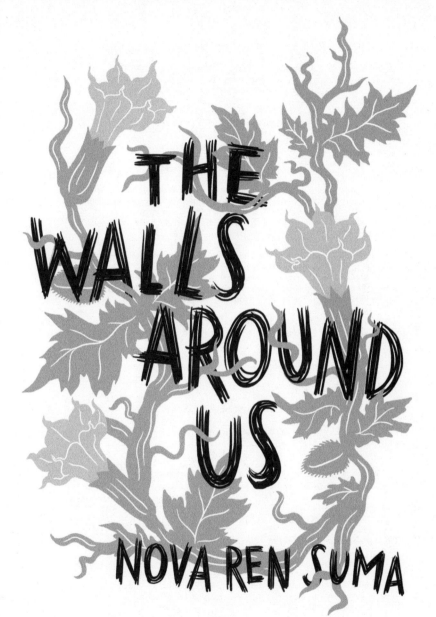

THE WALLS AROUND US

NOVA REN SUMA

ALGONQUIN 2016

Published by
ALGONQUIN YOUNG READERS
an imprint of Algonquin Books of Chapel Hill
Post Office Box 2225
Chapel Hill, North Carolina 27515-2225

a division of
WORKMAN PUBLISHING
225 Varick Street
New York, New York 10014

LIBRARY OF CONGRESS CATALOGING-IN-PUBLICATION DATA
Suma, Nova Ren.
The walls around us : a novel / by Nova Ren Suma.—First edition.
        pages cm
Summary: Orianna and Violet are ballet dancers and best friends, but when the ballerinas who have been harassing Violet are murdered, Orianna is accused of the crime and sent to a juvenile detention center where she meets Amber and they experience supernatural events linking the girls together.
ISBN 978-1-61620-372-6 (HC)
[1. Juvenile detention homes—Fiction. 2. Ballet dancers—Fiction. 3. Supernatural—Fiction.] I. Title.
PZ7.S95388Wal 2015
[Fic]—dc23   2014031972

ISBN 978-1-61620-590-4 (PB)

10 9 8 7 6 5 4 3 2 1
First Paperback Edition

For the girl who needs to hide her diary
For the girl who doesn't think she's worth so much

And again, and always, for E

THE WALLS AROUND US

PART I:
Saturday Night

It isn't running away they're afraid of.
We wouldn't get far. It's those other
escapes, the ones you can open in yourself,
given a cutting edge.

—Margaret Atwood,
The Handmaid's Tale

Amber:

WE WENT WILD

WE WENT WILD that hot night. We howled, we raged, we screamed. We were girls—some of us fourteen and fifteen; some sixteen, seventeen—but when the locks came undone, the doors of our cells gaping open and no one to shove us back in, we made the noise of savage animals, of men.

We flooded the corridors, crowding together in the clammy, cooped-up dark. We abandoned our assigned colors—green for most of us, yellow for those of us in segregation, traffic-cone orange for anyone unlucky enough to be new. We left behind our jumpsuit skins. We showed off our angry, wobbly tattoos.

When outside the thunder crashed, we overtook A-wing and B-wing. When lightning flashed, we mobbed C-wing.

We even took our chances in D-wing, which held Suicide Watch and Solitary.

We were gasoline rushing for a lit match. We were bared teeth. Balled fists. A stampede of slick feet. We went wild, like anyone would. We lost our fool heads.

Just try to understand. After the crimes that had put us inside, after all the hideous things we were accused of and convicted of, the things some of us had done without apology and the things some of us had sworn we were innocent of doing (sworn on our mothers if we had mothers, sworn on our pets if we ever had a puppy dog or a scrawny cat, sworn on our own measly lives if we had nobody), after all that time behind bars, on this night we were free we were free we were free.

Some of us found that terrifying.

On this night, the first Saturday of that now-infamous August, there were forty-one girls locked up in the Aurora Hills Secure Juvenile Detention Center in the far northern reaches of the state, which meant we were one shy of full capacity. We weren't yet forty-two.

To our surprise, to our wide-eyed delight, the cells of B-wing and C-wing, of A-wing and even D-wing, had come open, and there we stood, a thunder of thudding hearts in the darkness. We stood outside our cages. We stood outside.

We looked to the guards' stations: They were unmanned.

We looked to the sliding gates at the end of our corridors: They were wide-open.

We looked to the floodlights ringing the high ceiling: The bulbs had gone dim.

We looked (or we tried to look; it was the way our bodies

pulled) through the window slits and into the storm pounding outside, all across the compound. If only we could see
past the triple-fenced perimeter, over and beyond the coils
of barbed wire. Past the guards' tower. Past the steep road
that plunged downhill to the tall iron gate at the bottom.
We remembered, from when the blue-painted short bus
from the county jail had carried us up here. We remembered
we weren't so far from the public road.

That was when it hit us—how little time we were sure
to have before the corrections officers returned to their posts.
Maybe we should have been sensible about our sudden freedom, cautious. We weren't. We didn't stop to question the
open locks. Not then. We didn't pause to wonder why the
emergency lights hadn't blinked on, why the alarms didn't
blare. We didn't think, either, about the COs who were supposed to be on night duty—where they could have gone,
why their booths were empty, their chairs bare.

We scattered. We spread out. We pushed through barri-
ers that were always locked to us before. We ran.

The night burst open the way a good riot tends to, when
it takes over the yard and no one knows who started what,
or cares. The shouts and screams, the whoops and wails.
Forty-one of the worst female juvenile offenders in the state
set loose without warning or reason or armed guards to take
us down. It was beautiful and it was powerful, like lightning
in our hands.

Some of us weren't thinking and only wanted to kick in
the glass fronts of the vending machines in the canteen for
snacks or pillage pills from the clinic to get a fix. Some of us
wanted to pound a face in and jump someone, jump anyone;

it didn't matter who. A couple of us simply wanted to slip out back under the murky cloud covering and shoot some hoops in the rain.

Then there were those of us, the ones with brains, who took a breath. And considered. Because, with no COs coming at us with clubs out, no alarms bleating or intercoms crackling commands to herd us back to our cells, the night really was ours, for the first time in days. Weeks. Months. Years.

And what's a girl to do with her first free night in years?

The most violent among us—the daddy killers, the slitters of strangers' throats, the point-blank shooters of pleading gas-station attendants—would later admit to finding a sense of peace in the plush darkness, a kind of justice not offered by the juvenile courts.

Sure, some of us knew we didn't deserve this reprieve. Not one of us was truly innocent, not when we were made to stand in the light, our bits and cavities and cavity fillings exposed. When we faced this truth inside ourselves, it somehow felt more ugly than the day we witnessed the judge say "guilty" and heard the courtroom cheer.

That was why a few of us hung back. Didn't leave our cells, where we kept our drawings and our love letters. Where we stowed our one good comb and stashed all our Reese's Peanut Butter Cups, which were like gold doubloons up in Aurora Hills, since we didn't have access to cash. Some of us stayed put in the place we knew.

Because what was out there? Who would keep us safe, on the outside?

Where, really, would a girl from Aurora Hills, who'd disappointed her family and scared off English teachers and social workers and public defenders and anyone who tried to help her, a girl who'd terrorized her neighborhood, who was as good as garbage (she'd been told), who was probably best left forgotten (she'd read this in letters from home), where would a girl like that go?

A lot of us did try to run—even if it was only habit. Some of us had been running all our lives. We ran because we could and because we couldn't not. We ran for our lives. We still thought they were worth running for.

Most of us didn't get far. We got distracted. Overexcited. Overcome. A couple of us came to a stop somewhere in one of the hallways outside our designated wing and sank to the cracked and pitted floor in gratitude, as if we'd been acquitted of all our crimes, our records expunged.

This felt like everything we'd dared let ourselves dream up, when the taunting fantasies slipped in between the bars. Wishes for fast getaway cars or Rapunzel ropes to climb out the narrow window openings. Pleas for forgiveness, for vengeance, for glittery new lives on some far-off riviera where we'd never again have to face hate or law or pain. It was happening. To us. We never did believe it could happen to kids like us.

Some of us cried.

There we were, set loose on the defenseless night, instantly wanting everything we could imagine: To thumb a ride at the nearest freeway. To call an old boyfriend and get laid. To have a never-ending breadstick feast at the

Olive Garden. To sleep under fluffy covers in a large, soft bed.

That August marked my third summer at Aurora Hills. I'd been locked up here since I was fourteen (manslaughter; I pled innocent; I stuffed myself into a skirt and sheer hose for trial; my mother turned her face away when I was found guilty and hasn't looked my way since). But it's not my arrival I find myself thinking about, now that we have so much time to sit here thinking. It's not the judge's ruling and the deafening years of my sentence and how I landed here because not one person believed me when I said I didn't do it. I let go of all that a long time ago.

It's this one night that I keep coming back to. That first Saturday in August, when the locks couldn't hold us. That brief gift of freedom we'd take to our graves.

I get hung up on it sometimes, on what if things had gone another way. If I'd made it past the gates and gotten out. If I'd run.

Maybe I would have made it over the three sets of fencing and down the hill to the free patch of road and my part in this story would be over. Maybe all that was about to come tumbling at us after this, someone else would have to bear witness to. Someone else would have to do the remembering.

Because that was the night we went wild. I remember how we fought and we cried and we hid and we flung ourselves through windows and we pumped our legs with everything we had and we went running as far as we could make it, which wasn't far.

On that night, we felt emotions we hadn't had a taste

of for six months, twelve months, eleven and a half weeks, nine hundred and nine days.

We were alive. I remember it that way. We were still alive, and we couldn't make heads or tails of the darkness, so we couldn't see how close we were to the end.

Violet:

___

STANDING O

___

I SLIP BEHIND the curtain—it's almost time, get the spotlight ready, soon I'll be on.

This'll be my last dance before I leave town. My last chance to make them remember me, and remember me they will.

When I'm onstage, I'm all for them, and they're all for me. I feed off what they give me, and they bask in what I give them.

When I'm offstage, these people are nothing to me. I've got some level of hate for practically almost everyone I run into on any given day. But in the midst of dancing? When they're watching me and I'm letting them watch? I've got so much love, I'm like a whole different person.

After tonight, the final Saturday performance, I'll be packing my bags for Juilliard, for the city. I got in. I graduated high school two months ago. I sold my car as of last week. I have my dorm assignment. My roommate's a modern-contemporary dancer from Oklahoma or some tornado state. I've stocked up on Grishkos in the size and style I like, since I have strong feet and high arches and can kill a pair of pointe shoes every ten days. I've been tracking the time left like this is a prison sentence and by the end of August the cuffs will come off and I'll be free.

I shouldn't say that. I shouldn't even think it. Not after what happened to her, where they sent her. Aurora Hills is a real and actual prison, with barbed wire and chains and those baggy orange puff suits you see on TV, though they don't call it a prison. Since it's for under-eighteens, they say it's a "detention center" instead.

It was August when she got bussed up there. Early August, almost exactly three years ago.

I should stay positioned in the wings, since my solo is the second number after intermission, but I pull on some socks over my pointe shoes and cruise away from the stage area. I head for the exit out back, like I've got something radioactive to chuck in the Dumpster.

Back behind the Dumpster is what the older girls called the smoking tunnel, for obvious reasons. The thing is, it's not technically a tunnel. The trees are thick overhead, and the branches hang low, playing ceiling. But it dead-ends against a thicket of trees, so if it's a tunnel headed somewhere, I've never seen where.

The tunnel is all entirely green inside, and in August surely infested with deerflies and mosquitoes. You'd think someone would have chopped down these trees since, made a memorial like a park bench with the girls' names engraved on it or at least a fountain, but I guess people don't do that with places they'd rather not remember.

I don't go in, but I don't leave, either. I throw a backward glance at the theater door.

If anyone notices the cinder block propping it open, I'll say I'm getting fresh air before my solo. Could be that all the most elite soloists, from the New York City Ballet and ABT to the Royal Ballet and Bolshoi and beyond, go out to grab a few breaths behind the Dumpster before dazzling everyone onstage. No one at our studio is near as good as I am anymore, so they wouldn't know.

It's not air I need. It's to take one last look inside.

No one's in the tunnel. No one's huddled under the web of tree branches, only leg warmers and crisscrossed pink ribbons visible from the outside. No vicious little titters. No smoke. No giggle fits. No toe shoe slamming down on a blazing butt, crushing it in the dirt. There's nothing. There's nobody.

I can't even explain why I thought there might be. Why I keep looking for her, everywhere, why any sudden noise or shadow-shift gives me the creeps.

Every August it's like Orianna Speerling forces her way up through my brain. Every August it feels like Ori's back—I'm the one who gave her that nickname, Ori—but she's not here in the smoking tunnel, there's no trace of her anywhere out here, and why would there be?

Intermission's over, and I've got to get to stage. It's when I'm circling the Dumpster again that I catch sight of the exit door swinging shut. Someone's kicked out the cinder block. But whoever's done it isn't fast enough for me, because I leap for the door with all I've got, crossing space and time like I do in my choreography, and the door's in my hands before it hits the jamb, and I coast through it, and they thought they could get me to miss my solo, and they were wrong.

Fast before anyone spots me, I'm in place, in the wings. I don't know who was messing with me, but I do know no one's looking at me, not directly. All the other dancers, they're avoiding eye contact, they're not even wishing me to break a leg. This tells me everyone's guilty, every last one.

It occurs to me as I hear the hush of the audience members taking their seats after intermission. It occurs to me. Everyone here *wants* me to go away, don't they? They can't wait to be rid of me.

So let them be rid of me. Let them wish they never met me. I'm up next, after this medley.

The curtain sweeps open. Some predictable music, some off-count blur of movement—nothing worth watching like I'm about to be.

I shift in the wings and peek through the hanging velvet to scan the seats at orchestra level. Miss Willow, my dance instructor, has rented this theater for the studio's showcase as she does every season, and I forget, each time, how big the place is, how many seats. I spot my mother. My father. My aunt and cousins, who probably got forced to be here tonight, and I don't even care. My mother's friends, too, a whole row of them. My dance coaches—the old one my parents fired when I didn't get into the summer intensive and the new one I've had since. I spot my boyfriend, Tommy, yawning and playing some game on his phone. Some of the older girls have even snuck out from backstage to watch me, slipping into aisle seats so they can rush back in when my piece is done. I see Sarabeth, sitting alone. In another row I see Ivana and Renata and Chelsea P. and Chelsea C. I see people from town, like the handsy lady from the flower shop, the nosy guy from the coffee place. I see my math teacher. I see my mailman, though he has to be here because his daughter is a tulip in beginning ballet. But most of these people have come here tonight to see me off. I'd say the great majority of the audience is here for me.

Besides the people I know, I also see strangers, a whole bunch of strangers, out into the back row and up into the mezzanine. I've never performed for this many people before. Even in court during Ori's trial there weren't this many people. The music stops, and horsey Bianca—she shouldn't have had a solo, but she's a graduated senior, too, and off to SUNY Nowhere where they don't even have a dance program—tramples offstage into the wings. The applause is faint, polite. "Good luck out there, Vee!" she says as she passes, though "luck" is the last thing you should ever wish an oncoming dancer.

Vee is the nickname Ori gave to me.

The lights go down before I can check the nosebleeds, which tells me that's where she'd be seated if she were here, up as high as the rows go, looking down on me.

But she's not here. Of course she's not. The reality is she's dead, and she's been dead going on three years.

Ori's dead because of what happened out behind the theater, in the tunnel made out of trees. She's dead because she got sent to that place upstate, locked up with those monsters. And she got sent there because of me.

Besides, if she hadn't, she wouldn't be watching from the audience. No, she'd be here at my side, in costume like I am, backstage with me.

We'd be together in the wings, about to go on. It'd be a duet instead of two separate solos. If this were our last performance here in town before college, I know she would have wanted it that way.

I'd get anxious, and she'd take my shoulders—she was taller, and her hands were thinner, but with surprising grip—and she'd hold me in place to keep my nerves in check and she'd tell me, *Breathe, Vee, breathe.*

She wouldn't be feeling any of this pressure to be perfect, like I am. She'd be relaxed, loose, even smiling. She would've told horsey Bianca she was wonderful, and that it didn't matter how hard she stomped when she torpedoed through her grand jetés. She would have gone and wished every dancer here to break a leg, even the bitches, and she wouldn't have meant it with any sort of malice, the way I would've.

I know she would have talked me out of this plain costume, the simple white tutu I've got on, the white tights, the small white flower pinned in my hair. She would have wanted to go out in color. Bright, bold. As many colors as she could get away with—that was Ori. For class, she used to pair a red leg warmer with a blue one, pulled up high on her thighs over pale pink tights, a purple leotard with a green tank on top, a fuchsia bra, straps showing. The band holding her black hair off her face would be yellow maybe, with polka dots. I thought she looked kind of ridiculous, and I don't know why Miss Willow let her get away with it. But then Ori would dance, and when she danced, you forgot things like mismatched leg warmers and too many colors clashing. You could only watch what she could do, you had to see.

For Ori, dancing came naturally, without a nervous stomach or worries she'd forget the steps. She danced like it was meant to be, in a way that couldn't be copied, no matter how carefully I watched her move, mirroring my body after hers and trying to get my limbs to loosen up and act more free.

She had this vivid spark of life in her, wanting out, and you could see it clear when she took the floor. I'd never witnessed anyone move like that—I guess I won't ever again.

If Ori and I were dancing a duet tonight, she for sure would have been better than me. The audience would have basked in *her,* loved *her,* followed *her* light across the stage. My light would have been background.

That's the truth, or it could have been. It's no longer the truth anymore.

I let the curtain drop.

I'm on, I hear my cue. I take my first steps out onto the stage, and next I hear her voice, what she would have said to me, had she been here.

Breathe, Vee. Go be amazing. Go show them. Let them all see.

She used to say things like that all the time.

I'm at my mark. The darkness lifts, and my body lifts with it, and I'm tall now, as tall as Ori because she had only a couple inches on me, taller even, because maybe since she's been gone I grew. I'm balanced on pointe, on one leg, without a tremor, without sway. The spot of light circles me, and I'm growing warm inside it.

I wonder how I look, from out there in the audience, to those strangers in the seats who know me this way only, who have no idea.

I don't need a mirror to tell me. I look like I belong up here. I've got new Grishkos on, broken in this morning by massaging the shank and slamming the hard cast of the box into a door. My mother sewed on the ribbons with the tiniest stitches—no one could ever hope to see them. My hair is pinned slick with shine to my head, and the tutu is a rigid ring around my middle, not as flimsy as it might seem. I'm entirely in white. I wanted it that color. I asked for it.

The audience holds its breath for me. Ori's not the one up here, I am. The audience eyes my bent and poised leg, my arms molded in a graceful line over my head, my lifted and lengthened spine. All my weight is on a single toe. I hold. At least a dozen people watching from the wings want me to fall, and I'm not falling.

Now comes the building crescendo of music, every little increment of movement from my body studied in mirrored reflection, coached and corrected into place. It may not be as free-form as Ori would have done it, but it's impressive because I'm so precise. I make no mistakes, not a single one. People in the audience can't hear the clomp of the brand-new shoes as I touch my weight to ground between each whip-fast pirouette. Or if they do hear, if they're seated close enough to the stage to hear, they ignore it. They want it our secret. They want me to win.

But there's another secret. Inside, past the tulle and the skintight stretch of fabric going three layers deep, I've got things I can't talk about. Things Ori knew, and only Ori knew. If you peel away the first layer, and the second layer and the third layer, underneath would be something ugly. Something broken. Eyes clawed out and blood still clinging to her neck, her arms, her face. Sometimes I think I still have the blood on my face. There's this thumping, and it's not my pristine pair of pointe shoes touching floor for the first night in their short lives. It's what's going on in my head. It's a stampede.

It may look like I'm dancing, but I'm somewhere else. I'm out there behind the Dumpster, in the tunnel of trees, and I'm screaming and flinging my arms, and dirt is everywhere, and rocks and twigs and leaves and blackness, the whole world getting knocked out like a set of teeth. I'm out there even now, as much as I'm in here.

Before I know it, I reach the end of the choreography. I can barely keep it together, but still I finish my solo with a flourish, poised on one rock-solid leg.

Silence.

They say nothing, do nothing. I can hear them all breathe.

Then it happens. The seats creak and shift and people rise to their feet. I've given them everything, I've given them too much this time, and then I realize, it takes me a moment to realize. These people really have no idea, do they? I showed them, and they couldn't see. They start cheering for me. These people—family, friends, strangers, all those innocent strangers—they stand on their feet for me and their hands smack and smack with increasing violence, and they shower me with noise like they wish I never had to leave this town or this stage. They're praising me. They're showing me how much they love me and have always loved me, no matter what. Look how blind they are. They're giving me a standing O.

PART II:
Inmate #91188-38

*We were just acting out the strangest,
tragic little roles, pretending to be criminals
in order to get by. We gave very
convincing performances.*

—Heather O'Neill,
Lullabies for Little Criminals

Amber:

———

IT WAS TOO LATE

———

IT WAS TOO late in the night for any wishful thinking. Past midnight. Past hoping. None of us was lying around in bed, holding our breath, willing the nearest CO on night duty to have a heart and let us out. That was not how it happened.

We never would have guessed at what was coming, not that night and not on our first day at the Aurora Hills Secure Juvenile Detention Center, when we emerged from the blue-painted bus from the county jail and looked up at these gray walls, this gray place.

Because this was true even when we stepped through the gate for processing: Even when we were stripped and searched and deloused and dressed in the orange jumpsuit and photographed and shackled to the wall while they chose a wing among A or B or C or even D in which to put us. Even when they determined our gang affiliation (I had none) and calculated our threat to the open population (mine was moderate). Even when they diagnosed, in seconds, whether or not we were suicidal, which meant restrictions on privileges like getting to keep our glasses outside the classroom or being allowed to sleep with the lights off or be civilized and wear a bra. (I could keep my reading glasses and was issued two identical sad, gray bras.) Even when we were shoved in the cage, our wrists freed and the barred door closed, and we heard the lock turning and making the choking sound that stopped hard in that last, low clunk, and that was it, we were inside, we were done. Even then, we never thought we'd see it all get reversed, in an instant.

We never thought the locks would decide to open on their own.

We were on our bed slabs, sandwiched in our bunks, which was where we spent all our nights and where we woke, trapped, on all our mornings. We slept, those of us who could sleep. We drifted, those of us who couldn't sink into full, eyes-closed unconsciousness. We did what we could to make it through another night inside.

Some of us knew for sure it was a Saturday, the first one of August. Some of us kept track of days, as Lian did (her charge was manslaughter, like mine, though her weapon was a handgun and she had only ninety-nine days remaining on her sentence; I had far more). There were those of us, like Lian, who kept track of every passing hour, notching the wall beside our bunks or carving up the private patches of our bodies beneath scratchy, state-issued underclothes.

Some of our thighs and cinder blocks said we had two months left; some said two years.

Then there were those of us who didn't want to keep track, whose sentences ran as long as a set of train tracks to all the places we'd never been. We pretended weeks were days, and years were weeks. That we still got to live our lives out in the sunshine.

There was Annemarie, held for her own protection in D-wing. (Murder in the first degree; chef's knife; once she turned eighteen, she'd get sent downstate, to an adult correctional facility, to serve out the rest of her time with other full-grown murderers.) For some of us, like baby-faced Annemarie, a girl so tiny she barely grazed my shoulders, it was simply thinking of the nights left, the time still to do, that made her go gray.

Some of us didn't have that much time left on our sentences, but still we felt like every hour was stolen from us, like the branches had been ripped clean off our growing trees. Over in C-wing, Little T. was cranky, even though she had less than a month left. (Her conviction was for assault, in the play yard at school; she said the girl had it coming.) Little T. was always cranky, but on that night she was more so. There was a leak dripping down from the ceiling, which meant it was raining.

This was why, when we argued over it later, when it was only us and our memories of the night to pry open, we were divided. Not everyone agreed it was August, and calendars were no help to us anymore. Annemarie was convinced it was still July, and Lian wished it were already September. Little T. could say only that it was raining.

What we did agree on was that it was hot and it was dark. It was a deep, sweat-drenched night sometime in the worst stink of summer when the locks came open. None of us could argue over that.

The gray stone building that housed us was more than a century old and was so far north, its shadow practically fell on foreign land. Like every detention center, every stop on the chain between jail and long-term juvie, Aurora Hills had its quirks that only those of us inside could know and appreciate. We knew the way the heating vents were situated, so a girl in A-wing could speak in a low, clear voice to a girl in C-wing simply by pressing her mouth to the wall and letting her words scurry off into the ducts and dusty airways that connected the wings. We knew that the hallway outside the woodshop was out of reach of surveillance cameras, so if a girl wanted to cut another girl, or press her up against the wall and slip her some tongue, that would be where to do it.

There were other details, small secrets, like the way sugar-soft snowflakes landed on our upturned faces from the sprinkler system in B-wing during wintertime. Like how sometimes, without the excuse of a holiday, what the cafeteria served as meat loaf tasted to us like a fudgy, springy slice of devil's food cake baked by one of our dead grandmas if eaten with our eyes closed. Any place can be made to feel like home. And one thing many of us had in common was how we'd dreaded living at home and desperately needed to escape that sinking ship. Home is where the heart is, and where the hell is, and where the hate is, and where the hopelessness is. Which made Aurora Hills pretty much like home.

We were each assigned to one of the four wings, and each wing had two tiers. The cells were arranged in an even square, the top tier lined with guardrails, each cell facing its mirror opposite across the way. Sound carried, voices juggling back and forth across the gathering space on the first floor. That space was where we spent our free time when we weren't made to sit through classes, forced to learn out of gnarled books so old whole generations above us had napped and drooled all over them. In the gathering space near our cells, we gambled over worn decks of cards and told stories about our former lives on the outside—exaggerating our virgin acts with boys and with crime.

Inside our cells, if we'd made friends with our cellies, we could choose or not choose to share our secrets.

We were kept two to a cell, sleeping one above the other with the low, scratched ceiling looming over the one who got top.

Our small rooms, longer than they were wide, contained two desks barely large enough to hold a sheet of paper, and two sets of shelves sturdy enough to contain two books each, if the books were skimpy and thin. There were two squares of mirror, made of an unknown metallic substance that wouldn't shatter. These poor excuses for mirrors reflected smears of our faces, in chunks, and not a whole head.

We had two lockers and two hooks. We were always asking for more hooks. We had one toilet and one shrunken sink. We had a door that was green-painted and walls that were mildew-blossomed and always growing new blooms.

We had cockroaches. We had ants. There were rats in the walls, and mice in the ceilings. We had plastic tubs outside our doors in which to stow our canvas slip-ons, so whenever we were inside our rooms, we didn't have shoes.

There were two windows. One was in the door, facing the hallway; the other was in the wall, looking toward the outside.

The first window was covered in wire mesh and belonged to the COs; that window was molded into each heavy cell door so our guards had a way to check on us, whenever they wanted, when we were undressing or napping or doing push-ups with one arm bent behind our backs, or when we were jammed flat against the door, glaring back at them through the hole.

But the second window was ours. It was a horizontal gash high up in the wall. Through it, we saw a wash of green if we were on the bottom tier of the wing, and that green was the surrounding forest beyond the fence lines. If we were on the upper deck, one floor above, we saw sky.

D'amour (smuggling of a controlled substance, on behalf of a very persuasive boyfriend; eighteen months) had the top bunk above mine. We were in B-wing. D'amour slept facing the window, eyes on the moon if she could find it, as she did on all nights.

We slept while it rained, those of us who could sleep. We counted mistakes like sheep, those of us, like me, and like D'amour, who couldn't sleep.

Then the deadbolts came open.

I'd like to say there was something to alert us, a certain charge in the air that caught our unsuspecting toes. But that would be romantic, and that would be a lie. There was nothing apart from time passing. The minutes moving forward, giving no warning.

Lola was the first of us to shout out, from the bottom floor of C-wing. She'd been jolted awake, once again, to see her cellmate standing like a stop sign in the darkness, as immobile as the stones wedged together to make the walls.

Kennedy was the cellmate no one wanted, known for her creepy habits, like munching her fingers and eating her own hair. She also had a habit of sleepwalking, though there wasn't far, in a locked compartment as tight as ours, to go walking. She wouldn't reveal her reasons for being here, but we could imagine: obsessive trespassing; cannibalizing *other* people's hair.

Lately she'd started watching Lola sleep. It wasn't that she touched or made threats. She simply stood, silent, inches from her cellie's slack, unconscious face, and let her eyes do the wandering.

We couldn't blame Lola for reacting the way she did.

Lola had a good number of months left for holding up a corner store and beating the clerk to unconsciousness. The judge found her so remorseless, so lacking in empathy, that he threw the book at her. But—she believed and we agreed with her—she'd calmed that raging part of her since then, tamped it down and tied it up in her own private basement, until this night, when she woke to find Cannibal Kennedy's eyes all over her. Again.

What we heard was shouting. Then the quake and shudder of a body being slammed against a cinder-block wall. We heard a gurgle and a crack and a squash and a thump.

What wasn't strange was hearing noise from Lola's cell at night. We'd gotten used to her shouting at Kennedy, just as we were used to a new girl whimpering when the first hours of the first long night set in—and how it was often the ones who looked the toughest, and acted the hardest, who cried out for their mommies.

What was strange was that no CO came to investigate. Kennedy crumpled down the wall until she made a slack pile of limbs at the bottom. Lola went back to bed and didn't help her up.

If the locks were open then, Lola wasn't the one to notice, and Kennedy was out cold at that point, so it wasn't like she would have known.

It happened to be a girl on B-wing—my wing—who was the first to make the discovery. Jody, down on the bottom deck.

Jody got up in the middle of the night, as she did most nights. She had this pastime she enjoyed, a kind of hobby. It involving ramming herself into the door of her cell, butting her head against the cold, rock-hard surface like a bull wired up for a fight. She liked the crash of impact and the shaken rush to the skull, then falling back, dazed and nursing a new goose egg on her forehead. It was a comfort to her, a hurt she looked forward to because she was in control of its coming. Like nothing else in her life, this was something she owned all to herself. *She* chose when.

She climbed down off the top bunk and took position. She lunged, poised, like a sprinter. She kicked off the steel toilet and set herself flying. All that stood between her and feeling something was the gap of air before the closed door.

She wanted that hit. She was expecting it. She didn't expect to find little resistance and have the door swing outward and tumble her through to the slippery tiled floor on the other side.

Had a CO been huddling outside her door, playing a trick on her? That was something Rafferty might pull, but he only worked days.

When she looked up, dizzy with the spins and slumped on her knees, Jody saw there was no guard. Even the booth that Woolings, the night CO, napped in when he was supposed to be watching us was empty.

She knew she'd been locked in at the start of the night— as we all were, on every wing, every night. But, somehow, the electronic deadbolts on Jody's barred door were undone. And not just hers; all the deadbolts on all the doors had come open.

When the new lock system had been installed earlier that summer—fully electronic and controlled from a command center in the deep heart of the facility—we had entertained a host of teasing thoughts; we couldn't help it. In our fantasies (which starred ourselves, of course, as superheroes instead of criminals), the door leading to the command center didn't hold. How easily we could sneak in to push the red button (we pictured a single red button that controlled every last lock, a red button begging to be pounded and right there in the open for us to find).

We imagined it. We wished for it. We played it out in our minds. If we were the type to pray, we prayed. But the power of those locks, and of the juvenile detention system, was stronger than any of our fantasies.

Until that August night.

Jody was the first of us to step out of her cell. But even cruel, boorish Jody (sentenced to a solid year, for stomping a rival gang member's head) knew freedom was meant to be shared with those around her.

She had a reputation among us, and it wasn't for being kind. She once shanked a new girl with a sharpened piece of fork plastic for daring to arrive with cheerful, Easter egg hair. But when it came down to it, in the moments that mattered, it was all of us against the corrections officers. Us against the warden. Us against the state. Us against the whole world.

Jody yelled out to her neighbors, who got up to try their doors. Then they yelled to the others, and they tried their doors. More and more of us, breath held, pins and needles cascading through our arms, hope trilling through our hearts, we went to our doors and we reached out and we gave a push.

The doors opened. And, just like that, we realized it was true. We'd been set free.

I HELD BACK

I HELD BACK in the doorway of my cell in B-wing, below the sign that said 91188-38 SMITH, which had followed me to every cell I'd been assigned to these past three years. This exact spot was where we stood to be counted by the COs, every morning and again at midday, after academic classes, and one last time, to cap off the night, before being caged into a small compartment of stale air with our cellmate.

But no one was attempting to count or corral us now, and any CO who showed up to try would have failed. I may have been the one inmate in B-wing who wasn't moving. Jody, once she alerted us to the open locks, gave a war cry and went rampaging out of the wing. I caught sight of Mississippi (possession of a loaded firearm; seven months) and Cherie (sixteen weeks for soliciting an undercover officer and resisting arrest; lies, she insisted, dirty lies!) bolting into the shadows. And other girls—faceless in the dark, numberless—shoved past and exploded out of the open exit at the end of our wing.

Behind me, still inside our shared cell, inmate number 98307-25—D'amour Wyatt—was rummaging through her foot locker, the small, combination-secured box where we kept our private items. (Probably, knowing D'amour, she was digging out some stash of drugs she bought off Peaches, our resident dealer ever since the last one got released.) But I couldn't know for sure. D'amour never showed me the contents of her box, and I never showed her mine. When we were searched by guards, randomly, every few weeks or so, I noticed how little she'd collected over her months inside. She didn't even have her own comb.

D'amour had been rooming in my cell since she got here. In the beginning, she was leaking shock at being locked up with the likes of us, practically comatose her first week and needing me to explain every last thing. I remember how she'd shuffled in, as if dragging herself on clubfeet. Her glazed eyes, pale as green bottle glass, her sniffle-squeaks. She sweated up her one set of bedsheets the first few nights, like she'd caught some kind of third-world fever from being near us. During the day, she walked around, a frazzled, whimpering mess of yellow-white hair and pink, flushed cheeks, even without the help of borrowed Maybelline (contraband, worth a whole heaping handful of Reese's Cups). She stood out.

As D'amour's cellmate, I was responsible for her. If she cried too much, I was expected to quiet her. If she stared too hard or for too long at someone like Lola, I had to explain the workings of this place and who shouldn't be looked directly in the eyes unless she acknowledged you first. It was a matter of respect.

Soon enough, D'amour did get her bearings. She found her place here, in the way most of us did, once we accepted that our freedom had been stolen and our every move watched, and that now we were forced to dress alike in a baggy wardrobe that was orange for the first few weeks and then yellow or, in most cases, green. Once we made it to greens, most of us stopped kicking and screaming and crying at night.

D'amour also stopped listening to me.

It came to a head last August, when the girls of Aurora Hills discovered that the vines growing on the outside of our facility's gray stone walls were creeping ever closer to one of our cell windows, and could be grabbed at by a skinny-wristed arm plunged through the bars. Those bars and that window happened to be in the very cell I shared with D'amour. Our window had somehow wedged itself open, and D'amour said there was no reason to point that out to the COs. What the girls of Aurora Hills wanted were those vines and the flowers that grew on them. And D'amour had scrawny arms. And she was willing to be dangled, armpit wedged against the bars, fingers stretching, reaching, for however long it took.

Some of us said the vines kind of looked like jimsonweed, which we'd witnessed growing in wild patches on the sides of highways and in unmowed fields behind our high schools. Some of us had ideas. We were also desperate to escape this place, however and in whatever fraction of a way we could.

And so the experimentation began. The vine's leaves were gen-pop green; they tasted disgusting. But in late summer, in the nighttime when the COs had the lights down, the blooms opened. They were shaped like alien heads, the petals pink and thick and sweaty and a bear to pluck off. At least they were edible, to those of us who could stomach something so sweet, like a pulpy gumdrop laced with corn syrup. Some of us spat it out and suggested that smoking or snorting might be a better way to get a buzz.

D'amour was the first volunteer. She smoked the first batch. Then she snorted way too much and turned green (a noxious contrast to her already pink cheeks) and started retching. Before that, though, her eyes had sparkled like diamonds, her pupils exploded, and she said she saw creatures floating over our heads, gassy-gray and smoke-breathing, and they were talking to her, telling her nice things, and singing her songs sometimes, and the songs were beautiful, even more beautiful than when Natty sang to us before the COs told her to shut her trap. That was how we discovered that the unidentified climbing plant growing on the stone walls of the building was a pretty potent hallucinogen.

We waited for the COs to put a stop to it, to command that the vines be cut down and burned in a pit in the yard, but they didn't notice. And soon enough, September came, and the blooms closed up, shrinking in on themselves like shriveled beetles.

D'amour turned to other options. She became known for being willing to try anything. Lately, there were more visits from Peaches (her crime possession with intent to sell; her sentence a year and nine months—sometimes we were only what we were on the outside, not less, and not more). Some nights I checked D'amour's pulse in the bunk above mine, simply to be sure her heart was still beating.

Thirteen months I spent in a cell with D'amour, breathing her air as she breathed mine. I didn't judge her for her habits. I didn't nag her to please at least run a comb through her hair. I even let her keep her drawings on the walls, the deformed dragons she said she'd seen in her hallucinations. She collared and named them like dogs: Horace and Gladys. Boris and Lazarus and Mazzy Star. I thought we had a bond, after thirteen months. Some kind of understanding.

But, as soon as the lock on our shared door came open, as soon as she heard Jody yelling that we'd been set free, she turned on me.

She rummaged in her foot locker and then burst out of our cell. She paused for a moment in our doorway, but not to share a word with me.

"Hey," I started, "where do you think you're going?"

She didn't acknowledge me. All she did was grab her canvas slip-on shoes from the plastic tub, shoving them on her feet. Then she bolted.

I guess the sudden open darkness didn't frighten her. I guess nothing did. With one last streak of pale hair—the palest on the unit—my cellmate was gone.

That was how I ended up alone, with nobody watching out for me, and me not needing to watch out for anybody else. All of B-wing had been emptied. There was nothing to do but wait for a CO to find me. Or start running. I took off.

If a CO appeared out of thin air and caught me—two rough hands shoving me to ground, or, worse, no hands and instead the swing of a baton—they'd assume I was like the others. Heading for trouble. Aching for it. All around me, girls were shrieking and careening down corridors, out for blood and out for the nearest exit. Every last one of us needed to be contained.

But I had a different purpose, a sudden destination in mind. I wanted to make sure it was still there, I told myself, that's all. It had nothing to do with how I felt safer there than even inside my cell. It wasn't pathetic. It didn't prove I was a coward. It was where I should have known I'd end up.

The prisoners' library was in the corridor outside the cafeteria. It was never locked, and there wasn't even a door to close it off, so none of the books were safe from looters, or from anyone else who wanted to destroy something dear to someone else. I expected to come upon a spill of books, from here to at least the end of the hallway. Every shelf to be toppled, book covers stomped on, pages pissed on and spat on, torn skins dropping down from the black sky. I came, expecting some touch of chaos, but I guess that would have meant someone else besides me cared.

The books were on the shelves, still alphabetized, thanks to me. My eyes adjusted to the low light, and as best as I could, I checked their home spaces on each shelf by touch and by memory. Nothing was missing.

Zora Neale Hurston was in her place under H. Under B, as she should be, was Libba Bray. Sylvia Plath and Francine Pascal took up an entire shelf of P. The dusty Dreiser was under D, though no one but me had read *Sister Carrie*. I'd read everything here, sometimes twice.

I sank to the floor. Crawled behind the desk and tucked my knees in, though the space was too tight for me and my shins and bare feet stuck out. No matter how well I thought I knew all the girls here, I was still separate from them. Always would be. Hearing the frenzy in the distance, being unable to not hear it, made me aware of the divide all the more.

On the afternoons I wheeled the library cart around to each wing—every wing except D-wing, which lost all privileges, the least of which was book-borrowing—I always knew the titles certain girls would want. Jody loved bodice rippers and any romance (you'd never guess it to hear her mouth), and Peaches was using her time inside to study up on the law. Little T.'s taste in novels leaned toward the classics, and she was always hogging our one copy of *Jane Eyre*.

Our private taste in books showed a hint of our secret selves, and sometimes I was the only one who got to see those secrets.

Of course I'd skim the books later, after they were returned, searching for smudges and feeling for turned corners, and thinking maybe there'd be a message inside for me. There never was.

There *were* messages—just for everyone else. For girls on A-wing and B-wing, for a girl on C who'd been on B just a month before. Whole conversations I wasn't a part of. Coded messages I couldn't hope to unravel.

On library days, when I doled out the books as part of

my life-skills job in the afternoons (we all had to have them; I was lucky), I could be counted on to deliver an important message written in tiny script on a small square of toilet paper, secreted in my cart and wheeled from one wing to another. Some of the notes were intimate, blush-worthy, girl on girl, and for no one else's eyes but theirs.

Then there were the nasty notes. Hate so fine-tuned and full of passion, it could get confused for something else. The usual bodily threats. Graphic descriptions of disembowelment and shit-slinging. Mother-insults. Creative cursing. I read those notes, too.

No one could have known if I read the message I was passing, fast, if I maybe memorized it and ran through its words later, gaining access to confidences and dingy, unspoken secrets.

No one knew how much I remembered. How I thought it was important that someone here made an effort to remember.

I couldn't even remember why, but I knew I should.

There were other ways to gather information outside the library, apart from the usual eavesdropping in the cafeteria or slow-drifting past a heated conversation in the yard. The beauty salon was another setup inside Aurora Hills meant to teach us "life skills," for our eventual release. Only those of us without any strikes for three months running could stand with a pair of scissors against the nape of another girl's neck, or let ourselves be scissored. All under adult supervision, obviously. And when a girl was in the chair, her hair wet and combed for cutting, she tended to talk. Anyone could have been in the next chair getting a trim and pretending not to listen. Anyone.

It was a good thing my hair grew out so quickly.

Still, for all my ways, and with all my chances to over-hear something worth hearing, I hadn't caught a single piece of information about a jailbreak, even from the girls who made friendly with the COs. No one was talking. No one hinted that something this big was coming, something this glorious. No one knew.

So how come I had this prickly feeling? This scratching at me from deep inside?

Like we'd run these halls before, on a night just like this one. Like we'd pushed open our unlocked doors and we'd gazed in equal parts joy and confusion and knee-knocking fear at the empty guards' stations, and we'd taken our chances, and we'd thrown those chances to the wind, and we'd kept on running. All of this was familiar.

Like we'd lived this night already. Like we'd live it again, after this. We'd eternally be circling back around to relive it, and we'd never make it out, and we'd never stop running, and I couldn't fathom how I knew this or why it would be so, even if I did.

I was huddled behind the library desk, hoping the dark-ness would shield my legs and all the rest of me, feeling no small comfort from the surrounding shelves containing all my books. And I was asking myself, Could I be right? What if I was? What if this had happened already, and this space behind the desk was waiting for me to fill it, as I always did and always would?

If I was right, then I could predict what would come next. I centered in on myself, and dug around, and let my mind swing open. It came to me.

Right about now, I'd hear a song.

It'd be Natty (fourteen months; domestic assault against her mother—they were arguing over the use of a curling iron). Natty would come sailing through this corridor any moment now, and she'd be singing something familiar. Her voice would carry, and anyone nearby would hear it and hush for a moment, forgetting where they were, forgetting *who* they were, needing a listen. Natty was the only inmate here who could make every last one of us stop and pay attention without threat of violence. Pop stars had nothing on Natty, except their freedom.

I held my breath, waiting. The distant noise shifted, same as before. The darkness kept its shape. Maybe I was wrong.

Then I heard her. Natty came bounding around the bend in the corridor, sailing past the bookcases and the library desk where I was huddled, belting out Beyoncé for no apparent reason.

It was just as I remembered: hiding here, catching Natty's passing song. A glimmer of memory. A warmth filling me as I recognized the song—I'd heard it on the outside, before I came to be in here, and Natty had brought that all back to me, as she always could—and then the warmth sinking and leaking out my toes when I realized what it meant.

I knew what was coming. This night would end, and soon. Which meant I had somewhere to be.

Something rolled over to me on the floor, a flashlight one of the COs must have dropped, only it looked different from the usual black flashlights they kept clipped to their belts with their weapons. This one was made of cheap yellow plastic, like something someone would pack for a camping trip, if that someone was out in the world the way I wasn't and could sleep a whole night under the stars.

I kept the yellow light, gripped it tight in my hand. I squeezed out from behind the library desk and made myself stand up. I found my footing and wished that I'd thought, like D'amour, to grab my canvas slip-on shoes.

Something was pulling me down the corridor, after Natty and toward the heart of the noise. I remembered now. Something was about to happen, and I was meant to be its witness.

I LET IT CARRY ME

I LET IT carry me. The noise. The loud rush of inmates felt like something liquid and fast-moving enough to pull me along with them, and I didn't fight it. I felt it—them, all of them—pushing me forward, wanting me to be the one.

Then it—they—let go.

I landed on the stairwell between B-wing and the store window of the canteen, which was closed off with a grate for the night. This spot, which offered a wide view of the facility from the protection of a wall to lean against, secure from sneak attacks, was usually taken in daytime by an armed guard. I kept the found flashlight dark, not wanting to call attention to myself. I waited. Watched.

Natty was long gone, and she'd taken the shivery notes of her song with her. Now in her place was the girl who didn't wait for me to follow. My cellmate, D'amour.

I caught sight of her in the dim fizz of light from the
EXIT sign that hung over the fire door. A devil-red glow, still
faintly lit from the building's emergency backup system, occasionally flickered. She was a crimson chalk outline moving
with purpose. And calm.

She seemed to know exactly where she was going.

The fire door was a door we'd never seen opened. It
wasn't an emergency exit we were allowed to step through,
even during emergencies. We assumed it shot straight out-
doors, to the side yard, the staff parking lot, and all the fresh,
free air beyond. This was the door D'amour tried to pull
open. When it wouldn't pull, she tried to kick it down.

D'amour was slight, and she didn't weigh all that much. She
was flighty and kind of vapid and, we suspected, quite dumb.

Now she was something else. She wasn't acting dumb.
She didn't seem numbed up or high off whatever new substance Peaches was peddling. She seemed hell-bent. The
light in her eyes was red with determination.

She shoved her body against the steel-gray expanse of
the door, yellow hair flying. She wanted out. I'd never seen
anyone want out as badly as she did right then. But the door
wouldn't budge.

Then she spotted the unbarred window.

I caught the rest in flashes. It wasn't that I couldn't focus;
it was the lightning, the summer storm raging through the
window. She'd be dark, and then she'd go bright. Her yellow
hair black, her yellow hair white. I caught her, foot kicking
out and the perfect hit in the center of the glass that caved it
in. Then came the second and third kicks that made it shatter. She'd gouged open the window into the night.

This window was narrow, but so was D'amour. She was inside with us, breaking glass with her feet, and then she was outside apart from us, braving the wind and the rain.

She bent down to untangle a chunk of long, sloppy hair from the window frame. Her hair came free, and then she was also. Free and running for the first set of gates.

Thunder shook the scene. But it was only weather. At some point the storm would stop, and the sun would come out, and the whole world would then be there at D'amour's fingertips. That was how we imagined escape to be, in the most blinding of our getaway fantasies. We had so many.

Any inmate held here at the Aurora Hills Secure Juvenile Detention Center would have rushed that open window. It was our dream, come to life. So why wasn't I following D'amour? Why wasn't I trying to escape along with her? I had a real way out now, open and calling me closer. I took a step, stumbled. I switched on the flashlight to find the stairs. No one was there to stop me—no one but myself.

I should have run to it. Dived through, hoping the hole would fit me, kicking out more glass to make room if it didn't. I should have been out there, in the storm, speeding for the closest gate. Any one of us would have abandoned whoever was left and gone running.

Sometimes I'm sure I did do it. That maybe I buried it, blocked it out.

I have this distant memory, hanging on a ratty clothesline in the backyard of my mind, and in this memory, I *am* running. There I am, running fast and hard for that window as if it's a set of doors that will soon be slamming closed to passengers and I'll lose my chance. I will lose at all chances forever. That feels real enough.

Glass. Shards of it. The edge of the window slicing me with its teeth. Then pain.

The pain tells me I really did do this; the pain is too precise for this not to have happened.

And the storm. The storm, now that I'm out in it, pounds like an alarm of some kind, but not one shutting me down, face mashed to the ground, hands in surrender on my head. It calls me closer. Says it's my time now; the whole rest of my life could be found on the other side of that gate. I'm not afraid. That's why it feels so artificial. How could I not be afraid?

I don't remember much more, because, next, something slams against me, as heavy as a sack of stones. Reality.

That memory—the pain and the wet and the getting closer, the shaky view of the approaching gate, the yellow-haired girl racing for it, and me on her heels, but clumsy on my feet, slipping in the mud, unsteady, about to go down—that memory blinks back. Blinks away. Gone.

No matter how I may have pictured myself escaping this place—face-first or feet-first—truth is, I can't leave it. I would never.

That's my real secret.

If D'amour had made it out, and I mean for good, we may well have forgotten her. We always forgot girls, once they left us. A girl could be a legend among us for months, even years, but once she was transferred or—worse—released, we didn't like to think so much about her. She got blacked out of our imaginary photos, erased from around our tables. We'd recite her stories until the names and specific characteristics faded away, until it was that-girl-in-green, that-girl-in-yellow. Until it was somegirl, which may as well have been any one of us.

But this is what happened, instead, to inmate number 98307-25, the girl we knew as D'amour:

She reached the first fence. She went for it across the mud, and she did make it, soaking wet and shaking. She grabbed her hands to the metal rungs and started to climb. She slipped a few times in the mud, and she lost a canvas shoe, but she kept climbing.

She was a pinprick of movement rising up the length of the fence. We expected shots to ring out. The air horn. At the very least, we expected the release of the dogs.

But it seemed the only eyes on her escape were our eyes. My eyes.

My flashlight beam didn't reach out there, but still I could see her. The lightning made it so I could.

She was nearing the top of the fence. And we knew what was up there. Razor wire. Hadn't I explained this to D'amour when she first got here? Didn't I tell her what happened to the last girl who tried? A girl (we misplaced her name after she got transferred) made the climb during rec in the yard when the COs' backs were turned. Broad daylight, in view of anyone and everyone, and she'd thought it a good idea to try her fate at the fence.

We watched for a while, chuckling to ourselves, critiquing her moves, until, on delay, the COs caught on. They observed her climbing, and only looked on, weapons not even raised. I guess they knew what the razor wire had in store for her, and they had hushed to silence, waiting for the touch, and then the screams.

D'amour didn't scream when she reached the top of the fence. She was tougher than I'd given her credit for. She flinched and then, somehow, she vaulted herself up and over, with a blast of energy I hadn't seen in all the months we'd shared a cell. She was covered in mud and almost impossible to make out in the dark storm. Or that could have been blood. Maybe the sharp barbs on the wire coils had sliced her clean through. But she did keep going, running for the second fence like she wouldn't need her liver or her spleen on the outside if she could only make it.

Here was another thing I'm not sure D'amour knew: The second fence was electrified.

She might have assumed the storm had knocked out all the power on the property, including outside, so the second fence would be cold and climbable and not mortally armed to zap her like a third rail. It would have been a logical assumption after the locks had opened.

She was wrong, though, and all it took was a single running leap for the fence without testing it first. One touch and that fence came alive.

D'amour took every volt it had to give her. The sound was a sizzling snap booming through the night. The stink, which reached me, even as far away as I was standing, was like a burning tower of tires.

It was the brightest light I'd ever seen.

Then that light fell, fast, like a meteor into mud, dropping down into darkness.

It was in that exact instant when it happened. And this can't be explained to any of the other inmates when they ask if I saw D'amour get electrocuted, if I saw her go up in a white-blond burst of flames, and if it was awesome. Because, yes, I did see all that—and then I saw something else.

Someone else.

When D'amour went down in that flash of light, the walls shifted around us. A different kind of window came open. And someone just as bright slipped in.

THERE WAS A FACE

THERE WAS A face in the darkness, down the stairs in the open area near the canteen, a face I'd never seen before, and I found myself drawn to it. I'd had my flashlight trained on the window, but this face had gotten caught in the beam.

I knew every face at Aurora Hills—the girls on C-wing and B-wing, on A-wing and even D-wing. The warden, at least from a distance, when we caught him through the window, getting in or out of his nice car. I knew the COs by their fat cheeks or their beard shapes, not to mention their knuckles on the crook of a shoulder, the certain kind of way they grabbed.

This, though, was a face I couldn't identify.

She was a girl, but she wasn't one of us. She was an outsider. A civilian. I'd been out with the book cart Thursday afternoon and would have noticed someone new being admitted. On Friday I'd kept my ears open, my head down. No one mentioned a new inmate. And she couldn't have arrived today, because we never got new inmates on Saturdays. Every single day we talked of our comings and goings, who was being released, who was about to be transferred somewhere worse or somewhere worlds nicer and lucky them (we didn't really mean that), who got sent to the hole and for what, who was moving wings and getting a new cellie, who wanted to move but got denied (Lola, again), and I listened to every word because I was always listening. I knew every name, every face, almost every crime confessed to and even some crimes best kept hidden. I had a good memory for details. Before my arrest, I made As in school.

This wasn't one of the girls I'd seen step off the blue bus from county jail. She was someone who didn't belong. Someone from the outside who'd gotten in.

I could tell just by looking at her. She had her hair up in a way we didn't wear it here, a neat knot on the crown of her head held back with shiny clips that would get confiscated within seconds inside these walls. She wore jeans, actual blue jeans, tight enough to fit her, and a sleek little shirt in turquoise, a color not allowed on anyone visiting, since at a distance it blended with our greens. She wore jewelry—in her ears, around her neck and fingers, a circle of gold attached to one wrist. She looked well cared for. And exceptionally clean.

I couldn't fathom how she'd gotten herself in here in the middle of the night. Had she stowed away during visiting hours? Was she related to one of the COs?

The outsider's eyes drifted. At first I assumed she was taking us all in, but then I realized. When one of us lunged at another girl, the outsider didn't flinch. And when one of us wailed close enough to burst the outsider's eardrum, she didn't shrink back. A gang of us crashed through the corridor, and the outsider didn't turn to see, didn't make a break for it, didn't run with us or away from us. Didn't do a single thing.

She acted as if she couldn't even see us. She was unfazed by the flashlight beam dancing all over her body, shining right in between her eyes.

I left my safe, shielded spot by the wall and stepped closer to the railing, risking being seen. The outsider was down below, in the wide-open space between gated entrances to the different wings. We were often lined up there, on the way to rec or to class, and once or twice, after a violent incident they thought might inspire us, we were chained ankle to ankle, like a slow, sad train.

The crowd had dispersed. The rest of us had gone off and left me here, with whoever this was. Their noise—our noise, because I belonged with them more than I did with her—shifted to the other side of the facility. Still, my eyes couldn't leave her, and my feet wouldn't take me from where my eyes held.

She turned in a swift circle, like she'd heard me. But she didn't look up. She didn't raise her eyes to find me staring down on the crown of her barrette-filled head.

I was about to call out to get her attention, when everything got confused. The flashlight in my hand started acting crazy. Everything its light touched was changing in the room around us. The walls were no longer the plain, sick-colored green I knew and the green they should have been. They were a riot of spray paint, filled with color.

All around, on every wall and standing structure, were spray-painted tags, bright bubbles of letters, scribbles, swirls, sloppy and angry and awful all at once. It reminded me of something from outside: the graffiti found under a highway overpass, when passing through, fast, in a moving car. My mother used to say bums did it, but it was kids, I was sure of it, kids who wanted to be remembered, like I did.

I used to find it beautiful, when I'd spy a patch of graffiti from the window of the car. Now I did not. Now it was everywhere, on our walls and marking up this place we knew. Too many colors. Ugly colors. I got woozy just from looking. It didn't belong.

Many of the tags were hard to read, but I could make out some. *Stevi + Baby* crawled up one wall (none of us were named Stevi or called Baby, at least by anyone locked up in here), and I wondered about them, if they were still together, Stevi and Baby, and I hoped they destroyed each other, that they broke up and got restraining orders. I hoped they never found true love.

Many sets of initials, scrawled one over the other, cascaded from one side of the wide space to the other. Someone named Bridget Love had inscribed her name on every available surface, and someone else named Monster had taken it upon him- or herself to cover it up. I wanted to cover Monster who'd covered Bridget. I wanted to get rid of every last one of them. None of the names on the wall said Amber Smith. None said Mississippi or Lola or Little T.

(we'd been teasing her for months, trying to dig out what the T stood for). None said Cherie or Jody or D'amour. Those were some of our names—and none of our names were anywhere I could see.

I wouldn't have known where I was, if not for the single painted letter high up on the wall, higher than even the highest tag of graffiti reached. A black-blocked stencil that said only B. That meant we were just outside B-wing.

Nearby was a black piece of graffiti so enormous, my flashlight could barely catch it in one sweep. It said *RIP*.

I closed my eyes. When I opened them, I noticed even more things wrong.

The sign noting directions to the visiting area was gone. The postings about the rules we needed to obey (NO RUNNING, HANDS IN VIEW AT ALL TIMES) had been taken down. The grate blocking the canteen was broken clean off, and where the canteen should have been was a dark hole in the wall with nothing for sale.

The only other thing the same was the window D'amour had thrown herself through to get outside. It was still broken.

As I watched, a gust of wind blew what appeared to be a bundle of loose twigs and leaves across the grimy floor. It looked like no one had cleaned the floor in years.

I didn't think, not consciously, about what I did next. I started down the stairs, straight for the intruder. She was connected to this, somehow. She'd made this happen. I reached flat ground and went running. I sped up so much that I couldn't get my feet to stop and almost rammed into her, and I wanted her to fall, wanted her flat on her back doing some explaining.

Except there was no her.

I rammed through air.

I turned around.

She wavered before me. Her face was urgent and stark white, like a face of the dead. So far, neither of us had said one word.

She had these dark blue eyes, much like the sky outside, which had been filled with pounding rain and clapping thunder, but now I couldn't hear the rain out there anymore. Or the thunder. I couldn't hear anything at all, apart from her breathing. Blue like some kind of warning. No, we were beyond warning. Blue like being thrown off a cliff and sunk in the deep of the sea.

That was what I saw when I looked at her. I had no idea what she saw when she looked at me. Especially after what she said next.

"Ori?" she said.

I shook my head, confused.

"Ori? Is that you?" she said, muffled and mush-mouthed, like she was communicating through the paint and plaster and insulation of a wall between rooms, and I was on the other side, in that other room, my ear pressed to the wall, trying to catch what she said.

She reached out, like to touch me, but I wouldn't let her. *Who* did she think I was?

She said it again—that name. And it was the sound of the name that brought it on again, that inside-itching, the prickling electricity in a quiet section of my brain.

Then, yes.

Yes, Ori. Remember? Yes, I remembered. Inmate number

47709-01. Her favorite book off the shelves was going to be the thick, chewed-up paperback we had of *One Hundred Years of Solitude*. She was going to say she'd be here long enough to read it one hundred times. She would wear her hair much like this stranger, tight and in a knot on the top of her head, but without barrettes because we weren't allowed to have anything with sharp, stabbing ends. She'd have mangled feet that she never wanted any of us to see, and a thousand-yard stare. She'd have a kindness in her that would be foreign to us—and within a week or so, there wouldn't be a girl among us who wanted her dead.

She wasn't here yet, but she would be soon. She'd have to be. She was our forty-second.

But how did this intruder know who Ori was? And how did I, if Ori hadn't come up our hill and stepped off the blue-painted bus to join us yet?

A shift in the intruder's face. I must have done something to frighten her, in the way I've always frightened people even when I don't mean to. By my size maybe, since I know I'm a lot bigger than most girls, or by the scowl that's always on my face, only it's not a scowl, it's just my face. But she didn't know that, because she backed away, put up her hands as if to protect herself from me, and opened her small screw of a mouth. She let a sound come out, and the sound was even smaller, even more pathetic, than I expected. Her whole body was shivering like I was something revolting, and then I guess she knew exactly who and what I was, because she did what I should have done.

She ran.

WE LOST

WE LOST THE connection. I lost my sense of time. This could have lasted a few seconds. It could have been a whole hour frozen in the summer heat.

She'd gone running, and all that was left was this raw feeling inside me. This burn going all down my throat until it met my stomach and turned heavy, dangerous. Until it became a bomb.

I'd felt this before.

The first time was the day of my mother's wedding, when I was in grade school. She'd worn a white dress for him, which was bursting at the seams thanks to him, seeing as she was months into carrying his child. She'd said yes. She'd made her choice, which involved plugging up her ears and covering her eyes. The choice of telling the ER doctor I'd slammed my arm into the kitchen door, or calling herself so very clumsy as to knock a bar of soap into her own eye while taking a shower. The choice of him over me, over herself, and that day at city hall would seal it.

I gave her warnings: I puked on the floor of the car on the way over, and that was why I was walking into the courthouse without socks or shoes. I grabbed her arm in the parking lot—she'd made me wear lacy, white gloves to go with my scratchy, too-tight dress. I yanked her arm, holding her back, pulling so hard, the lace webbing between my fingers ripped apart and my bare skin was exposed.

I didn't want to go in, I told her. Could I stay in the car?

I remembered what she'd said to me and the way she'd said it, with an intense, blinding light in her eyes. She'd said, "Do something for me this once. Make me happy." And she went off without me, the white veil slipping off the back of her head as she walked straight up the steps and into the courthouse, where my soon-to-be stepfather was waiting. She knew I'd follow. A feeling came over me. Fury, roiling in my gut. Fury mixed up with a tinge of fear, rising and rising as I took the stairs. It was because I knew, even then, that she couldn't hear me. She wasn't listening.

The second time was the week after my stepfather's accident, years later. When the two police officers called me out of first-period language arts class at school, the same feeling from the wedding day billowed around me as I walked up the aisle with my book held against my chest. (We were reading *Watership Down;* I wanted to like it more than I did.) I remembered little details like the turned-down corner of the page, so I could save my place. My dirty fingernails, blackened and oily like I'd been digging in wet earth. The thudding of my heart in my chest. I never did find out how that book ends.

Fury, mixed together with fear, because I was afraid I knew what they were going to tell me. They wouldn't believe me. No one ever did.

Everything I know about bombs tells me they are built to explode. But something must set them off first. There must be a trigger before the noise goes off, before the big burst of bright, choking smoke. Otherwise a girl could stay quiet for years.

When the intruder ran from me, she set something off in me.

Maybe it was how she'd been so close, her clean, bare shoulder in reaching distance of my hands. I'd gotten a good look at her. She had a bracelet on her wrist that caught my eye, a gold strand with tinkling charms. I could make out every last charm on that gold bracelet. A ballerina. A second ballerina. A third ballerina. And more. All ballerinas. All the gold charms were ballerinas. I'd never even seen a ballerina in real life. The miniature gold ballerinas had their legs flung out of their sockets. Their arms thrown up in the air, their miniature toes pointed. Every last one the same. She'd stroked the bracelet with her hand. She held one little gold figure tight in the palm of her hand like she could squeeze it to pulp, but when she'd opened her palm, it was still there.

This tugged at me.

The intruder looked like she had everything, and that bothered me. She wasn't pretty like her outside parts. Not smooth-skinned and high-cheek-boned and glossed like her thin lips, not made of tinkling gold. Inside she was swollen and ugly-red, inflamed with crusty secrets. There was a smell, too; she leaked it out each time she let out a breath. She was rotten.

All I know is when she started running, I, too, started running. I needed to get away from her—that wretched, white-faced thing who called me by the wrong name. I needed to get away from what she'd done to our corridor, our walls, our home. Now that the state had taken custody of us for the life of our sentences, it was our home even if we would never admit that out loud. She had no right.

I heard the pounding of feet behind me, and I was sure it was her chasing me. Had she gotten turned around? Decided to come back for me?

But I knew this facility better than she did, better than any person, apart from the COs. I'd been here since I was barely fourteen—longer than anyone.

I turned a corner. I took a right, a left, another right. She was coming fast behind me.

This passage took me into the back hallways that housed the laundry and then past the laundry itself, deeper into the center of the Aurora Hills Secure Juvenile Detention Center. I kept thinking that surely a CO would appear and I'd be caught, but there were no COs anywhere to stop us. There was no one except the two of us.

A gray steel door stood between me and turning back, and I shoved it open. The lock was undone, and when the door went slamming outward, the shock of what was there was more than I could take.

The fresh air hit like a fist to the eye, and I was down. On my back. In the gravel lot outside the detention center.

Above me was the stretch of sky, a clear view of a sliver of moon. Around me was tall grass, run wild with weeds and fallen vines and dropped trash. I'd made it outside. The entire sky was above me, the whole clear sky.

Only, no storm was raging, as there had been just minutes before. There wasn't even a sprinkle of rain. The gravel pellets beneath my body were bone-dry. The fencing in front of me had fallen over. A gust of summer wind cascaded past me, smelling sweet.

Any second now, she should come bursting out of the door behind me. If I looked up, she should be standing over me, wavering in the quiet night with her glimmering gold chain, her feet planted within kicking distance of my spinning head.

She didn't come.

I was alone, outside, in a dense thatch of silence that felt like my life before. Before I was accused, when the whole world, my mom and little half sister included, still thought me innocent. That kind of summer from childhood, when the sprinklers in the backyard come on all for you, and the ice pop on a stick is yours for the licking, and school hasn't started up again and it feels like it never will, and your mother hasn't married that man yet, your mother hasn't even met him yet, and it's still just your mother and you. What I mean is, it reminded me of one of the happiest moments of childhood, before broken wrists and purpling bruises and nasty names hissed when my mother's back was turned. Before "Who do you think you are? You're ugly. You're nobody." Before a hard, hot twist of a pinch under the dining room table and bursting into tears and being made to sit all night, for five hours, at the table in the dark room until I choked down the cold dinner because he told my mother I had to, because he'd said. I mean before. Before the accident they said wasn't an accident. Before I was charged and convicted. Before riding the blue-painted bus up this hill and being ushered inside this building. There was a time when I could have grown up to be almost anything I wanted, like some of the stories promise in our more happy, hopeful books. I did once have a future.

I pressed myself against the gray stone wall of the facility. The stones were cold, but dry and smooth, and they felt right against my back. They welcomed me. Told me to not let go, to stay.

Then the quiet bubble burst. A pop-popping and a slam shook the wall behind me, snaking up my back like an earthquake jolting from the calm.

Shouting. The piercing shriek of a whistle. The COs had come out from wherever they'd been. If they'd been sleeping, they'd awoken. If they'd been locked up, they'd broken free. The outdoor lights blazed up, aloft on poles and trained down on every entrance. A spotlight found my upturned face. It wasn't long before a CO discovered me on the ground, splayed out before the wide-open door. I was drenched from the pouring rain that was once again falling and puddling around me, soaking me through.

A thick trunk of an arm wound around my neck, and I was lifted up and plunked down inside the building, a bag of meat and bones more than a girl.

I met the concrete, face-first, as we were made to do whenever a group of us got out of hand. I had eyes to the floor, nose mashed to the ground. I kept still, hands on my head. But I could see out the still-open door if I lifted my head an inch, and what I saw wasn't the clear night I'd run out into.

The storm was raging. I guess it had never stopped.

And I guess, when I got lifted to my feet, that I began clawing and flailing and using my elbows. I was kicking and pounding my fists on the closest surface, which turned out to be the unyielding body of the guard. The bomb inside me had gone off, and I couldn't stop myself any longer; I couldn't keep it in. I didn't even know why or what I was fighting. This was familiar, safe. We knew that the why didn't matter sometimes, and if we wanted a fight, we could always find a what.

I was forced back through the familiar corridors, and in slow motion, as the plain green walls surrounded me, and the graffiti disappeared and I saw for sure everything was back to the way I remembered, I calmed. I loosened my clenched fists. My mouth closed, and at that point I heard an end to the screaming.

The only things moving through my mind were questions.

Who was that girl? How'd she get in? Did she have anything to do with the locks opening? With the night going so wild? With the rain stopping and starting again? With everything getting so confused and me caught up in it?

And why did the name Ori sound so familiar—so significant, like the right key slid into a rusted, forgotten lock?

I wouldn't find any answers in what remained of the night. I was secured in a chair as the COs herded down the rest of us, told to shut up, told to mind my own business, told to chill out and wait for my turn. It would take hours, but all of us did get caught. Not one of us made it past the perimeter, though quite a few of us had tried. All we knew was that we'd tasted it, hadn't we? Freedom. Free-floating air on our tongues.

What I'd seen was our after. I'd been allowed to witness what would become of this place, after we were gone.

Rest in Peace. Except none of us could do any resting.

For now, the electronic lock system had been resecured, and the power had come back on, so there was nothing hiding in the darkness anymore except the truth. A CO came to retrieve me, at last, but he led me to D-wing instead of B. That was bad, though it would get much worse.

As the gate to D-wing came into view, I knew that we had about three short weeks left. And then, nothing. At that, I was shoved in the hole and locked in.

PART III:
Vee

Justice. I've heard that word. I tried it out.
I wrote it down. I wrote it down several times and
always it looked like a damn cold lie to me.
There is no justice.

—Jean Rhys,
Wide Sargasso Sea

WORMS AND ROT

YEAH, THE AUDIENCE loved me.

I mean, *of course* they gave me a standing ovation. They practically ate me up, which was how they used to act with Ori, before all of what happened here more than three years ago, when she got arrested right before she was supposed to play the Firebird, the starring role in our spring showcase. Before everyone turned their backs on her and my parents made me cut ties with her and attend the other girls' funerals and the dance studio almost even got shut down. Before, I mean. People used to cheer for her onstage the way they now cheered for me.

So much is about how you look on the outside. That's what matters to most people. Smooth your hair and bobby-pin it down. Use as many pins as you need. Be sure to flick the eyeliner crumble out from the corners of your eyes.

Wear your prettiest clothes. Pale noncolor colors help, like powder pink. Keep that good-girl mask on and no one will see past it to the bad, unstable girl inside. At least they never did with me.

On the inside, if they could've seen, Ori was good. She loved to dance, and she didn't need music to do it, even on sidewalks or in the middle of the street. She despised wearing shoes, and didn't care what anyone thought of the oozing toe blisters on her busted-up ballerina feet. She once burst into heaving sobs when I accidentally ran over that cat in the road, and she stumbled out into the glare of the headlights and stripped off her own coat to bundle the animal in, holding its matted body in her arms until it stopped convulsing and finally was dead. She completely ruined her coat. I stayed at the wheel.

Those are some things that no one at the trial got to hear.

Because on the outside? After Harmony and Rachel were dead? Something went wrong with Ori's face. I try not to think too hard and remember too much about that day—it's best not to—but I do remember the change in her face and how sudden. Her cheeks sunk in. Her eye sockets hollowed, the whites gone yellow. Her mouth hung open in shock, I guess, and her dad couldn't afford a dentist, so anyone could see her crooked front teeth. When people decide there's ugliness inside you, they'll be looking to find it on your face.

Plus the practical matters, too, which made casting her as the enemy fit kind of nicely, in a world where people with sad home lives were the ones to do the sad, bad things. She wasn't from a decent family like mine, that was obvious from where she lived. She had no mom, and lots of people had questions about her dad. My own mother went around asking me, after, "When was the last time you saw her father? Is he ever home? Is anyone ever around to watch her?" like that would have made a difference. I tried to explain how her dad drove for a trucking company, and could be away sometimes for two weeks, or maybe I didn't explain. Maybe I just said I didn't know. Lack of parental supervision makes children into devils, my mother likes to say. Read the news, and you'll see so many abandoned young people doing horrible things.

"I had this girl at our house." My mother, again. "I fed her my food. I washed her sheets." My mother said a lot more than this—and she bought very expensive sheets—but the point is she spoke to what so many people were thinking. It was easy to find Ori bad in the days and weeks after, the clues suddenly there for the picking. It wasn't so easy with me.

It's curtain call now, when all the dancers of the night return to the stage for more applause, plus some flowers, I hope, if anyone thought to bring roses to toss at our feet.

I go out alone to gather my flowers. I try to remember how good it felt to dance for all these people, but I'm cold inside again, I'm an empty tunnel that meets a dead end.

After curtain call, the cast backs away from the swish of velvet that's swept in for the last time tonight, and everyone's still engulfed in that warm after-show glow from making it through a whole performance without disaster. The audience didn't dash for the exits when the long, boring adagio came on. None of the dancers fell and broke a tailbone. The little tulip in the first row didn't spin around and hit the little tulip in the second row, like she did during dress rehearsal, which got cut short because both tulips cried. No fires. No one puked. No dead bodies out behind the Dumpster and girls running in screaming that someone should call 911.

We did good. Now that the curtain's closed and the show's over, the older dancers give a big whoop and giggle and wrap arms around one another, kiss-kiss on both cheeks like they're in France, a twirl in the air, a ring-around-the-rosy like they're children. They are, basically.

I kiss no cheeks. I hug nobody.

What I do is back away, farther and deeper into the closest pocket of wings. In my arms are all my flowers. I need a moment to myself, and it's not to count my bouquets.

It's not until I'm out of view, in the backmost section of curtains at the rear wall of the stage, two velvet layers deep and only concrete beyond that, when I let myself hunch over and everything I've been holding in leaks out. It's the performance tonight that did it. How well it went, how every single thing is coming together for me, piece by piece, my dreams coming true, when I'm not sure I truly deserve to have these dreams.

I fold up my knees and press my face into my white tights, press it hard, grind it in, and I open my mouth. And nothing. No sound comes out. The ache is sharp, it burns, like maybe how it'd feel to be the one who got stabbed. Something sweeps me up in the thought of that, the powerful visual of the knife going in, the plunge-and-stick, because there would be bones and muscle and ligaments and squidgy, lumpy organs past the skin, and a blade wouldn't go in smooth, like into a plate of flan.

I'm on the floor, my back to the wall. I don't care that I'm getting the white costume grimy and crushing the tulle. I don't need this tutu. Juilliard has tutus. Everything is totally fine. No one knows.

Sarabeth is cursed with clown feet, so I know it's her on the other side of the curtain before she says my name.

"Vee?" she goes. "You dropped all your flowers." At some point I must have let the bouquets fall, because there are so many flowers scattered about, it's like someone ransacked some old lady's garden.

I kind of hum from behind the wall of curtain. I'm noticing how, back here, where the audience never goes, this side of the curtain is tattered and plain. No velvet shine. No glimmer and sparkle. It's moth-eaten. It's frayed. And it smells—like wet dog.

"My mom got me flowers just like you," Sarabeth babbles as she searches for a gap in the curtain. "I mean, not roses. Not like you have roses. I mean, I know I didn't have a solo, but it's still special that she got me flowers, don't you think, Vee?"

The thing about Sarabeth, who I know counts herself as my best friend now, though we've never had an out-loud conversation about it, is that she doesn't know when to let me be.

She doesn't understand me.

Being best friends with Ori wasn't ever like this. She once found me crying in the back rehearsal room after ballet class, and maybe we were twelve then, maybe we were thirteen, and she crept in, careful not to give me a scare, and she placed a hand on my back, drawing pictures along my spine, the way I liked her to during our sleepovers. "What's the matter, Vee?" she asked me. She knew that when I cried too hard I got the hiccups, and she didn't laugh when my ribs rocked as the hiccups came.

It was easy to know what was the matter, why I sobbed. Miss Willow had selected Ori to advance to pointe, which meant a whole new kind of training, plus separate special classes three times a week, and she hadn't selected me. I needed more time to strengthen my ankles, she'd said. But Ori's ankles were ready. Mine were still the wimpy spaghetti ankles of a little girl.

Any other friend would have patted me on the back and assured me my time would be soon, but Ori made a promise, and she always kept her promises. She said she wouldn't go on pointe until the day I got to. She wouldn't wear the perfect pointe shoes Miss Willow had gifted her in charity because her dad wouldn't have paid a dime for them until I had my own pink satin pair.

I remember her fingers drawing down my spine. I remember her cheek on my cheek. I remember how she said, "Anything I do, you'll get to do, too." How she said, "I won't do it until Miss Willow says you're ready. I'll wait for you."

She did wait. She waited six and a half months for me and my ankles to catch up to hers.

And she didn't bug me about it even once.

Sarabeth is still fumbling with the velvet. She's going off about all my roses. Apparently I have quite a lot, because so many people came to see me.

"Sarabeth, stop. I don't care about the flowers."

"Oh okay. You did wonderful, Vee. Everybody was saying."

"I know."

"Oh yeah, of course you know." She quiets as I finger the back of the curtain, its ugly side only I can see. "Are you coming out? Tommy's here. But I thought you said you were breaking up with him? But he's here. And we've got the cast party, you know. And since it's your last show, you're a guest of honor . . ."

Every graduating senior would be a guest of supposed honor at that cast party. Sarabeth was only a junior.

I find the gap in the curtain and open it up and let her fill my arms again with all my bouquets. But as we're gathering the last of my bouquets, Sarabeth lets out an earsplitting squeak. She starts swatting at me with sloppy, panicked hands like she does at the air when she sees a moth, instead of being normal and opening a window.

Maybe Sarabeth has reason to freak out a little. One of the bouquets in my arms is leaking. And it's not water.

What's coming out the bottom end of the carefully wrapped bouquet is brilliant red and thick, like lukewarm syrup. It seeps and smears and screams all down the front of me, congealing on my white tights. The bouquet is bleeding. It's bleeding all over me.

With horror, I tilt my neck and look down. My eyes aren't sure what they're seeing at first, and then the picture sharpens and my brain makes sense of it. There, in my arms, stuffed into delicate pink tissue paper, is a bouquet of disgusting trash: balled-up tissues and a few rags and what looks like a guy's old white T-shirt, ripped into shreds but

Fruit of the Loom still on the decapitated collar, all covered, soaked, sopping really, with blood.

My arms go loose, and the bloody bouquet drops, spraying its contents everywhere. A hemorrhage. A nightmare. The blood spatters and clings to the curtain. It's sticky, webbing up my fingers like with snot. Sarabeth's bent over, gagging. A glop of thick, almost-black blood falls from my kneecap to the hard toe of my pointe shoe, and I stare at it, transfixed. I can tell by the smell it's not real blood, because I promise you don't ever forget the smell of *that*.

"Oh my gosh," Sarabeth squeaks. "Oh my gosh, Vee, oh my gosh." She lifts a bloody arm, slick and glistening, and she points a bloody finger at the floor.

A card has fallen out, one of those baby-size cards you get from the florist, but it's facedown in a goopy puddle, and neither of us is making a move to pick it up.

"Did someone really give you that bouquet?" Sarabeth says.

"No, I gave it to myself, what do you think? Some bitches thought it'd be funny, obviously. They can't say it to my face, so they do this."

"Say what to your face?" Sarabeth says, and I've never pitied her more for that pea brain she's carrying around in that head of marshmallow fluff than I do right now.

I stare at her until she glances away, flushing. *Now* she remembers.

This shouldn't be happening. None of this should. The girls who would have done something like this to me on my big night aren't around anymore. It doesn't connect.

Because Harmony and Rachel, they're gone. Ori got rid of them, everybody knows that. Ori got rid of them for me. And then Ori got gotten rid of, too, and now I'm the only one left.

The thing I can't get a grip on is how the bouquet ended up in my arms. Some bouquets were thrown at my feet, and some were handed directly to me, with an embrace, a congratulations. All this took place in front of everyone.

The faces blur. Smiling, everyone all smiles, so it's teeth and stretched lips and sour breath and sometimes whiffs of sucked-on mints or sneaked cigarettes. No one seemed cruel enough to present me with a bouquet filled with trick blood and grungy tissues and a sweaty gym shirt and then grin in my face and tell me congrats. No one who's still alive, anyway.

Cold creeps up my back. It reminds me of how I was looking for Ori—not the other two, only Ori—right before I went on, how something unspoken told me she might be out there, though she's long dead. I'm not sure what I believe, but I know what the little voice in my head believes.

She was here tonight, Vee. She came all the way here to see you.

She wanted me to have the messy, explosive gift so I wouldn't forget her, and so she wrapped it in pink paper, my favorite color, and into the pink folds she tucked a small card. From the ground, the side of the card that we can see says CONGRATULATIONS ON THIS JOYOUS DAY! It's white and silver, or it once was, like it was meant for an anniversary celebration or a wedding, the kind of thing you get for free if you actually buy flowers. But someone had to go to the trouble to buy this card—or at least swipe it—just to take credit. If anyone signed it, that would be on the other side, currently facedown in the puddle.

"Who's the card say it's from?" I ask.

"I don't want to touch it," Sarabeth says. But she sees I'm waiting for her to do just that, so she bends, delicately, and lifts it, warped and dripping. She turns it over and reads.

Her eyes tell all.

Sometimes I forget that she was there three years ago— not with us, I mean, but somewhere. She did take classes at the studio like we did, even though she was back-row bad and sluglike when it came to catching on to floor routines and any up-tempo combination. We ignored her, but she was around. She'd remember. Maybe she was one of the girls who'd been shattered by it and gone around wailing backstage—I seem to remember hearing a few banshee wails when the police escorted me home. Later I heard that there was one girl who came upon the bloody scene out back behind the theater and flat-out fainted, which contaminated the area. Maybe that had been Sarabeth? Could that explain why she's attached herself to me and blocked it all out?

It's funny how someone can witness the aftermath of a double murder, like after the bodies have gone cold and the scene's gone quiet, and someone's dropped a blanket over both corpses so all you can see are the pink feet, and that's enough to break them. She wasn't even there to see how it went down.

Sarabeth's eyes are very large and she says, "I think"—she gulps, she sniffles—"I think this is really nasty, whoever did this to you."

I don't nod to agree with her. I can't. I know this is only what I deserve.

"We can't go to the cast party like this, Vee," Sarabeth says, assuming I'm going and she's coming with. "It looks like we both got our periods at the same time."

It doesn't look like that at all. It looks like we committed a gruesome murder. And then decorated our bodies with the blood. It looks horrific.

"It's in your hair, Vee. Ick, it's in mine, too. We have to go shower and change. Let's go out the back way. I don't want my mom to see me like this—she'll freak. Why'd they write that on the card, anyways? Why'd they pretend to be her? Who'd be so mean?"

She waits for answers, like I'm some sort of psychology expert.

But this is not from the girls at the studio. I'd know Ori's handwriting anywhere.

I may have fooled the audience and my parents and Sarabeth and the admissions committee at Juilliard—I mean, how wowed were they by my audition? The ballet piece I prepared for them was the dance of the Firebird, from the Igor Stravinsky masterpiece, first performed in Paris in 1910, which had been Ori's solo those three years ago, which I'd learned from mirroring Ori, and which I'd forever know by heart.

But Ori wouldn't have been fooled for a second. She always did know me better than anyone else did. She didn't judge me, but she didn't shy away from me, either. She knew what I was and, still, for some unknown reason I'll be tossing over and over in my mind for my whole life, she stayed true to me, kept being my friend. I'm the one who turned away.

Like tonight. Ori would have seen through my once-white, now red-stained leotard and the white, now red-spattered froof of my tutu, to what's inside. Not the second leotard under the first one, but deeper, under my skin. The gross parts of the person I really am, the blood and guts, the ugliness, the slimy secrets, the liar I'm hiding in there, the true person I am, tangled up with the worms and rot.

NEVER AGAIN

THE DAY MY best friend got sent to prison, I was a hundred miles away, eating cheese.

That's all I like to eat on the day of an audition, for protein, for energy, and for luck. One piece of cheese in the morning. Another piece an hour before, to give it time to go down the tubes and digest, and a tiny piece minutes before, gobbled up so quick, I hardly bother chewing, so it gives me that last bump I need before going on. Cheese breath doesn't matter when your muscles are warm, your feet fast, and you dance like the star you are destined to be.

It was the first week of August, the summer I was fifteen. That was the same summer Ori spent in jail, the holding place where they kept her until she got sent to Aurora Hills. It was my first summer without her, when the hole in my life seemed too humongous to face by looking right at it, so

I didn't let myself look. I was at an audition. I was eating a hunk of cheese. I was lacing the ribbons of my pointe shoes, knotting them neat at the back and tucking the knot in. I was humming Stravinsky, and then when that got weird, I switched to Tchaikovsky. Her life was over that summer, but mine? Only just beginning.

I had my legs split, stomach pressed to floor, spine stretched as long as I could make it go. My arms were out, reaching. No one was on the other side, opposite me, to take my hands.

I closed my eyes and did the breathing thing, the one she taught me, where I visualized myself onstage in New York City, where else, with the roses at my feet, the roses at my feet the roses at my feet, until, finally, I was ready. I had my rituals, and I wasn't going to break them, even on the day she got shipped upstate.

That was what I heard someone call it: "upstate." Even though we already lived pretty far up. It was like she was being sent off to a work camp in Siberia—that was how far away it felt. Way too far to ever visit.

She should've been with me at the audition, slipping the bobby pins in my hair and then I'd do hers, wrinkling her nose when I took out my cheese. Then again, if she'd been at the audition and not headed to prison, she for sure would've gotten a role, and I for sure would've been passed over, told try again next year, and there'd have been no roses at my waiting feet.

I knew audition morning that it was the day they were announcing her sentencing. My parents made sure to tell me themselves. It was like they thought I'd feel better, knowing. Like I'd relax and sleep safer at night, knowing the exact number of days she'd be locked away.

No one needed to tell me it was the day. I was well aware already. I streamed it on my computer during morning pliés. I saw how they put her in orange, and perp-walked her away, and there were details the cameras caught like how she had more makeup on her left eye than her right, and I wondered if she ran out of mascara, and then I wondered if she even had mascara in jail and if not, what the gunk on her left eye could be. I also noticed that her thick, dark hair, which I kind of envied since it grew stick-straight from her head and didn't frizz, looked now like it was thinning and bits of her scalp peeked through. I wondered if it was possible to start going bald at fifteen, like from stress.

Also, she seemed kind of pale. It could've been the cameras, or the orange of her outfit glaring against her skin, but she was usually nice and brown, never needing to lie out for a suntan, and now it was high summer and she looked like a ghoul. The Ori I knew, the Ori everyone knew, or used to know, was the kind of girl who seemed sure of herself no matter how she looked. She never cared as much as I did. She'd come away from sweating buckets in advanced ballet, and she'd be all glowy and dewy and full of life like this was a tampon commercial, when all I wanted was to dunk my head in a cold sink of water and hug my knees till the shakes stopped.

But watching her there, live-streaming on the news, I was struck by what was missing. She was just putting one foot in front of the other, and barely. Her ankles were in chains, her arms behind her back. She was stringy-haired and wonky-eyed and alarmingly gray.

The news lady was talking about the details of the crime. I put her on mute.

I only wanted to see Ori. Now she was pushed through a door, and she didn't look back once, and the door closed behind her, and the camera held on the shut door like we were in some kind of European film, and then the camera swiveled and swooped in on the crowd, going in close on the victims' mothers, and I shut off the picture. I finished my last set of pliés.

At the audition I sat alone, apart from the other girls, and snarfed down the cheese from my bag. Then I stood up and shook out my limbs and cracked my neck and cracked my knuckles and tried not to think of her, didn't let myself think of her, got my number called, took my spot, didn't think of her, did the combination, did it spot-on, did it with every step precise, didn't think of her. Didn't think of anything. Didn't even feel my own feet, which was a miracle, because I had a pretty outrageous blister.

I got the part, obviously. Only a role in the corps, where you have to move exactly the same as everyone else and dance background, the lowest you can go in ballet unless you're on crew, carting around the scenery.

They said I got it because I had solid technique. I had the right body. I had decent feet. My extension was fine, my training up to level. I had a lot of potential. I had a future, if I wanted it and worked for it.

They didn't say they were overtaken by my performance,

that I took their breath away, made their hearts skip a beat, that I was unforgettable, astonishing even. If Ori had danced for them, those are things they might have said, once they got their breath back.

Still, I got the part. And I got it because after my best friend was sent away to the Aurora Hills Secure Juvenile Detention Center in wherever-it-was-I-needed-to-look-at-a-map upstate, my luck kind of changed. My life started looking up. Everything I did was something she wouldn't get to do, so I'd have to do it one better. I'd have to be her, in a way, because it wasn't like she could be herself anymore. I didn't have her natural talent, her spark. But I was *good*. And people started taking notice.

I couldn't help but think that by the time Ori got out, she'd be way too old and it would be way too late. She wouldn't dance on a stage again, ever.

Days passed after the audition, and after Ori was sentenced and sent to Aurora Hills, and I made a whole list of nevers in my head: Never again would Ori build a blanket fort with me. And never again would we hide under the blanket fort like little kids. Never again would Ori paint my toenails purple to match a purple bruise. Never again would Ori do one-bite, my-bite, two-bite, your-bite with a bowl of Cheerios. Never again would I catch Ori doing the sweet things she sometimes did for perfect strangers, and make fun of her for them, like holding doors for slow, decrepit randoms and looking all over the neighborhood for that whiny brat's overweight dog. Never again would Ori step on a stage and wow an audience to tears. Never again would Ori shake her head and get embarrassed when they said how perfect she was. How incredible. How stunning. How transcendent. *Transcendent*—they actually used that word. Never again would she ask me to please stop talking about it, and never again would I say, "Did you see how they looked at you? It's like you're the next Anna Pavlova." Never again would she ask me, hours later, timid and shaky voiced, "Vee, you're not feeling weird about what they said about me, are you? You'd tell me, wouldn't you?" And never again would I have to lie through my straight teeth—hers were crooked, she really should have gotten braces—and say, "I'm okay—don't worry about me. I'm fine." Never again.

I did plan to visit her up there, *someday*. And I did plan to write her back, *sometime*. I was thinking about what I'd say to her, since my attorney pulled me away after and told me not to speak a word to her, not just about the charges, but about anything at all.

I knew we'd have a chance to talk one day. We had to. But I guess I wasn't done with the never agains.

Because never again would Ori see me, and never would I see Ori. We wouldn't get to exchange a hello or good-bye or d'you want a piece of cheese or I like your leotard can I borrow it ever again. I wouldn't get to look into her eyes and see if she hated me. If she deep down despised me. If she dreamed of getting out and murdering me with an ax or a gun point-blank at my temple, or if she'd choose to shoot me in the back like cowards in old Westerns got to make someone die. If she dreamed of doing to me what I woke up, sweating, flailing, heart pounding, dreaming she'd already done.

The worst was this: Never again would I get to see Ori alive.

I will always remember where I was the day she got sent to Aurora Hills—the audition, doing my cheese ritual, snagging that role in the corps—but I don't know where I was when she, and all those other girls with her, died. I wouldn't have been back in school yet, because it was still August. Probably I was at the ballet studio, because where else would I have been, testing out the limits of my body, as I liked to when I had the studio to myself, trying to perfect a step, or get my leaps to go even higher or my split to go down even farther, or trying for a triple pirouette because I hadn't mastered that yet, but soon I would.

Our ballet studio's spring showcase had been postponed that year, as anyone would have expected after losing three featured dancers in the cast, but when I took the stage at some point that summer as the Firebird, the role that had originally been hers, I was better than anyone expected. My costume wasn't as elaborate as hers had been, but I was enchanting, I heard someone say. Unforgettable.

I could have been doing any number of ordinary things the day she died: Taking my second or third shower of the day. Breaking in a new pair of pointe shoes. Watching old Bolshoi performances on YouTube. Sitting through another meal with my parents, then going up to the barre installed in my suite to work it off after. Draining my toe blisters. Cleaning my room.

All I know is that I wasn't thinking of her. I kept myself busy to make sure.

My mother and father were the ones who gave me the news, together, one weekend on the white couch in the living room even though we didn't ever sit on that couch, or go in that room, unless we had the excuse of company. I heard odd phrases, confusing patches of sentences that didn't connect to anything, so I had to piece the whole truth together later, from a few choice Google searches.

". . . mass poisoning . . . ," my father said.

". . . the lord works in mysterious ways . . . ," my mother said.

". . . I'm sure there was quite a lot of vomiting. Honey, do you need some water?"

". . . right near the Falls, such lovely wine country . . ."

". . . why, yes, dear, some of them were gangerbangers, or is it gangbangers?"

". . . forty-two dead . . ."

". . . forty-two girls . . ."

". . . suicide pact, you'd expect . . ."

". . . no one knows for sure . . ."

". . . how about some pâté for lunch?" That last bit was my mother.

And because I didn't see it for myself, I don't think I let myself believe. She was in that place not even a month. She couldn't be gone for good. I still hadn't come to visit.

I turned sixteen that fall after Ori died, and that was the year I danced the part of Odette in our school's showcase at the community theater. And I felt fine. I turned seventeen, the following fall, and danced the part of Giselle, which would have been a feat if Jon hadn't dropped me during our pas de deux and the audience hushed to a deadening silence, and I tried not to think how that's what she hears, now, every day. I still felt fine. I turned eighteen. She'd never get to. I felt fine. I auditioned for two summer intensives, and for a few repertory companies, to be a trainee, had some hiccups, some bad luck, some morons not letting me in, but then I saw the call for Juilliard auditions.

The school was known for not just ballet but contemporary, which made my coach say it wasn't the ideal fit, but there was something that spoke to me. Ori, maybe. Ori's eyes I was seeing through. So I tried to channel her, I tried to *be* her on the dance floor, I expanded my practice hours, I doubled up on my cubes of cheese.

Even though I hadn't danced the role of the Firebird since I was fifteen, that was what I chose to embody for the solo I prepared for the Juilliard audition. I danced what haunted me. I owed her this acknowledgment. Whenever I practiced it, in the studio or at home, with my coach adjusting me or all alone in the mirror, I felt her there with me, shadowing my every move. I felt her inside me sometimes. She breathed when I breathed. Her body stretched when mine stretched. I felt the blisters on her toes pop when mine popped.

When I got in, it's like we both got in. The months went on. Had a little scare with Achilles tendinitis, but I got over it, it wasn't so bad, I felt fine. Started hooking up with Jon, dumped him, felt fine, ended up with Tommy, who didn't even study ballet, which was fine. Let Sarabeth from our ballet studio hang around. Let her think we were best friends. Graduated high school. GPA: perfectly fine. Summer started, my last summer at home. Knew I'd get around to dumping Tommy sooner or later. Let life happen, I guess, and in between, practiced at the barre every day, looked in the mirror every day to see if I looked okay, if I looked fine.

Because what's inside is getting harder to hide.

After my standing ovation and the bouquet full of blood that had me and Sarabeth sneaking out of the theater and going back to my house to change before the cast party, I find myself doing it again. Looking. I've washed my face for the third time and lifted up my neck, dripping, to study myself in the mirror. At first I look decent. Wet, but fine. Then I see it. There's a speck of red I didn't catch, a droplet of fake blood on my earlobe. I wipe it off and take a taste of my finger. Like candy.

Sarabeth hovers in the doorway. "Vee? D'you have any clothes I could borrow?"

"You can wear whatever's in the tall dresser, or what's on the left side of the closet. That's the stuff I'm not taking with me."

She waits. It's like she's afraid or something.

"And just go ahead and keep it," I say. "Whatever it is."

"Really? You sure?"

"Keep whatever you want." I'm never coming back, I feel it.

Her face creases. "Okay. I don't know what'll fit me, but okay."

She drifts out of sight, and then I look again in the mirror to see if the guilt is written all over my face. No matter how many times I wash it, I keep seeing red.

"We're not going to the cast party, are we?" she calls.

"Nah," I say, even though I know my parents are there,

my coaches are there, Miss Willow, who's been my instructor all these years, is there. My mother's called twice already, and I'm waiting for her to call again.

I wash my face one more time. When I come out of the bathroom, Sarabeth's been digging in my closet and has a take-pile started on the floor. It happens in slow motion, when she reaches up to remove a shirt from a hanger and the sleeve gets caught on the shelf above. She gives a tug, and that's the jolt that does it.

It drops from the heights of the walk-in closet directly onto me, its sharp, pointy end striking me between the eyes, dead on, like there's some red-circled target on me I wasn't able to wash off with soap.

I'm down, now, on the carpeted floor of the walk-in closet, on my knees, the gaudy red costume feather crushed in my hand, and I see another trace of her, though I was so sure I'd gotten rid of them all. But there, lined up with all the old pairs of pointe shoes I'd crashed through, worn out, grown out of, broken a little, broken clean in half, got bored of, spilled cola on, their shredded toes, their blackened bottoms, their scraggly ribbons, there. A pair of hers I missed. I know they're hers because of the initials marked on the inside of the satin sheath: Not VAD, for Violet Allegra Dumont. I always use my middle initial so no one can say I have VD on my toe shoes. Ori copied me and used hers, too. OCS. That's what it says on the satin. O for Orianna. C for Catherine. S for Speerling. Blood pulsing in my arms. Blood pounding in my head.

I remove a shoe and hold it. The box has been softened to mush, the ribbons are frayed, and the satin on the bottom of the toe, where it touches floor, is peeled open. It smells dreadful, like it's been rotting six feet underground for years.

The shank, the hard bottom piece that runs along the sole, has been cut three-quarters of the way down with a box cutter to give the shoes new life after the shanks got broken from dancing, which happens. Ori and I read about this shanking method online, how real-life ballerinas adjust their shoes so they can use them for longer. Ori didn't have the money to keep buying new pairs, and she felt funny when I tricked my parents into paying for hers, so we'd make these adjustments. She'd hold the shoe steady for the operation. I'd slice.

And it's the cut that sends me back. I can see the ridge, the line we made with the Sharpie, the deep carving. I can remember the feel of the box cutter in my hand. We were in the studio's dressing room, the two of us in a corner, and the others, a whole group of them, were hissing and laughing across the way.

I made a deep, straight cut, and I wanted to ask her, *Why are you here, with me? Why aren't you with them, over there?*

I sliced too hard, with too much force, and nipped my finger. She wrapped a tourniquet of tissue around my injured hand, and a drop of my blood got on her tights. The tiniest fleck.

But that was later, closer to the end.

She could have chosen anybody. But I had nobody in the beginning, and she wanted somebody even if she didn't know it. The moment was cemented one evening, early on in our ballet training, when no one came to pick her up when class was over. My mother was inside, discussing making a donation to the dance studio, as she would begin to do each year, and she'd told me to wait out front, in the car. Instead, I'd gone wandering.

That was when I spotted the girl from class: the one with the very, very long hair, like no one ever took her to get it cut at a salon, and her funny, made-up-sounding name, Orianna, like two names squashed together. We got to talking. We were about eight years old then, I'd say. Even then, I had ideas.

"I'm gonna be a prima ballerina someday," I told her. It was something I used to tell everyone back then, until it became so obvious, years later, and everyone started telling me.

"You will," she said. She didn't announce that she was, too.

"I'm gonna be famous. I write it down every night, so in the morning it knows to come true."

"That's a good idea," she said.

"What about you?"

She looked at me oddly, and now it hangs heavy over me, like even then she knew she had no future. "I don't know yet," was all she said.

She checked the parking lot again. No cars were slowing on the road.

"He's not coming," she said. "Probably he forgot."

"C'mon," I said, and I took her hand. I had no siblings, no close friends at school, no one I touched like this before, apart from my parents when they used to make me hold on to them when crossing a street.

Her palm was thin and felt so soft. Her skin was cool, like she never got sweaty. She let me pull for a moment, and didn't stand up, so I thought she wouldn't come with me, and I was about to let go. Then she stood and my hand was in her hand and we went running. A brown car shrieked over the curb, coming to a hard stop right before us and almost clipping our legs, ending our dance careers before they even got started. It wasn't her dad. The driver honked at us, blasting his horn and yelling out the window. What were we trying to do, kill ourselves and everyone around us? But we were children then, and we were just figuring out how to live. The car finished its U-turn and headed back for the road. I laughed. I believed in writing down my future, but I didn't know to keep an eye on hers.

I led my new friend to my mom's car, and I opened the door and showed her the backseat. "Come on," I said. "Get in."

I still wonder what would have happened if that car had hit us, or if her dad had showed up on time, or if she hadn't climbed into the backseat and we hadn't ended up taking her home.

Now she's gone. I'm in my bedroom with Sarabeth ten years later, and I turn and I swear, it's like Ori's back in the room, lounging out on my bed behind me, a waterfall of dark pin-straight hair, muscled legs, and blazing toe blisters. The awareness of her is back. The loss of her is back. The heavy weight of what was done, too, is back, in my bed, and I'll have to sleep with it every night until I do something and face what I've done.

I never visited her, never had the chance. Ask me and that's what I'll say to the question. The truth is, even if I'd had the chance, even if there hadn't been that freak accident or suicide pact or bad batch of dinner in the cafeteria that of-fed the whole population less than a month after she got put away, I'm not sure I would've gone to visit her behind bars.

What would I have said?

What would it have looked like, that reunion?

I heard about Aurora Hills. It's closed now. Vandals have had their way with it—I read that somewhere online. Graffiti and broken windows and fires set in the hallways.

People who knew the girl prisoners who died are drawn to the gate outside Aurora Hills, down at the bottom of the hill. There was a photo on some website—that's how I know. Family members go there, friends. Sometimes the curious, or a morbid freak who gets hot off the idea of all those dead girls. It's August now, the third summer, and soon, people will be gathering to remember. I have an urge that's sudden. I want to get up there before the families do, before the candles and the singing and the prayers, before the anniversary, before August 30. Before I leave for New York City. I can see it now. In that pile of rotting stuffed-bear corpses I saw online, bow-tied bears and fairy bears and chubster bears and puny baby bears, the runts no one wanted. At the gate with the bears and the cards poorly drawn by children at some demented elementary school, and the flowers, the mass grave of rotting flowers, yeah, down somewhere in all that, dug in deep, I might have to leave a little something.

There's nowhere else to do it—she wasn't buried in a cemetery, so there's no grave to visit. Her dad had her cre-mated, right before he moved away.

Sarabeth is hovering over me, bug-eyed. I barely have to turn to let her know I'm speaking to her now. "You up for a little road trip?"

"How long a drive? I get carsick . . . Can I pick the music?" she starts, but then she gets it. My hand has come open and the bright, crimson-dyed feather is visible on my palm. Does she remember? I do.

It's from the headpiece of the Firebird costume, the last costume Ori ever wore, and the last connecting link between her and me. Ori's telling me it's not something I'll be able to put away and forget, like I tried to do with her. Never again, she's saying. Never again.

THE HOLE IN THE FENCE

IT'S THE NEXT day, and I get Tommy to drive.
He'll be over soon.

Sarabeth assures me she's coming, even though she gets
carsick and I won't let her pick the music, and we have to
wait to leave until after she gets off work. Then she wants
to borrow a sweater because she's cold, constantly, even in
summer, and I tell her to see what's left in the tall dresser.
Then we have to make up a story for my parents, and it's
already afternoon by the time we go downstairs to meet
Tommy, who's parked outside but doesn't want to come in
for some reason he won't say.

Sarabeth and I head down and spot his car at the curb,
but it's empty. We find him in the rock garden, directly below my bedroom, like he's keeping tabs on me. He's not
alone.

Tommy's leaning against the lattice and kind of gives me a nod when I approach, which isn't his usual. Maybe I should've texted him back after the showcase last night. But the shape lurking in the shadows behind Tommy is what makes me grab for a hold of the wall to steady myself. I can't let them see that, though, so I act like I've got an itch on my ankle.

I scratch a few times and straighten up. "Miles," I say, nodding.

Just look who it is. Ori's Miles, the one and only, all in black, surprise, and sporting his usual cowlick like he doesn't own a hairbrush to his name. Years have passed since I last had to look at him, and he seems taller now, scowlier.

He nods back, doesn't meet my eyes. No hello. I look between Miles and Tommy, Tommy and Miles. What, they're buddies now? Where Tommy goes, Miles goes, too?

Tommy won't meet my eyes. His gaze holds steady on my feet. It's summer and I'm in sandals, though my toes are completely covered. He knows I hate when he looks too closely at my feet. His ball cap is on backward, begging for an adjustment, and there's something like moss growing on his cheeks, which I realize, with dull horror, is his attempt at growing a beard. Ballet dancers never have beards.

"Hi, Tommy! Hi, Miles. I didn't know you were coming!" Sarabeth says, ever oblivious.

"Tommy?" I want his explanation. I want him to tell me why he's brought that kid here to my property tonight, letting him tag along on our drive up to the prison, which is my personal expedition and nothing to do with anybody else, apart from Tommy being the one to drive because I already sold my car and Sarabeth can't use her parents' SUV. I told him it was private. None of his business. And his response was to invite Ori's ex?

Tommy pulls me aside against the lattice, so we can have a moment alone.

I think he's going to stutter out an apology maybe, try to explain. But no. He gives me a kiss, and I wonder if it's hit him yet, that I have so many important things all about to start happening for me, and I'm not going to spend any time looking backward. Does he get that? There are things he doesn't ask of me, ever: Like, *Are we breaking up or what?* Or even, *Hey, weren't you best friends with a convicted murderer, and weren't you a witness on the case, and didn't she die in some bizarre poisoning, and now, suddenly, you want to go visit the scene of the accident—and, hey, what's up with that?*

Nothing. The boy has asked me nothing.

I give him a little shove so he gets his scratchy face away from mine. "What is *he* doing here?" Out of the corner of my eye, I notice Sarabeth smiling and attempting to make small talk with Miles, and I'll have to set her straight on who we're speaking to later.

"I asked him to come," Tommy says.

"Why," I say dully.

"He knows how to find the place. He's been up there before, you know."

"There's GPS in your phone."

Tommy gets defensive. You'd think his loyalties are all with Miles instead of with me. Miles wants to see her, too, Tommy goes, and I'm like, we're not *seeing* anybody, she's not there to see. Then he's like, doesn't Miles deserve to come, because *he* wrote her letters, and *he* even visited her up there, one time with his stepdad, before she died, and I never got on her visiting list, did I? This is the most Tommy has ever said on the subject of Orianna Speerling, who he didn't even know when she was alive. I had no idea he had this much information.

I zip my mouth, keep it in. "Fine, Tommy. Let's just go, then."

I snap my fingers at Sarabeth, causing her to step on a rock sideways and flail and fumble, the graceful thing that she is.

Miles smirks. He heads for the curb, opening the garden gate without having to search around for the hidden latch first, because he knows where it's hiding. He used to come here all the time, but never to see me.

Maybe that was when things shifted, between Ori and me. She got with Miles, for no good reason I could put a finger on, and she wasn't always around like she'd been before him.

Ori used to peek out the window and communicate with him—they had a set of hand signals, ones she never shared with me—and then she'd turn to me, in my bedroom, and she'd say, "Miles just wants to talk. I'm going down for a few minutes." At some point between slipping on a pair of shoes and finding a hoodie, she'd pause. Then she'd have to say it, because this was my house. "Want to come with?" Of course I never wanted to go down there and watch her make out with him on my patio furniture. "Nah," I'd say. "Go. I'll be fine."

She'd tiptoe back up my staircase after I stopped waiting

for her. She'd slip in under the covers, because by then I'd be in bed, making my breaths even so it seemed like I was asleep. She'd whisper my name, but it'd be a quiet whisper, halfhearted. She'd sigh. She'd flop over a few times on the mattress, shuffle the pillows, try to get comfortable. Then she'd sigh again, and I'd hear it, I couldn't *not* hear it, it would fill up the room in the dark night: the contented sigh of her happiness. I kept my eyes closed.

"Let's go," I say. We all head for Tommy's ridiculous green car, with the too-big tires and the white racing stripe. Before I can call out a claim for it, Miles is taking shotgun and I have to squeeze in the tight backseat with Sarabeth, who's reminding us she might get a little queasy and it's no big deal, but if she asks Tommy to pull over, that's why.

Miles sits face-forward, playing with his phone. That was how I found out about him and Ori in the first place— those text messages he was sending and the messages she was sending back. She was trying to hide it from me, as if I wouldn't like it. She was right.

"You good up there?" I call out to Miles. "Got enough room to stretch your legs?" The driver's seat is wedged into my knees, so I sure don't.

Miles doesn't respond. He doesn't need to. The seething hatred coming off him is so strong, I half expect the windows to fog over, frogs to rain down, a crack to open up in the cul-de-sac and take me. And maybe after that a tornado.

As we start moving, I feel, distantly, a spot of warmth on my body. I realize it's Sarabeth's hand. She is patting my arm. I think she's trying to comfort me.

It brings me back.

Not to any warm and shimmering memory between me and Sarabeth—she's nothing to me. More to a warm hand on my shoulder. Two warm hands. If Ori were here, she'd tell me to ignore him. She'd shove her head between the two front seats and demand that he be nice to me. Why? Because she said.

Then again, the thought of Ori being here and not nowhere, which is where she is, makes my conscience rumble.

She didn't like it when people were mean to me. Way back when we were girls, she could have slipped into any of the cliques at our dance studio and stalked off, smiling. It could have been Harmony, Rachel, and Orianna. Or Harmony and Orianna, with Rachel kicked to the curb, and maybe Harmony would have been the one to start calling her Ori. I wouldn't have known her, apart from having to stand next to her at the barre to do demonstrations, or sometimes sharing the floor during a group combination and avoiding her kicks to the shins. But she chose me and only me—maybe because she saw no one else had.

She had a way of seeking out the weirdo, like she wanted to be some kind of protector. The outcast no one else was conversing with, she'd go over and sit next to, make it less awkward for everyone, help that freak feel less alone. Look at Miles. He was a nobody she plucked from nothingness.

I glare at him in the passenger seat, narrow my eyes, thinking this. Until the thought about-faces and I realize what it might say: Out of everyone Ori could have been friends with, charity cases and otherwise, she zeroed in on me.

The drive isn't so long. The way I've acted, anyone

would've thought the detention center was days and days away, practically in another country. It's up north near Lake Ontario and the Canadian border, sure, but we don't live so far from the border ourselves. At most, if Tommy follows the speed limit, the drive is three hours, a day trip closer than Niagara Falls.

"You shouldn't be wearing that," Miles says, from out of nowhere. These are the first words he's spoken in nearly an hour, since we left my cul-de-sac and hit I-90. His words aren't aimed at me but at Sarabeth, who he must know from school, since they both go to public.

She turns crimson. It's what she does at the slightest push. When we're doing barre work and Miss Willow adjusts Sarabeth's arms or makes a microscopic correction to her turnout, Sarabeth's cheeks flame. Her freckles pop like blood spatter. The only things not reddened on her whole body will be her hands, her feet, and the very tip of her nose. It's here I remember, randomly, for the first time in forever, that I used to call her Rooster, though Ori didn't seem to like when I did.

"What, why?" Sarabeth says. "What's wrong with what I'm wearing?"

I get it before she does. Miles only means the sweater she has on, borrowed from my room. It's striped and has a hood. Orange stripes, yellow stripes, blue stripes, green stripes. A black stripe here and there. It was a revolting number of colors to wear at once, and of course it wasn't mine. It was Ori's. Another thing of hers still mingled with the stuff in my room.

Miles would remember that sweater. He'd remember

Ori in it. He did seem like the kind of boyfriend who paid attention.

"He means your sweater," I tell Sarabeth.

"Oh," she says. "It's not mine. It's Vee's."

Miles's gaze lifts to my face. This is the first time he's met my eyes. "It's not yours. It's hers. Did you steal it from her before or after you got her sent to prison?"

I'm thrown for a loop, but then Tommy blasts the horn like there's a deer in the road, except there is no deer, there's only me now, Ori's not coming back, she's never coming back, she's gone.

And Miles is right. I did do that.

"Who cares whose shirt is whose!" Tommy shouts. "Miles, is this the exit?" And this draws Miles's attention back to the highway, to where we're headed, to the gate, the shrine for the girls who never got out.

I need to see it for myself, before I move on. I know we won't be able to get near the building where she was held—there are gates and chains and everything's all locked up, and we're not trespassing and getting ourselves arrested, because I've got Juilliard in a week. But maybe we'll see a guard tower. Some barbed wire. Something connected to her. Something.

Will that be enough?

We exit the first highway for a second highway, then finally swerve off all highways onto a wooded, increasingly narrow road. The place isn't at all familiar, but it's also everything I thought it would be. There are bumps and pits in the badly paved road, so my stomach lurches up to my throat, and Sarabeth hangs her head to her knees, saying she's queasy. We're going up and up, on a steady incline, but too many trees are in the way to see where. The sky is smaller above us, as the trees close in, and then the sky is cut out completely. We're close.

I get a chill. I almost want to ask for the sweater back. Other than that, I feel nothing.

We pass an old street sign, bent over and shrouded in hanging leaves. It says:

PRISON AREA

DO NOT PICK UP HITCHHIKERS

I still feel nothing.

Miles is the one who tells us where to stop before the gate is even in sight. He really has been here before. Tommy's not sure where to park his car. He's so precious about the paint job and doesn't want any passing cars to swipe it, but it's not like there's a parking lot here to welcome visitors. It's not like there's valet service.

Soon I'm standing in the backwoods on a one-lane road before the entrance to the girls' detention center. In one hand is a bouquet of drooping carnations that we bought at a supermarket on the way over, and in the other hand, clutched in my fist, is the feather from Ori's last-ever costume. Something tells me she wants me to leave it here.

She'll see it, somehow, this gesture I'm making. She's looking down from high up on that hill, and she'll understand. She'll see it and she'll let go. Of me. And we'll move on, to our two different futures. Mine involves the sparkle and lights of the city, and Juilliard, and the big stage, and fame and recognition and everything I've ever wanted. Hers involves eternity in a dark hole.

I approach the pathetic-looking shrine at the closed and chained gate. I appreciate that they stay back, letting me have my moment. We haven't seen one other car since making the turn at the first old sign that said AURORA HILLS DETENTION CENTER, 11 MILES. There are no mourners here. No tourists. No rubberneckers. No one to sideswipe Tommy's car.

There are the four of us and all those stuffed animals at the gate.

I go in close, crouch down on my knees. There are dry candles. None are lit. The pile of filthy teddy bears I saw in the photos online is still there. There are other things, too. A blue dolphin. A baby doll with a hard, plastic head and a soft, plush body. Her parts are all black with decay, and one leg has rotted all the way off.

There is a music box. The whirling ballerina inside is the size of the ones on my charm bracelet my parents got me, that bracelet Ori always loved, the one I still wear most every day, and when I open the box, it starts to spin; it starts its song, its dance. But this music-box ballerina is made of plastic and breaks off easily in my fingers. The box still sings and spins, but now there's no one to do the dancing. I palm the ballerina and slip it into my jeans pocket.

I start to read the cards, the ones that aren't too weathered. The three of them stand behind me, probably noticing what catches my attention, what I touch and don't touch, what I step on, squash, drop on the ground. I wish they'd leave me alone. There's something about being here that makes me want to be alone.

Off to the side, wedged into the iron grate, is a water-warped piece of paper. It's not colorful. The handwriting is small, contained, penned by an adult. When I get close, I can make out some of the words: *despicable, garbage, you monsters*. And I wonder who drove all the way up here to leave this piece of hate mail for the dead.

I close my eyes and do the breathing thing. I tell myself to think of New York. A gnat-size voice inside me wonders if I'd be headed to the city if Ori had never been sent here or—better? Worse?—if she'd been found innocent of all charges.

Then I hear him. Miles. "You know the way in is right over there? A hole in the fence. The prison is up that hill. It's not so far."

"No. Way," Tommy says, his voice booming. He's faking surprise. He knew.

"Wait, wait," Sarabeth says, because no one ever tells her anything. "I thought we were just stopping here to leave the flowers. We're going in?" She lowers her cell phone in the midst of taking a photo.

"You want to drive all the way up here, see some gate, then turn around and go home?" Tommy says. "Miles is saying there's a way up. So we're going up."

"There's a way," Miles mumbles. "I've done it before."

"But it'll be dark soon," Sarabeth says.

She turns to me. It's late afternoon now, creeping on into evening, since we had to wait forever for her to get off work.

"Then we'll take flashlights," Tommy says, like she's slow. "Doubt we'll need 'em."

"But it's illegal," Sarabeth goes, mostly to herself, because they're not even listening.

Tommy runs back to his car to dig in the trunk for flashlights. He finds only one and says the rest of us will have to use the light of our phones. He even has a few cans of spray paint, purchased, I assume, right before he came to pick us up.

Miles has turned all his attention to me. His eyes are as black as mud, his hair sticks up without a care, and his mouth is a small sneer, taunting me, twitching.

"Vee?" Sarabeth says from somewhere behind me. "Violet? Hey. Uh, are we really going up there? Do you think maybe I could wait in the car?"

I ignore her. We all do.

Miles has been close to Ori, and I haven't. He's been up there, and I haven't. He's seen what she's seen. He knows too many things I don't know.

And then I'm remembering things. More things. Like the things they had, between the two of them, together. That time she told me she slept with him in his parents' basement and how momentous it was and how he held her after. And I guess I was supposed to coo and say, "Aw," but I couldn't. Because why did everything come so easily for her but was such an effort for me? She barely practiced outside of class. She had the most perfect, flexible dancer's feet, and she didn't do strengthening exercises to work her ankles and metatarsals like I did. She didn't sleep in her pointe shoes to mold her arches—they were just built like that. She had a boyfriend, and he maybe even loved her.

"What?" she said, after she told me about Miles and I still hadn't said a word. "You don't think we should've waited, do you?"

"I can't tell you what to do. You always do what you want. When's the last time you thought about me first?"

It was a weird question, one she'd get a chance to answer for me later.

Now here's Miles, black eyes blazing and hands in knuckled fists, daring me to go up that hill like he knows something I don't.

"You coming?" he says. He doesn't ask Sarabeth, he doesn't ask Tommy. The person he's asking is me.

So am I? Will I go see where she lived her last days and ate her last poisoned meal and retched her last retch? Do I have the stomach for it? Do I have the strength? Do I have the heart? Which is funny, the kind of funny that's actually sad, because that was the last thing Ori said to me, in the courtroom. It was what she hissed at me when she was dragged past me by the court officers, with her face dripping snot, and a fury in her eyes I'd never seen before. These were her last words to me:

"You know what you did, Vee. Do you even have a heart?"

I do. I swear I do. Just show me the hole in the fence.

PUSH

IT LOOMS UP there. The place is so much bigger than I thought.

By the time we've climbed the hill, pushing through undergrowth and fallen razor wire and thorny sections of weeds to find ourselves in sight of the giant, gray stone structure that was shut down three summers ago by the state, we're panting. Our hearts are racing. Even mine, and I should have the stamina for a hike like this.

Miles takes charge at a section of fencing that's been knocked over. If we go through here, then weave back the other way and duck under there, he tells us, we can get in.

"It looks dangerous," I distantly hear Sarabeth protest as she points out a sign that says the fence is electric.

"The power's off to the whole place," Miles says. "They shut it down years ago. You're not going to fry."

Sarabeth squeaks.

Miles looks to me. I nod and take a step. I'm not getting stopped by a dead electric fence.

Tommy turns to me in surprise. "You didn't tell me she was in maximum security!"

"She killed two people. What do you expect?" I feel my mouth say. It almost hurts to say it, and hurts more to hear it. The patch of sky above us darkens, like a storm passing over our heads.

The way Miles glowers at me it's like, give him a rock from the ground at his feet or one of those cans of spray paint or any other object nearby that could be used as a weapon, and the body count will soon reach three. Four, his eyes correct me, if we're honest and include Ori.

I give him my back and head for the next fence.

The place looks like something from deep in the last century. The guards' towers are empty now, but they're menacing all the same, their watching eyes trained on us. The walls of the prison are gray. The trees are far away, kept back with gravel lots and layers of fencing. Just as far away is any sense of escape. The place looks like a fortress.

They used to lock up kids here, girls, I heard, as young as thirteen. I can't make sense of it. A flash of Ori comes at me. It's her ghost now looming in the gravel, one hand on the far fence, the way she was when I last saw her, at fifteen going on sixteen. But no, it's not the Ori I knew. It's an Ori I never knew. The Ori I made her into.

She wears a blazing orange outfit that hurts my eyes. The sinking afternoon sun is brighter than it was before, making her glow like a lit lantern. Her hair is greasy, parted crooked, stuffed sloppily behind her ears. She holds—it doesn't make sense, but it's what I see—a shovel. Wooden handle in her grip. The scoop propped in the dirt at her feet like she's been digging.

What is she trying to tell me? Her other hand opens, palm out, facing me. It presses against the fence. She might be waving me closer.

Is this happening? I think it is.

I take a step forward, and because I have my eyes on her, I don't see it and fall in.

There's a small ditch in the ground, and I've stumbled into it and rolled my ankle.

Miles laughs, and Tommy laughs with him at first, then sees my face and shuts up. He gives me his arm, to help me out, but I don't need him or anyone. I stretch out my ankle, massaging the tendon, and put some weight on my foot to make sure it's fine. It is. I'm fine.

When I look back at the far fence, of course that flash of her is gone. I don't ask if they saw it, too. They didn't. They couldn't. Not even Miles could.

"Let's go in," he says. He wants to prove something to me, like standing inside those walls will change me more than it can out here.

I don't need him to egg me on. I'm getting this tug, this desire to get closer. I'm finding all these questions, and they're wanting answers. What would it be like to walk through those heavy doors at the front and hear them slam shut behind you? What would it be like under that roof, inside those walls? Was it freezing cold? Did you get issued a sweater? Or were you sweaty all the time? How did you

sleep, did you get a pillow, were the beds long enough to
stretch out your legs, and did the guards shout at you to get
up in the morning, or did you have an alarm clock, could
you sleep in ever, like on Saturdays, or was every day the
same when you were jailed?

I hadn't let myself think this far before. Now I was wondering a whole ton of things. Underbelly things. Ignorant
things. Like, were there strip searches and did you have to
get naked and were there shower rapes, and if so, what did a
girl use to rape another girl? Were there riots and big, burly
guards beating prisoners with sticks? Or did they have stun
guns, and what did that feel like, getting stunned? I bet
there were whole new laws of civilization inside that you
had to follow. If you were white, did you have to join a
white gang, and if you were black, did you have to join a
black gang? And what gang was there to join if you were
neither, or if you were half one thing and half another, like
Ori was? It's not like I could ever have asked any of those
questions out loud, then or now.

Other things come at me, too. Because what would you
do if you were almost about to turn sixteen, and fresh off
the trial, the trial during which you refused to speak one
word on the stand, not even coming to your own defense
as a witness—that never made any sense to me, but I guess
Ori had her reasons—and you walked in this door we just
walked through and you stared down that hall we're staring
down now and then you realize? You realize. This is home
now.

It's dark, and smells rank, and there's water dripping
from somewhere, this endless constant leak, and there's

glass on the ground, and this uneven, shifting cold making it so that one second you're wet with humidity and the
next you're shivering. Everything is broken. Busted doors,
shattered windows. The walls are painted over with graffiti
splotches, and it looks like it's been this way for a few years.
But I know the hallway we're standing in looked like something else entirely, when she was here.

Sarabeth and Miles and Tommy, they're around somewhere, but I don't care. I'm trying to relive it, trying to walk
her walk, wear her shoes or whatever, but there's nothing I
can do to put myself in her place. Not anymore.

If I'd been on trial, I wouldn't have ended up here. My
parents wouldn't have let it happen. But no one fought for
Orianna Catherine Speerling.

I'm thinking about that now. I'm thinking a lot about
it. She had a patch of wildflowers and weeds somewhere in
the back of her house, and she liked to dig in it. She often
had dirty knees when my mother picked her up for ballet. A
few times Ori brought my parents fresh-picked bouquets to
put out in the foyer, but they were scraggly and too brightly
colored for my mother, so she'd let the flowers die in a dry
vase and then ditch them after a day. A nice gesture, my
mom would say in the voice that said she didn't think it was
so nice at all, seeing as we were feeding Ori breakfast and
dinner four, five times a week, which meant we were basically raising her.

Ori didn't know my mom said any of that. She only
knew the flowers were gone, and so she'd bring along more
next time she came over. I didn't care what my mother said

when Ori wasn't around. "You can stay over anytime," I told her, and I meant it more for me than for her. My suite of rooms upstairs was less lonely when she slept over.

So she had me then. But without me, once I turned my back on her, because my attorney said I had to, she had practically nobody.

Miles is up ahead. He seems to know his way around. "This way," he says. "Over here."

Tommy is reading aloud snippets from the patches of graffiti we pass on the walls, spotlighting them with the flashlight, since it's almost pitch-dark inside. *"Ray Ray Six Oh Nine,"* Tommy reads off the walls. *"Holla K, love you, bitches."*

I follow Tommy, and close behind us is Sarabeth, chirping at our heels.

"Bridget Love, Bridget Love," Tommy reads. *"Monster. Monster. Monster."*

It's all nonsense that has nothing to do with Ori.

"You think there are *vagrants* here?" Sarabeth says in a mouse voice at my ear. "Think they'll come out and protect their home with baseball bats? Like, they've lived in the dark so long, the skin's grown over their eyes?"

I'm not sure what movie *she's* been watching, so I ignore her. She doesn't hear it. None of them hear it. I mean, how could they with Tommy? Now he's jumping on things and kicking open doors and grandstanding in the guards' booths, pretending he's the sadist in charge of a prison full of naughty girls.

What I hear is a rumbling hum. A faraway rumble.

Miles has led us to a wing of cells, a lower deck and an upper deck of steel doors, all ringing some tables in the center of the room. The tables are bolted to the floor. As are the benches. There's nothing here that hasn't been bolted down and made permanent.

It feels important that I say something, but only the most random thing pops into my head, like how cold it is, now that we've entered this area of the prison, though I seem to be the only one with the shivers, rubbing my exposed arms in my tank top, goose bumps rising.

Up at the top of the room, if this gray void of space could be called a room, far over our heads and impossible to reach without a ladder, are the windows. Really, they're gashes in the concrete. These gashes filter in some of the remaining light from outside, but very little, not enough to brighten the place.

"So she was in here, this wing," Miles says. He points to a specific green door. "That one. B-three. In her last letter she told me."

He wants me to react to the words *last letter,* but I don't. I won't. He wants me to ask what she told him in those letters, and I'm not going to give him that pleasure.

The door to B-3 is wide-open. On the cinder-block wall beside the door there's an old, torn piece of paper mounted in a plastic sleeve. It hangs upside down, about to come loose. I lift it up to see what it says, but all I can make out is one word and a couple numbers: 38 SMITH, which doesn't in any way point to Ori.

"That's not her name," I say, stepping away. "This isn't her room."

"Hello, she had a cellmate," he says. "Name could've been Smith something . . . I think it was Ashley? Amy? Anne? Something with an A."

Sarabeth studies the name, touches the two numbers with a finger. "Thirty-eight," she says, musing like it means something. "What do you think her roommate did? Was she a murderer, too, you think?"

Miles glares.

"Probably," I say. "Most of the girls here were." I've done more reading about the accident, if it could be called that, than anyone knows.

I push past Sarabeth and Miles and enter. Tommy is off behind us, climbing a table.

The room is ridiculously small. My walk-in closet could fit two of these rooms with a little foyer area for stowing all my shoes. The window in the wall is tiny, and a carpet of vines is in the way, so the room is darker than it should be, even at the end of the day. I'd already grabbed the flashlight from Tommy—the way he was acting, he didn't deserve it—so I let the beam of the flashlight explore every crevice while I stand in the doorway, only my toes edging in. I point my toes reflexively inside my covered sandals. There is a kind of power in an aggressively pointed foot, especially when nobody can see it.

Behind me is a hush as we all let the flashlight do the work of showing us what had been hers in that last week, those last days, three Augusts ago. Even Tommy climbs off the table to join us at the edge, peering in.

There's a bunk bed, like you'd find at summer camp, but this one is the width of a tanning bed and looks as hard as actual stone. The bunk bed is bolted to the cinder-block wall, the way the benches and tables outside are. Most everything in here is a part of the walls, locked together and unable to be moved. I do see one loose chair, though, toppled over, and I find myself reaching over to right it. Ori sat on this chair. Maybe, if this really was her room. I carefully push the chair under the bolted-down desk. Ori wrote letters to Miles at that desk. Maybe, if that was her desk. Either way, she didn't sit at this desk and write a letter to me.

There is a horrid toilet, one that doesn't even have a seat, one she'd have to use in front of her roommate, and in front of the guards and everyone else who could watch her through the door, and the smells, and the shame, and the inhumanity of it. I back away from the toilet, but there isn't far to go. No one could dance in a room like this. If I extended a leg, it would hit hard wall.

The microscopic window is open, but there are bars in front, so it's not like anyone could've squeezed through. Brown leaves and fresh green leaves and dank water and a random scattering of twigs cover the top bunk bed. The bushy vines grow in through the bars, ragged green and reaching. A pink flower pulses off the end of one of the vines, bright like poison. It's not a rose like the ones that were thrown at my feet. I don't know what it is. I touch it and a buried thorn nips me.

Miles hovers behind me, too near in this small space. There isn't enough air for the both of us. There never was. But he's not leaving, and I'm not leaving, and one of us will have to say something, one of us will have to say get out of the way, let me out.

I don't see Tommy anymore, so I figure he's gone off somewhere, entertaining himself with more things to climb on or crash into or break. I don't see Sarabeth, so she must have followed, and I make a mental note to check up on her spending voluntary alone time with my boyfriend, even though I have full plans to dump him before I leave for New York next week.

"Can't picture her in here, can you?" Miles says.

I hear the faint rumble in the distance again. Now it's far-off shouting and what sounds like chanting, like there's a football game going on outside. Very low. Very hard to make out. But Miles has asked me a question, and by the way he stares, watching my mouth, waiting for it to open and reveal my answer, I know he won't let us go anywhere until I've told him.

"No, I can't," I say. I can't picture any person I've ever known in here. And it's not that I don't have an imagination. It's that I never thought I would know people who would do the kind of things that would get them locked up in a detention center like this one. It looks like a real prison, for real criminals. Then I remember and curl my toes.

"Yeah," he says. I've given the right answer.

Sometimes I wonder about him, about how trusting he is when it comes to Ori. I wonder if he really thinks she was innocent. I wonder if he would fight to prove her innocence. I wonder, if he saw a blade aimed at him, a bloody blade grasped in a bloody hand, what he'd do. Like if he'd try to take it or shout for me to stop. Like if he'd run.

"But I'm trying to picture it," he goes, and where he's pacing is blocking my way out. His legs are so long, he only

needs to make one step back and forth in front of the doorway, one step, again and again, one step. "I need to, I think.
That's why I've come up here. Three times now—this is the
third. I thought being up here would make it make more
sense."

"Does it?" I say quietly.

Miles and I were always kind of alike in some ways—how
serious we'd get, how we'd shrink into ourselves and only
Ori could make us come out. She used to say so. If Miles had
gotten himself in trouble, I wonder what she would have
done to protect him. How far she would have gone, I mean.
Far enough to not come back? As far as she went for me?

"No," he spits out. "It doesn't make any sense."

If I have to, I can see what Ori liked in this boy. It's hard
not to. There's the liquid way he moves, which any dancer
would notice, and the intense focus in his eyes when you're
the one he's looking at. It's like being cradled in the white-
hot center of your very own spotlight.

I'm drawn to it, the way I always am to that sort of light,
which is kind of wicked of me, but if he put his hand on my
shoulder and it slipped, or if he turned and his mouth got
close to where my mouth was, I mean I wouldn't be the one
to stop it.

"I was hoping," I say. "I thought being here would make
it easier to, you know . . ." I don't know a thing. I don't even
know what I'm saying. "To have all this make sense."

"No." He turns, and I can no longer see his face. "The
only person who can make it make sense is you."

I feel a Sarabeth-like heat in my cheeks and have to
glance away.

"You," he repeats.

There's something taped to the wall, and barely hanging on, crooked and tipped over on one side, blocked in part by the bed frame, and I distract myself with it. A piece of paper that's held fast to this wall for three years. I reach out to see what it is.

"Violet." I hate the way he says my name just now. He makes it sound like *violent*.

I've retrieved the piece of paper and make myself busy smoothing it out. I couldn't picture Ori in here, not on that bed, top or bottom, not in this corner or that corner, not standing in the tiny patch of space taken up by Miles, not in the chair, not on the toilet, not the wall, pressed up against it, not sunk down on the concrete floor. But all of a sudden I can picture her with this piece of paper I've rescued, this drawing, and I feel sure she had her hands on it.

It's a head. A head without even a pair of its own shoulders.

Something about the face strikes me. The mouth is tight. The eyes are mean. The ears stick out. It's simple, it's honest, it's startling. I shut off the flashlight so I can't see it.

Miles says what I'm thinking. "Sure looks a lot like you."

It's when he says it that I know it's true. It's a picture of me. She's been in this cell and she's drawn a picture of me and she's left it here for me to find it. My hands can't grip anymore and I drop it. And it's when I'm bent down to the floor with my back turned. That's when.

The door to the room slams shut.

Miles is on the other side of it—outside. I'm the only one still in the room.

There can't be more than a few steps between me and the door, but in the sudden darkness that falls like a sack's been shoved down over my head, all sense of direction is meaningless. I push forward and knock my shin into what might be the toilet. A splash of something lukewarm, something slimy and wet. I retreat and hit wall. I step to the side and a wedge of what feels like steel cuts into my neck. That might be the bed. I whip backward, holding my throat. A whisper that seems to come from inside the walls swirls around me, like it's slipping in from the rooms next door, the rooms around and above, through the cinder block somehow, creeping in.

Is she gonna cry? Wait for it, wait for it. Ten on the bitch to flip her shit.

Who? Do they mean me?

"Stop it," I shriek. "Stop."

I'm cramped, I'm cut in on all sides, I'm caught. In the smoking tunnel, we both were. Then she told me to go. She told me to get out of there, she'd take care of it, she'd be the one. She told me to run, and I did run, and a part of me has been running ever since.

If I told that story in the courtroom, would it have made a difference? Would I have landed here, with her? Would we both have eaten the poison and be remembered by a rotting teddy bear at the gate?

I pull myself back and the whispers grind to a halt, the walls take a breath and settle, and there's silence again. Complete silence and the lingering scent of dust. I sneeze.

Somehow, with my arms stretched out in front of me, I reach the door. I think it's the door. I look up, and it's not as dark as it was a moment ago, and there's a pane of glass cut into the door, and I can see out. Which means someone can see in. I can't get the flashlight to stay on.

Miles's face is framed in the hole. The sound of his laughter is muffled, but I can tell by the shapes his mouth makes that he's cracking up.

I try to pull the door open, but it won't give. "Very funny. Let me out, Miles. Open the door."

"How's it feel?" he says through the face-hole. "Getting used to it?"

"The door, Miles." I say it up against the glass, my mouth mashed against it.

"How many years you think you could handle?" he says. "In a cell like this?"

"Miles. Just open the door."

He closes his eyes first, like a slow blink, as if he's considering, and then he closes the hole. He does something, I don't know what, to cover it so I can't see out through the door. It could be that he's holding his hand over the opening, or it could be that he's slid shut the steel trap.

It's dark again. I'm pulling and pulling on the door, and I'm using all my weight, and there isn't anything I can do to get it to come open.

I can't hear him on the other side. This room is that insulated, the door that thick. He's shut me in and left me. He's left me in her small, dark room.

The cold grows more intense, prickling at me the way a swarm of mosquitoes and deerflies would, except there's no summer heat. I'm afraid I'm going to hear those taunting whispers again. Hear them call me a bitch. I'm shaking now, and my breath makes crystal fumes around me, and the chill leaches into my bones, and I wonder if this is what it feels like to die alone.

"Let me out!" I scream.

Then I hear the strangest thing: the solid clonk and clank of a lock being turned. The door seems to vibrate, though no one said anything about Miles's having a key. There's a moment when I forget where I am, who I am, what I did.

I'm at the door. I touch the ice-cold surface and feel it hum.

I give it a shove. It opens outward. It wasn't locked at all, was it? All I had to do was push.

RUN

HAS IT GOTTEN darker?

I was in Ori's cell with the door shut on me for a few minutes, and now the large space outside is flooded with blackness, warm and tacky like tar, making me sweat and my clothes stick to my already sticky skin. I can feel the thick droplets slink down my spine, pooling in the small of my back. The dampness leaks down out of my hair, stinging as it reaches my eyes. I'm embarrassed at how I acted in there, how I screamed. Plus, my neck is sore from where I walked into the hard bunk, my hip aches from where I hit the wall, and there's a pulsing swell on my shin.

"Tommy? Sarabeth?"

There's a distant sound, a far-reaching echo, but it may just be my own voice battling against the walls.

No Tommy. No Sarabeth.

Though I kind of hate myself for it, I yell for him. "Miles?"

I'm disturbed I even thought for one single beat of a second that he might kiss me, and, worse, that I was about to kiss him back. That I wasn't even considering shoving him away.

There's no answer. Nothing. No Miles. No Sarabeth, no Tommy. No anybody.

I start walking, the flashlight on and out. Now it decides to start working again.

I can't trust my ears. I keep hearing these whorls of sound, but when I stop, and try to listen, they're gone. Is that Sarabeth shouting? Tommy? No, too much noise for it to be just one person. And those gashes of windows give barely any light, and my flashlight shows only the smallest, dimmest circle. All I can do is keep going down this corridor.

A Beyoncé song comes into my head randomly, and I don't even like Beyoncé. It takes hold of me, and then I lose it, the melody, the lyrics. I don't even know what song it was.

The walls in this section of hallway have fallen. There are shelves, knocked over and spilling onto the floor. It takes me a moment to realize that the squishy, mossy ground I'm walking on isn't grass but is made of damp, rotting paper. These are books. A piece of furniture blocks the way forward like a fallen tree—another bookshelf—and I have to scale it. My sandal gets caught in a mound of waterlogged books, and what had once been a copy of *Breakfast at Tiffany's* sticks to the sole of my shoe. I kick it off. It's not until I'm past all that when I realize the flashlight isn't in my hand anymore, that I must've let it fall.

I hear Tommy. He's shouting that he's found the power supply—he's always had a thing for playing with plugs and coming dangerously close to getting himself electrocuted—and he's trying to see what will happen if he hits the switch. I call out to him, around that corner or the next, to quit messing around, but it's too late. He's gone and flipped the switch. He's made the power come on.

A whole series of lights blaze. But the glow is sick-green and soupy, and the sound is blaring, earsplitting—an air-raid siren, like we're under attack.

I hear cursing. Tommy's screwed something up. Lights flash and bulbs seem to pop and there's a charred, throat-burning stink in the air. There's a spark in the room, quick and gone, like lightning. My gold charm bracelet catches the light.

I feel for the bracelet around my wrist. It's still there. Ori didn't crave expensive things, but she always had her eye on this bracelet. She liked to tinker with the little ballerinas hung all around the chain, dancing them on my wrist. She knew I got a new charm each year from my dad for my birthday, 24 karat, and she knew I wouldn't miss a charm or two, because by now there were so many, but I never detached one and let her have it. I never let her borrow the bracelet, either, to try on her graceful wrist, not even in the safety of my bedroom so she wouldn't lose it.

I'm in a wide-open space. It's quiet now. My eyes have adjusted enough so I can make out what's on the walls: patches of graffiti and crumbling dust and hanging pipes and dangling pillows of what's probably asbestos. I lift my hand to cover my mouth and nose.

Then I'm hit. Something rushes through me. A shock of cold, face-first, and then gone. This is another thing that makes no sense. And I know that I can't tell anyone, not Sarabeth, not Tommy, especially not Miles, because none of them would believe me, and I don't want to be questioned. I don't want to question myself.

The thing is, I see her. Or someone. I swear on my life that I see someone who wasn't there just two seconds before. I step forward. I know this doesn't make any sense, but I say her name. I say, "Ori? Is that you?" And she doesn't say anything back, but there's this shuffling, this shift-and-shuffle in the dark, and then quick movement, fast, faster, a dance I can't keep up with, and I'm the one who can always keep up.

She's coming for me, the pieces and particles of her are connecting together in a hazy shaft of gray light, the particles and pieces are walking on human legs. She's wearing green. She's seen me, and she's coming down the stairs toward me, and she's wearing green, and she's come out.

She's reached me now, is inches away, and says, in a low voice, almost a growl, "Who are you? How'd you get in here?"

And then I see all these things at once: The green is army-drab, not a bright, happy color that Ori would like, not at all. The figure isn't as tall as Ori used to be, since she'd always been taller than me, by a couple inches at least. The figure isn't as thin as Ori—whoever this is, it's thick and barrel-chested, practically a bulldozer. The voice sounds nothing at all like hers.

I don't know who this is. Or *what*.

I step back, sputtering. "Who are you?"

"Who are *you*?"

"What are you doing here?"

"What are *you* doing here?"

I'm trying to communicate with a ghost.

My legs take over, the way they do after I've memorized a combination and there's my cue. They know what they're doing, my legs. I've trained them well. Here they go, but not in a pas de bourrée or a pas de chat or any quick-moving step my feet could shuffle through from memory. They do what I need them to do, the most basic action. They run.

PART IV:
Amber and Orianna

She is happy where she lies
With the dust upon her eyes.

—Edna St. Vincent Millay, "Epitaph"

I FOUND MYSELF

I FOUND MYSELF alone for the first time in three years, one month, and thirteen days. (I was counting.) I had a cell of my own, with the door sealed closed, its window hole covered and dark. I had privacy.

Only, we all knew to be careful what we wished for. Maybe to not do so much wishing after all. Because this wasn't a gift; it was Solitary, in D-wing, a section of the Aurora Hills Secure Juvenile Detention Center I'd only heard about, through passed-along stories and a few bold lies. (We'd heard there was a girl who tried to eat other girls' ears off, and that, after two separate ear incidents, she was housed in D and never saw sunlight, like a carnivorous mole. The Suicides, as we called them, were also housed in this wing, where the nightly rounds were constant. Officially this was known as Suicide Watch. The Suicides were strip-searched for pens or pencils at the end of each school session, every single day, all because one Suicide tried to gouge a hole in her own throat with a blue-inked Bic way back in 1993. Only one of these stories was a lie.)

In my years at Aurora Hills, I'd wheeled my book cart past the entrance to D-wing many times. I'd detour on purpose. I'd let the wheels slow, the cart stutter, and I'd take the opportunity to peek in. It looked grayer than our other three wings, and there was more howling. In my travels, that was all I could hear or see.

Now, though, I was inside, and I didn't know how long I'd be staying. When one of us was brought to Solitary, otherwise known as the hole, none of us knew when she'd be getting out. I'd heard rumors the ear-eater was still here.

The doors in Solitary were different from the green doors on the regular wings. As were my clothes, now caution yellow and easy to spot in a shadowed hallway, if the locks let themselves go again and I got out for a second time in one weekend. The doors were thicker here and built with reinforced panels, like armored barricades. They were stone gray, as if someone thought they weren't even worth painting a real color. The surface was scratchy, and rough against skin, I discovered, after shoving myself against my door, trying to get someone's attention through the closed hole. My face and neck came away stippled in raised dots. Scrapes on my forearms and the palms of my hands oozed and stung.

That was my first night. And the floor was where I must have spent it.

Outside D-wing, most of us had been returned to our

cells. The last sound of the night that most of us heard was the clank and crank of the locks as each of our steel doors resealed behind us. Our hearts sank, our spirits dropped. Our guts tied themselves back up into their familiar knots. The night came to an end.

We heard other things, too, since we were wide awake and wanting answers. We heard the COs' muffled talk from behind our locked doors. We couldn't make out all the words but could sense the shock in their voices, the confusion, maybe even the fear. It wasn't often that we sensed fear coming from our captors.

The COs were recounting what happened to them when the locks came open—how they all had their backs turned at the same moment, how each one of them on night duty, all across the compound, had been caught unawares. One had been in the toilet. Two had stepped out for a smoke. One was checking fuses and got stuck in the dark basement, feeling for a way out. This grand coincidence felt to us like magic, or like a miracle—either/or, because in the end it gave us the same thing.

We didn't feel sorry for the COs, not one bit. We hoped they'd be reprimanded for losing track of us, punished, and severely. Some of us wanted them all fired. A couple of us fantasized they'd be lined up against the wall out behind the facility and beaten with chains.

Some of us had their hand marks still on us, from when they grabbed us, our eardrums burst from their machine-gun shouts when they yelled for us to get down on the ground. One of us had gotten caught with Minko, the worst of the COs, on the stairwell, and thanks to him, she wouldn't be able to sit comfortably in a chair for days.

We were collecting all our own stories. They were ours to share, not theirs.

The last thing Jody, in B-wing, remembered from our hour outside our cells was a closed door rammed in her face by one of the COs. He grinned when he sent the door swinging. It knocked her clean out, and didn't feel as good as when she did it to herself.

Others of us turned ourselves around when we heard the COs coming, like Cherie, who raced back to her cell in B-wing like she'd never left it, and hid her face under her pillow as if she'd kept it there all night. Peaches played statue in a dark corner, until it was safe to come out. A-wing was there for her when she got back. Natty sang quietly to herself, eyes on the floor so she wouldn't be accused of insubordination, and sang louder when she went wandering, but scooted back to A-wing the second she was told she was out of bounds.

A couple of us didn't even take part, so we couldn't be blamed.

In C-wing, Mack had used the opportunity to daydream. She imagined her life in rewind: starting with *not* hiding that stash in her school locker and *not* elbowing the vice principal in the face, which got her expelled and then locked up, to rewinding all the way back in time, back five years, six years, seven, eight, nine years, to the first mistake she believed set her fate in motion. She was eight, little beaded braids and squeaky-new sneakers, walking right on past that pink bike on the sidewalk and *not* swiping it for her own. She pictured—and was still picturing, when her cellmate returned—just leaving that bike be.

Lola returned to a swift reminder. When she'd ditched the cell and gone running, she'd given one quick glance back at Kennedy—a sack of frizz on the floor, barely recognizable as human—and then she got caught up in the crowd, her body surging through corridors with our bodies, her feet hitting concrete with our stampeding feet, and she forgot how she'd left Kennedy unconscious or maybe even dead, and how much more time would be added to her sentence if Kennedy *was* dead.

Lola checked the floor as soon as she entered her cell, but Kennedy was not where she'd left her. Lola choked on the envious thought that maybe hair-eating Kennedy, out of all of us, Kennedy, the least deserving, Kennedy, the most despised, the most pathetic, had been the one to get free. Then she choked on laughter when she realized that Kennedy had simply dragged herself, like a wounded animal going off into the fields to croak, under the bed.

D'amour was discovered by a CO outside, one charred hand fused to the electric fence, but that news wouldn't make the rounds until later.

Most of us were back in our usual cells. Still, some of us wore our smiles to sleep, our jaw muscles aching from perma-grin. Some of us heard the whimpers of our cellmates in the bunks above or below, and told them to shut up or felt the tears coming and couldn't say a word because we were too choked up ourselves.

It took hours to corral us all, to count us, to come back around and count us again. We thought that would be the big event of our summer—the night everyone would be talking about for years to come, a legend in these walls, a brilliant glimpse of the passing sun. We had no idea.

After the COs completed their rounds, we did our own kind of counting.

We had roll call in the darkness, from inside our cells. If anyone was missing, we wanted to know about it first, before the morning bell and the fluorescent lights flared.

"You there?" said a voice through the heating vents in C-wing.

The vents of A-wing answered, "I'm here." And more and more of us, "Here. Here. Here."

We said our names. We claimed our spaces.

In B-wing the vents were set low to the floor and hissed clouds of dust in summer (though they stayed quiet when we needed that hiss for warmth in winter), but at a certain angle, once our vision adjusted to the low light, a blur of movement could be made out from the cell next door. There was next door's eye. Next door's mouth. The voice clear as crystal, even if the face looked diced and sliced through the grate.

Here. We made it back. We didn't get far. Disappointment was in our voices as we said it. Here, here, still here.

That night, all through Aurora Hills, we spoke to one another. We checked up. We checked in. The COs couldn't have stopped us if they tried.

"How far did you get?" we all wanted to know.

Those of us who had stayed put in our bed slabs were quiet. Those of us who made it only as far as the visiting

room, and broke the glass mask of the vending machine
and gorged on salty snacks till our tongues blistered, said
as much, but it was the girls who tried for the doors, who
tried to lift the gates, eyes set on the road, those were the
girls who spoke of their adventures with true pride.

Had I been in my usual cell in B-wing, I would have
communicated through the vents like the others. I would
have wondered about D'amour and asked if anyone else had
seen her. We would have made a few guesses, among us,
to how much electricity could run through a living body
before it took too much and got itself dead. But mostly I
would have listened to what everyone else said. I wouldn't
have gone to sleep until I'd heard absolutely everything.

But in D-wing, I discovered, there was no way to communicate except by pounding something heavy against the
wall. There wasn't much to pound, since no unattached
chairs or personal items were allowed, but there were hands
attached to arms, and attached to legs there were feet. There
was always something to slam against a wall, once a girl got
to looking.

D-wing had its own kind of Morse code, and I'd pick
it up quickly, though I might not have been clear on what
the codes meant. I assumed that three short pounds meant
we were making it through the abyss alive and kicking, and
other sets of pounds and rhythms meant *Stay strong, sister*
and *Are you awake?* and *Fuck the police.* Two slams meant that
we were hungry, not like our neighbors could do anything
about that. One slam, made with the whole body, could
mean a number of things: *Let me out,* which was obvious.

*Weren't those tuna fish guts they called a sandwich disgusting? I'm
protesting by throwing my entire being at this wall.* Or, say if a girl
keeled over and her body slammed against the wall, it meant,
possibly, that she passed out. I couldn't be sure.

I tried to communicate with thumps and slaps from my
feet and hands, but they got sore after a while.

Amber.

B-wing.

I made it outside.

I think.

I saw someone who shouldn't be here.

I swear.

I had a chance to run, but I didn't take it.

Don't know why.

This turned to gibberish against the wall, but that
didn't stop me from trying. Usually I felt connected to the
other girls, even if they didn't acknowledge me at lunch or
bumped my shoulder in the hallway and went on walking.
Now I felt entirely separate.

After a while, all attempts at communication faded out.
We were tired.

In the harsh light of morning, when we awoke behind
our locked doors, this would feel like a massacre.

I knew that better than any of us. I'd been wet from rain,
my throat all screamed out, mud in my hair and mud in my
eyelashes, the grit of mud in my mouth, when they caught
me. I was outside the facility. I think it was Long who had
me, or it was Marbleson. At some point when I was kicking, there were two of them holding me, keeping count of
my legs, and it wasn't my fault they lost track of one and

Marbleson (or was it Long?) got the black eye. All for this, I was accused of assaulting a guard.

One thing I knew for sure was that our walls were green again, and clean. The way they should be. And even in the stress of spending a night in the hole, this was a small comfort I clutched close to me, the way I used to have a stuffed lamb I slept with every night, before my mother married him, when I was still happy, and a kid.

Morning came. Sunday morning. Or, wait, was it Monday now? It couldn't already be Tuesday, could it?

I sat up, on the floor in my cell in Solitary. I found my feet. My throat scratched from old screams, so I kept it quiet, rubbing it from the outside, over the skin, as if that might help. My skin was raw from the sandpaper walls. I stood. Then I got dizzy and sat back down.

Here in Solitary, the lights were on at all hours, which meant the hours spun without my being able to keep track. Only meals shoved through the food slot let me know time was actually passing. If I happened to sleep through it—on the mattress against the wall, gray, and also as cold and hard as the door—the tray of food would be taken back, like I'd rejected it. I couldn't be sure how many meals I missed.

My memory was a distant boat I'd set sail in the river, and the current was too strong to snatch it back. Though I'd never had a little boat; I'd never lived near a river. I'd never even been the kind of girl who'd play near raging, flighty things. My outside life, cut short at the age of thirteen, when I was arrested, had been far more careful.

This carefulness, noticed by all my teachers in school and always mentioned on my report cards, ended up being held against me in court. I seemed calculated, they said. It spoke of premeditation in my stepfather's death, they said. It was in my diary.

"A thirteen-year-old is absolutely capable of planning the perfect murder." Someone in court said that.

My hands were folded on the table as those words were said. I wouldn't look at any faces, but I couldn't close my ears. A so-called expert witness spoke of what a young mind is able to understand, its sense of right and wrong, and how we lived solely in the moment, without thought of consequence, as the frontal lobe is not fully developed until age twenty-five.

I didn't know anything about any frontal lobes. As I listened, I thought, How could it be called the "perfect" murder if I am sitting here right now, accused? I wondered how they could know so much about my brain without lifting open my skull and poking through it. I expected my lawyer, a pale pinch-faced woman who'd been assigned to me by the court, to speak up. But my hands were folded so carefully. And my shoes were laced up nice, with one knot each. And if my clothes were too tight, I didn't fidget and let it show.

Behind me, across the aisle of the small courtroom, sitting for the other side, the side seeking justice for her dead husband, was my mother.

Pearl wasn't in the room, of course, since she was only seven then. I've wondered ever since, wondered at night in B-wing and wondered now, in the forced solitude and under the bright lights in D-wing, what my little half sister had been told about me, what she understood. It was her father who was taken from her, a man she happily called

"Daddy" while I'd spat at the ground when my mother said I should start calling him "Dad."

I weighed less, back then. I hadn't yet had my growth spurt. My shoulders hadn't filled out. Still, there was something menacing they saw in me, even at that size. If I stood before the judge now, this big, my jaw set by my habit of tightening it, he would have handed me a guilty conviction in ten seconds instead of taking a recess and coming back with it in an hour and ten minutes.

People can't move on until the finger is pointed, and the gavel's come down. This is called closure, and it's also called justice, and they are not always the same thing.

I thought for sure I was in Solitary for days on end, maybe even a week. My leg hairs grew, my stomach shrank. But when the door at last opened, it hadn't been a full seventy-two hours. I'd made it to Tuesday.

The lock turned, and the hole in the door—down low, to traffic the food trays—flopped open, and I could see two gray-clad legs. A CO.

I didn't know which guard was assigned to D-wing that week. It could have been Long or Marbleson, sporting the black eye I'd gifted one of them. It could have been Minko. None of us wanted to be trapped alone with Minko.

I retreated against the wall as the locks—more installed on this door than in other wings—snapped open.

If those two gray legs did belong to Minko, I had to be ready. My mind spun over how I might be able to injure him, hoping permanently. If it would be better to use my knuckles, or get some leverage and kick with my foot. (One of us—Polly, in A-wing—once fought off a would-be rapist with a hockey stick to the solar plexus. When she reenacted the scene for us, making do with an invisible weapon, she mimicked the sound of his pain and defeat and shame, a deep soul-crushing whimper. We loved to picture her assaulter going down, fish-eyed and flopping on the sidewalk, so we asked her to act out this story again and again.)

I would be like Polly if I had to be, though I had no sports equipment with which to take him down.

But no. It wasn't Minko. The door cranked open, and the CO who entered was Santosusso. He was practically as young as we were, and cheery, no matter the day. Of course, he was also new. I couldn't have been more lucky.

"Hey there," he said. He glanced at a clipboard. "Amber, right?"

His eyes skittered around the pitiful space, avoiding me and mine. He seemed ashamed at having to witness me in here. This was his first summer, and we'd caught him acting like he cared. It gave some of us the heebie-jeebies. Others found it endearing. Mississippi was in love with him, and so was Lian. But Peaches warned he might snap at any moment, as it was always the nice ones who had the sickest of the sick stuff buried behind their big blue eyes—and we should watch our backs with him.

"Yeah," I said weakly, acknowledging my name.

It was weird that he called us by our first names; most COs used last names for us as if we were enlisted in the military, and a few just called us "Inmate," as they were used to working at adult maximum-security facilities, where the prisoners didn't even deserve names.

"Time to go back to B-wing, Amber," he said, actually

smiling at me. He even had two identical dimples, one on each side of his face. He looked like a boy at my old school. Like a civilian, offering to take a walk with another civilian.

When I didn't come forward, when I didn't immediately offer up my wrists so he could cuff them for the walk home, he softened further. "How're you doing? What's going on?"

These questions confused and disturbed me. Maybe it would have been better to be confronted with Minko—at least I knew what he wanted. I would have known I was right to be on guard.

I shrugged. He flashed his dimples.

Except, now that we were talking, now that the door was open, and air was coming in, I remembered I had so many questions. First I needed to know the day. It was Tuesday, he said, which felt impossible in every way, but I went with it. Questions dropped from my mouth, one after the other, faster than the one before. "What happened?" I wanted to know. "Were you there? Did you see? Did they catch everyone? What was it? What went wrong? Could it happen again?"

He interrupted to explain that this was his first shift since Friday, so he wasn't clear on what happened Saturday night, if that's what I was asking.

But he must know *something*.

"Is she dead?" I said. "D'amour."

"The blonde?" he said, not unkindly. "Drug trafficking, right?"

I didn't take the bait. We don't talk about one another's crimes to anyone in authority. We know what we know, and we don't ask after what we don't know. I wouldn't agree

or deny that I was aware of what she'd done to get her eighteen months—and I wouldn't put in an opinion on if she
was guilty or if she was innocent. It's best to say we're all
innocent.

"I saw her at the fence," I said. "I saw her go up in lights."
That was the only way I could think to describe it, like she
was a fireworks show for the Fourth of July, a holiday we
didn't get to celebrate in here.

"She's okay," he said. "In the infirmary. Second-degree
burns, I think I heard. But she's not bad off enough to be
transferred."

I guess I didn't react.

"She's alive," he continued, assuring me. "That fence
is electric, you know. But she's okay. Really." Maybe he
thought I cared more about her well-being than I did. That
I'd been crying over her in here. For D'amour, I hadn't shed
one tear.

He secured my wrists—the usual protocol when being transported from one cell to another; we got used to
it—and we started out the door.

"I'll tell D'amour you were asking about her," he said
casually as he shuffled me forward. "She's not coming back
to B-wing."

"What? Why not?"

"She's moving to A-wing. You're getting a new roomie
today."

"Who's getting transferred? Lola? Kennedy?"

"Oh no. Yeah, that's a whole other story. You're getting
someone brand-new."

I was made to walk ahead of him, and I considered this

piece of information. The prick of memory nipped me. We were passing the stairwell between B-wing and the canteen. The sensation of having known what he was telling me, known it was coming because I'd lived it before, grabbed me.

She was coming. She was the next thing to come, after the locks. Once she was here, everything would go wrong. Of that I felt certain.

I jolted in Santosusso's grasp. We'd reached the entry gate to B-wing. We were almost home.

"Cuffs too tight?" he asked.

I shook my head. I knew I shouldn't ask, shouldn't let him in on anything more than I had already because he wasn't one of us, no matter how young he was and how nice he seemed with his dimples. I asked anyway. "Does her name"—it was coming to me, there it was—"start with an O?"

"You been watching the news? I thought they monitored what played on the rec TVs. But yeah. You know who I mean, then. It's in all the papers, too. Keep an eye on yourself, all right?"

"What'd she do?"

Even as I said it, I felt I should know the answer. Something in his face said so, too. Then his face shifted, and darkened, and I lost the two dimples, and everything else was a blur. I felt his hands turning the handcuffs lock to let mine go, and I sensed him drifting off, leaving me before the open door to my cell as if I'd wandered here all alone without needing permission from anybody.

It was an odd moment, and that was only the beginning. The sign that said WYATT had been removed from the cinder-block wall outside my cell, and a new sign, one that said SPEERLING, was attached in its place.

D'amour's things had been cleared out of our shared cell, and the top bunk was stripped, indicating a new arrival would show up soon.

This new arrival would be our forty-second.

SHE WAS SURROUNDED

SHE WAS SURROUNDED by guards. She came in under siege, as if she might lunge and go for the closest throat. But, from our vantage point, from our place of wisdom and experience and occasional regret, she looked nothing like the rumors made her out to be, so much so that I began to wonder if they'd been mistaken. If they'd caught the wrong girl.

She was known by the state as inmate number 47709-01, and known by the public as Orianna Speerling, but if we'd followed the sensationalized news stories, we'd have heard the press call her the "Bloody Ballerina," and we would have come up with a few pictures of our own thanks to that.

I watched—many of us were watching—from my cell window as the short blue bus from the county jail approached the curb. The COs converged before the bus door even opened.

We always made an effort to check out the new arrivals, but something about today drew more of us than ever before. We looked down from above, from our cells, as those of us on the south side of the facility always did when the bus was due to arrive. Sometimes we were looking for family: long-lost cousins and half sisters from estranged, despised fathers we wished were dead (the fathers, not the sisters). Or we'd see a friend we didn't want joining us here, so witnessing her step off the bus with her ankles in chains broke another jagged bit off what remained of our hearts. Sometimes, on good days when the sun was shining for us, we would spot an enemy from outside emerging from that bus. This was a gift from the universe, a reason to fold our hands in the night and mutter our thank-yous because she'd been handed over, like a sweet treat on a plate. No matter who it was, the fact is it could always be someone.

That day, the blue bus held just one girl.

"D'you think she'll get her own room and no one'll ever see her, like with Annemarie?"

Many of us had heard of little Annemarie, and some of us had spotted her from a distance. No one relished the idea of her getting released into the general population.

"Nah, I heard she's in B-wing. With Amber."

They spoke about me as if I weren't right there.

"Think she'll go psycho killer and slit Amber's throat in the night?"

"Oh, sure. If she can find something sharp."

"If not, she could just strangle her."

"True. You can do that with your bare hands."

"Or a bedsheet."

They then discussed all the other everyday weapons we had available, for those with a creative streak and a worthy target.

I kept any reactions to myself. It was so rare to hear my name aloud, spoken by another girl here, that I felt my cheeks heating up more than they were already, which was to a slow boil, thanks to the upstate August humidity. I wanted to cover my whole face with my hands.

The other girls often didn't speak to me directly, unless they had to when I wheeled around the library cart. It was more like they spoke near me and I listened in. I thought of us together as one, and included myself in their conversations, like a silent partner hovering behind their chairs.

But all that changed as the other girls gathered at my window, peering down. It was hearing my name aloud, being acknowledged in a way I often wasn't. That was when it settled over me. The feeling of being included. Of belonging. Like we were family now, more than ever before.

Someone poked me hard in the ribs, indicating I should move over, and my side pulsed from the pain, but I didn't mind. I wasn't used to being touched. This new girl, this Orianna Speerling, she'd turned me into a celebrity simply because she was one. Any girl made to share a cell with her would have been treated the same.

"Watch your back," a voice said in my ear, and the guffaw told me it was Jody.

"I'm not scared," I said, and a bunch of them laughed, thumping me on the back and massaging my shoulders like they were going to push me to the center of the ring for a boxing bout.

We returned our attention to the new inmate down below. Three COs were waiting to receive her from the county guys.

She paused on the lip of the sidewalk—she actually stopped moving, as if she had all day to dawdle and wanted to check out the view first—and we watched her. We watched her gaze at our gray stone walls, which we knew rose like a fortress. We watched her take a breath in the thin air and gaze upward, at our windows, and we wondered if she could see our peering eyes.

She was tall, and maybe too thin, from what we could tell, with her wearing the shapeless jumpsuit from jail. On the back it claimed her county: Saratoga. We whispered that rich girls lived there, in big fat houses, with their fancy cars; there weren't many of us, inside, who came from money, and we immediately disliked anyone who did. But none of us had ever been to Saratoga, so we didn't know for sure.

The new girl had medium-brown skin and thick, straight black hair too long to keep in here—she'd learn that soon enough. None of us could tell if she was Latina or mixed. Some of us thought that mattered, but others of us said it didn't matter what you looked like in here. You were here, after all.

The ugliest of us, and those who didn't waste their canteen accounts on items that could be substituted for eyeliner or mascara, said this all the time.

Mirabel started taking bets. The odds were stacked against anyone who thought the new girl wouldn't put up a fight. Most everyone assumed she was taking a moment before an exciting, explosive show of violence. They bet their Reese's on it.

Other bets went down saying at least she'd cry.

A few of us thought she'd try to make a run for it, but that was only wishful thinking, because it was kind of funny when a girl thought she'd get anywhere with her ankles in chains.

I didn't place a bet. I knew I'd be alone with her soon enough. It felt like playing a trick on your own dog.

We waited, and watched. And nothing.

She didn't try to raise a buckled fist. She didn't sob. She didn't make even one attempt at a shackled, running leap.

The longer we watched, the more we wanted to take back our bets, and save our Reese's Cups. Mirabel heaved a loud sigh and dropped her running tally. Cherie scarfed one of the Reese's she'd bet on the win, and the cramped space filled with the scent of peanut butter.

Down below, the new girl was taking her first steps onto the cracked sidewalk. There was something about the way she held her body, with a magnetic kind of grace that, if we ignored the telltale armed guards and the desolate barbed-wire fencing in the background, if we ignored the things we always tried to ignore, it made us forget where we were for a moment.

She didn't look foam-mouthed or haunted and on edge, her head full of razors. She didn't look like a killer at all to us, and this the opinion of killers.

She looked like a girl on a sunny sidewalk on a summer's day. Calm and at peace. Free.

We blinked. Was this the notorious criminal we'd over-heard the COs talking about? The girl whose face some of us had seen flash on the guards' TV?

Maybe she'd crumble before she got to us and by the time she reached B-wing, she'd be a shell of her former self. If not, reality would hit her fast once she was inside. We always said this when the rare princess arrived, and then a group of us would gang up on the girl out by the woodshop and make sure. Her dose of the real world. The floor meeting her face, hard.

But no one was threatening to hurt the new girl, not even Jody.

"Huh," one of us said. "So that's the big-time murderer."

"Booooor-ing," said another, with the yawp of a yawn.

"I could take her," mumbled one more.

They filtered away, losing interest, suggesting card games, slinging gossip, wondering what would be for dinner, until I was alone in my cell.

I was the only one still watching, but nothing more happened. She walked out of view, and I guess she was escorted inside, as we all had been. Next, I knew, came processing.

She'd join us in B-wing within hours. She'd be wearing newbie orange. She'd sleep in the same kind of bed we slept in, count the mold flecks on the same stretch of ceiling that we'd been counting.

Just because the papers and the news shows had all those stories about her and showed slideshows of her pictures, it didn't make her special. We were, all of us, the exact oppo-site of special. We were bad. Broken. It was up to the state to rehabilitate us into something worthy, if it even could.

Maybe, long ago, we used to be good. Maybe all little girls are good in the beginning. There might even be pictures of us from those easy days, when we wore braids and colorful barrettes, and played in sandboxes and on swing sets, if we knew days so easy or wore such barrettes. There was a photo of me in a red-checked shirt and two braids at the neighborhood park. I had a raised shovel and had lost a tooth, but I smiled anyway. My mother used to have that photo in a frame. But something happened to us between then and now. Something threw sand in our eyes, ground it in, and we couldn't get it out. We still can't.

Orianna Speerling was shipped up here like anyone else. She was guilty; the juvenile justice system said so. So that had to mean she belonged.

I COULD WAIT

I COULD WAIT for her to show up in my cell, bundled blanket in her arms like a refugee, and make our introductions, try to be welcoming, the way I was with D'amour. But it was Tuesday afternoon, and on Tuesday and Thursday afternoons I wheeled the book cart through the wings. I had to go.

Most girls weren't too interested in spending voluntary time flapping the pages of some stale, old book, but there was always someone needing the escape like a gulp of fresh water in the desert. Besides, not every book in our library was old. Some were fresh faced and still had the new-paper smell, and reading a new book before anyone else got to was like getting the first hot lunch and not the murky, lukewarm depths of the middle of the line, or, worse, canned-bean cold like the last few trays.

Some were books we shouldn't have even had, judging by the well-thumbed sections paged down for sharing, but thinking of what some girls did under cover of a strategically draped blanket while reading a certain section of *The Clan of the Cave Bear* made me squeamish. The point is, every book we had could save us in a different way—only, we had to open it. We had to drop our eyes to the page and drink in the words that were there.

I'd wheel my cart onto a wing, top tier first, then bottom. I'd slow in cell doorways—this was during free time when we were allowed to drift around and have open doors, even allowed to have guests (no more than two at a time) in our small cells—and all I'd do was make my presence known, my cart seen. Someone on each wing always wanted something.

I'd hand a book over, and it would be grabbed from my hand with something like hunger. I'd seen this happen with *Anne of Green Gables* and with every volume of Vampire Academy. With ragged, well-read copies of *The Catcher in the Rye* and with *Speak*. With the Bible and the Bhagavad Gita and a manual for repairing the engine of a 1982 Mustang. I'd seen an obscure, dust-encrusted edition of *Good Morning, Midnight* slipped inside a green jumpsuit, as if to keep it as close as possible, and come to think of it, I haven't seen that book since.

It was important, what I did. Necessary. And even for the arrival of my new cellmate, I couldn't miss it.

That was why, when I reported for duty and discovered my book cart missing, I wasn't sure what to do. The library (technically a patch of hallway, but I insisted on calling it the library as if it were its own room) had been ransacked.

Whole gaps of books were missing from the shelves I'd organized, and the cards on which I kept the borrowers' names
were tossed aside, the As with the Es, the Cs on the floor.
But it was the cart that unhinged me. The cart was made of
pale, glossy wood and built with shelves, two tiers like in
our cell blocks, and with four rubber wheels, even though
one of the wheels didn't take to ground so well and spun
and spun, making it difficult to steer. Not finding the cart
made me want to howl. Made me want to scream.

No one had messed with my cart before, or taken so
many books with so much recklessness. We'd never had such
an enthusiastic reader.

Or worse. What if no one was even reading?

There were a number of places the books could have
made off to: a vat of rancid sauce in the kitchen; that bathroom outside D-wing no one could use because the toilets
were eternally blocked up with chunks of concrete and gray
silt. That was where my mind went. To destruction.

I marched over to the closest CO's office: I registered a
small disappointment at seeing Blitt at the helm, all coffee
breath and sneer. She could not be made to joke with us,
like Marbleson could, like sometimes Long could, if hanging out with Marbleson. She didn't bend to our wills after a
peep down an open shirt, like Minko might, but that was a
whole other dangerous game I wouldn't play.

"I was just in the library," I said, knocking on the door
jamb and jolting Blitt to attention. She'd been watching a
rerun of the Orianna Speerling trial on TV.

She smirked, and shut off the picture. "You mean the
hallway, Inmate."

She never called us by our given names, last or first. We knew what she meant by it, hoping we'd feel like a scuffed ant under the sole of a shoe, but I suspected she was kind of slow in the head and just couldn't remember our names.

Refusing to call the library a library was a sticking point with me. The official books that belonged to the detention center, the regulation ones we used for our classes and had to read, by order of the Department of Education, were not shelved in what I knew as my library. They were on the other side of the facility, where we had school.

We weren't allowed to take those books back to our cells. Those books were for learning only. They couldn't be used to carry messages or love notes, couldn't snuggle up in bed or inspire a happy dream or a decent orgasm (some girls bragged—most were suspected of faking). The books in my hallway library were our own collection, and all from donations, often from church groups or private schools ditching their dog-eared copies for pristine new works. These books were ours and only ours.

Owning something while under detention gave the time less weight. And Blitt knew that; it was why she kept calling it the hallway.

"Where. Is. My. Cart?" I demanded. I didn't talk often—to inmates, especially to COs—but when I did, I had a whole lot of saved-up air in my lungs and I could be loud.

"My cart," I spat out, fist on glass that wasn't supposed to ever shatter, but maybe I could make it shatter, maybe my fist could. "What happened to my cart?"

"Inmate, settle down," Blitt said. "You want me to write you up for this? It's just a cart. It's a pile of books. Calm yourself."

It was the condescending act she used like a whip on a bare back. She had information, and I needed it. Steam shot from my ears, but I lowered my fist from the glass and my eyes from Blitt's helmet head, and I took myself to a calm place, a faraway place. Sometimes I tried to picture it, and it looked a lot like Florida.

"Want to lose your visiting privileges? No visitor next week or the week after? No visitor all month?"

This was the perfect thing to say to incite me, but for a whole host of other reasons. And she knew it.

"That's right. You don't get visitors, do you? You've never had a single one."

My eyes burned with a filmy liquid that could not be called tears. Finally I had my breathing under control. I loosened the set bomb that was my fist.

She waited. She waited a long time. Then she said, with a wink of her very tiny, very piglike eyes from behind her glasses, "I saw Ward wheeling your cart around over to C-wing."

"Cannibal Kennedy?" I roared, imagining all the stray hair I'd find in the pages after, wondering if she chewed on paper, too, if there'd be bite marks on the covers and gnawed pulp on the insides, wet slobber marks from her squicky tongue. I wondered, growing panicked, if there'd be smears.

Blitt shrugged. She was useless now; she didn't know anything else. "I figured she'd arranged something with you," she said. "Since you were late today."

I'd just gotten out of Solitary—I wasn't more than twenty minutes late for my usual shift. A half hour, tops.

Then I remembered—because I'd overheard some girls

talking. "Isn't Kennedy . . ." I searched for a good word to prove I hadn't seen the carnage at the hands of Lola the other night myself. "Uh, recovering?"

"And what would you know about that, Inmate?"

"Nothing."

"She got out of the infirmary this morning. Can't say the same for your French fry of a cellmate, though." She made a sizzling sound between her teeth.

"Didn't you hear? I'm getting someone else today." I waved at her dark TV. "The new girl. Remember?"

Maybe it was something I said, but the expression on her face was a funny one, a shifting and a sinking and a darkening. A blur. I couldn't look at her anymore.

It made me feel funny, too. Something about the word *remember*.

I took off for C-wing, hoping to catch Kennedy. I started to run, and Blitt didn't shout at me to stop running, as she lived to do. She didn't threaten me with privileges taken if I didn't slow down. She didn't shout after me at all.

I raced through the halls without passing another CO.

It wasn't long before I found Kennedy, exiting C-wing and heading for A. She was marked with bruises, her face the color of raw bacon, a meat item I hadn't tasted since I was thirteen. But she was upright and walking, and she was well enough to push the cart with a haphazard pile of books on it. She steered it clumsily into walls and then righted it, switching directions, hitting the wall opposite. A book of Rimbaud's collected poems dropped with his pretty-boy face to the floor tile, and she didn't even go back to pick him up.

It was a miracle she wasn't dead, or in a coma, after the number Lola did on her.

"Kennedy! Stop the cart."

She turned with what looked like a good amount of effort. She seemed to be having difficulty swiveling her swollen head on her swollen neck. Her ear was an eggplant, by color and almost by size. Kennedy always inspired sympathy—someone that pathetic had to, if we still bothered to care about worldly things like human suffering.

But I didn't care that Kennedy was a walking punching bag, her insides a sloppy soup from Lola's stomping feet. I didn't care that Lola had done this to her, and I didn't care that Lola could turn and do this to any one of us next. All I wanted was my books back. I wouldn't have minded if Kennedy dropped like a sack of potatoes, as she had the other night, just so she could get her grabby hands off my cart.

She didn't drop. Her fingers held fast to my cart though the whole rest of her wobbled.

"It's mine now, Amber," she eked out. "You got transferred. Yesterday." I stared at her as she spoke. The spittle at the corners of her mouth. The cut in her bottom lip that bloomed the red of a rose. She let go of the cart for a moment to wipe snot from her nose. "You're in the kitchen now. The book cart isn't yours anymore."

I didn't understand. Couldn't. Wouldn't. I wasn't even gone three days and I lost my life-skills job and got moved and Santosusso didn't tell me?

There wasn't much talking that could fix this.

The cart came at her like a semi skidding into the opposite lane in the icy night. The cart slammed her in the shins, and then the cart reversed and made a run for it, like a semi doubling back over a pair of legs.

It wasn't me doing it. It was the cart.

Then I was wrapped in a pair of thick arms, and I was flailing. Not Solitary again, not the hole, not more time on my sentence, because that was worse, we all knew that was the worst that could be thrown at us, more weeks, more months, more years.

But it wasn't a CO who had me; the arms holding me in place were in green.

Jody. The towering brick house that was Jody. She was even bigger than me.

She set me down and turned me to face her, hands still pressing on my shoulders to keep me glued to the floor. "She's had enough."

Our eyes, together, found the sniveling lump on the floor. The lump sat up and leaned against the cinder-block wall, heaving. Then the lump grabbed a hunk of hair and started chomping.

Between us—and unclaimed—was the book cart, splayed on its side, contents exploded, spines split and spilling, pages mashed up.

I reached out an arm for it, though it was too far away to grab even one book, but Jody took the arm in her large hand and lowered it to my side. Behind her came Peaches, all swagger. "Hey, bitches," she said, nodding to the lump on the floor and to me, still cradled in Jody's arms, like a mother and child who had love for each other. I didn't mind so much.

Peaches righted the cart and, generously, which was

unlike her since she never made any effort for anything that
didn't get her something in return, began to stack the books
on the tiered shelves. Kennedy whimpered. Jody smoothed
back my hair, straightened out my greens.

"Why'd you go and do that, Amber? You don't have
a violent bone in your body," Jody said. We all knew she
knew violence, had grown up with it in her house, had hidden from it in closets during the night, had then gotten up
in its face and run away from it, had modeled after it on the
streets, had made a name for herself with it, had let it carry
her all the way up here. She'd told all of us. Violence was
what she knew, so you'd think she would have recognized
it in me.

Peaches nodded, eyeing me up. "The only innocent
one here," she recited, like she'd heard it somewhere before.
That wasn't a compliment. She was calling me weak. Saying
I was a coward.

I took a step toward the books, but Jody kept me back.
What were they saying? That I wasn't really one of them,
that I didn't belong here with them? That it wasn't us against
the state, us against the world?

Peaches finished stacking the books and was now testing
out the wheels, kicking at the bad one, trying to get it to
spin all the way around. "This has nothing to do with you,
Amber. There's so much going on around here you don't
even know."

That couldn't be. She didn't have her ear to the ground
like I did; she wasn't always watching, absorbing, keeping
track. Didn't they know I was the one who kept track?

"Can I have my cart back now?" I asked.

They didn't answer.

"Can I have my cart?"

"Peaches is gonna do the books now," Jody said. "It makes sense. She's got things to run around. She's got things."

"Yeah," Peaches piped in. "I got things."

Jody rammed the cart into the wall beside Peaches, and Peaches got it in her grip before it bounced back.

We heard a miserable voice from the floor.

"But it's my job now," Kennedy said. "They said."

We ignored her, as always. At least we were united in that.

We heard the approaching thump of a CO, and we scattered. Peaches skated away on my book cart. Jody sped off, and for a giant, she vanished fast. Even Kennedy crawled a little ways, and then got to her feet and started lurching.

I headed another way, and not for the library, or Blitt in her booth, or for B-wing. Not for anywhere really, because if I went back to my cell, there'd be a stranger taking over my space. I didn't know where I was headed; all I knew was I had to force myself to think of Florida and I had to be calm. Kennedy—and then Jody and Peaches— had taken all I had. What was this place to me if now I had nothing?

I was outside the infirmary when I heard her. "Amber, Amber," she called. "Where were you? Where'd you go? You should be here. Come here." D'amour was inside, near the door. A few inmates were gathered at the foot of her bed. She was wrapped in white gauze all around her arms and legs, even covering patches of her face, mummified but still able to speak out of her throat, if a little raspily. Her once-blond hair, where it could be seen through the bandages, was the color of coal.

She beckoned me over and continued her spiel. I'd come in the middle of something.

"And everything we do, we'll do again," D'amour announced. She closed her eyes. She gestured at the air with her stiff, bandaged fingers.

"And everything we see, we've seen now three times. And the doors were opened. But they've been opened three times. We run, and we run again, and we run. And they catch you and you go away three times, Amber." She opened her eyes, nodded at me, kept on. "Then the new girl dances around the room three times, and three times Natty shouldn't trip her. Tell her. And the plants are growing in the windows, and you say no, D'amour, no. And next summer it's the same thing, except it's four. And the summer after it's five . . ."

She kept going. She reached seven, she reached eight, she reached nine. She was speaking like some kind of hokey visionary, and we were her flock who climbed the mountain to drink it in and maybe get our fortunes told next. It was a load of nonsense.

Or was it? A feeling tickled the bottoms of my feet, like something reaching up from deep down in me, wanting me to be reminded. To remember. Three times, D'amour had said at the beginning. I felt like I'd heard her say this already . . . three times.

I didn't want anyone to know that. "What's wrong with her?" I whispered.

"She got zapped in the head," Little T. whispered back. "Lightning."

"No, it was the fence. You think that's what did it?"

Little T. gave a shrug. "I got my meds. Got to go."

She crushed the tiny paper cup a nurse must have given her, though I didn't see any nurses, dropped it in the trash, and backed away. The rest of the girls drifted off, too, leaving me alone with D'amour, the two of us, the way I was used to, in the night, in our small shared space, where we huddled behind a barred door until our jailers said it could open.

"You understand, don't you, Amber?" she said.

"Yeah," I said. "I think so." I wasn't even lying. I'd witnessed some things she hadn't even mentioned.

I wanted to tell her about the intruder, but before I could, D'amour had her arm up, pointing with a rigid stabbing motion at the wall. She shook and shook her head, her bandages coming loose and revealing fried patches of skin. She covered her blinking eyes.

I turned, slowly, to see what had unsettled her so, expecting to find the white walls of the infirmary, this being the whitest room in the whole facility. Expecting to roll my eyes at her crazy, dismiss the ramblings of her sautéed brain. It would have been so much easier that way.

Instead, I saw what she saw.

Colors. Whorls and splashes and squiggles and scribbles and vacant, senseless streaks. The graffiti again. The unforgettable Bridget Love was here again, so-and-so plus so-and-so, and another RIP.

But more than that. Even worse. The cinder blocks of our walls were broken through, chipped out like kicked-in teeth, and the ceiling was crumbling down over our heads, shedding silt and concrete dust that was gray and sharper than sand. The floor was black with mold, and spongy with moss, so my feet sank. Through the gaping holes in the walls, I could see out. I could see as far as the parking lot, which had no vehicles in it and was taken over by weeds. Past that I could see that what surrounded us was edging in even closer than before. The forest was coming for our fences. The trees were growing through our gates. The vines hadn't stopped climbing. We were being swallowed. We were being choked in leaves and moss and living, searing green.

This was all that would be left of us in not so many years. Time didn't matter much in eternity. The days of this sentence couldn't be marked off on a wall and counted.

Through a gouge in the ceiling I could see up and up, to a picturesque piece of heaven, which was really only a chunk of blue sky. It was a perfectly nice August day, wherever we were. It always would be.

I rushed out of the infirmary.

And with that, with the simple act of leaving the room and getting away from D'amour, the walls in the corridor returned to their clean, solid color, their familiar green, which matched my jumpsuit, also green, the one I somehow knew would be the jumpsuit I'd forevermore be wearing. As I walked the hallway toward B-wing, I was only following steps I'd taken before. We all were. We always would be.

We kept forgetting. And we also couldn't let go.

WE WERE EYE-TO-EYE

WE WERE EYE-TO-EYE at the door to my cell. Our cell now. Her eyes were brown, and deep; mine were brown, too, but I hadn't looked in a workable mirror in some time, so maybe they'd changed. We met there in the doorway, staring at each other.

It was only a moment, but there was a flicker, some kind of connection, like the passing memory of having known each other before. Then it was snuffed out, like when the lights go down at night before we're ready, and all we can do is make the hatch mark in the cinder block to show one more day served toward release, toward our new life. It was hoped we might have two lives—the way cats are said to have nine. This life we ruined, and another, for after.

She dropped her gaze first. Then she stepped aside for me, so I could enter.

She'd claimed D'amour's top bunk and D'amour's shelves. Her canvas slip-ons were where D'amour's had been, in the tub outside the door, and her feet were socked and narrow and quite long. She'd already claimed D'amour's only hook. Now it was her hook. Now we would breathe the same air. She would sleep to the sound of my heart beating, and I'd sleep to the sound of hers.

Neither of us had spoken. I should have gone first. Said, *Welcome*. Or something shorter and more cryptic, like *Hey*. Here was the moment to drop some wisdom from my three years, one month, and fifteen days of being incarcerated at Aurora Hills, but I kept it back. I'd tried to be helpful the last time, with D'amour. And look where that got me.

Besides, I had other things on my mind. The loss of my book cart. The transfer to the kitchen, which was noted and official now, listed under my name outside the cell. All the rest—the sense of what was coming—seemed so far away. It was a forgetting like a heavy door being closed. It would take a lot of effort to push it open.

I sat on my bottom bunk, curled my knees in. A job in the kitchen would involve spills and smells that were sour, rancid, sickening. There would be burns from oven racks and hot plates. Wrinkled palms from searing dishwater. I'd be pruned after every shift. I'd stink.

What there wouldn't be were the books, the soothing sound as they cascaded open, a thumb flicked to give them a good, fast skim. There wouldn't be a way to travel from wing to wing, listening. No wheels on the cart spinning, carrying the stories, the words.

I felt gutted. Alone.

Alone like in the interrogation room at the police station, when they didn't bring me a glass of water, and they didn't let me leave the table, and they said they had my diary, and they said they saw what I wrote in it, and I asked for my mom, and I asked who gave them my diary, and I said I was thirsty, and I asked again for my mom, and they didn't bring me a glass of water, and my mom didn't come.

The new girl hovered near me.

"Did I do something?" she asked. "Are you upset you have to room with me?"

I grunted.

I'd been in long enough to know how to act around a cold-blooded killer. We could never be caught seeming nervous. We should always reveal only a small, tip-of-the-iceberg version of ourselves, and submerge the rest. The very last thing we should show is fear, and if we did, we were toast.

She didn't look so much like a cold-blooded killer, but still. This was better. Safe.

"Did they tell you who I am?" Her voice was the one shaking.

"Orianna," I said, the name bubbling up without any effort to grab it.

"Call me Ori. I don't mind."

Somehow I'd expected that. I gave her a nod. Her knees were jittering in her baggy orange pants—I could see the outlines of them beneath the thin fabric, rocking. She didn't ask if I knew what she had done.

"I guess I'm your new roommate," she said. It was funny the way she talked, as if the small space we were made to exist in could be called a room. That simple word could make it seem like we were anywhere but in a dank, dark prison.

"Cellmate," I corrected. She shouldn't sugarcoat it.

"That's what I meant."

"I'm Amber. You can call me Amber."

"I know. They told me. I heard you're innocent."

"Who said that?"

"The others."

Part of me bristled at the idea of being talked about behind my back, but I also liked it, liked being a topic of conversation, visible when I'd thought I wasn't. I kind of liked it a lot. If I could have smiled, I would have, but my face always seemed to contradict what I was thinking. I knew I looked angry when I was sad. I looked angry when I was happy. Angry when I was checking the clock on the wall to see what time it was. I'd been told I came out of the womb looking angry, my brows furrowed, my mouth like a knife. It was when I really was angry that I wondered if I finally looked like myself.

"What are you here for?" she asked. "I mean, what do they say you did?"

"You're not supposed to ask me that."

In the interrogation room at the police station, no one had thought me innocent. My own stepfather would have stood up out of his grave and pointed a crooked finger at me. (The fingers of his right hand were crooked in the sockets from a fist punched against unforgiving wood when he was aiming for a dodging head.) He would have declared me guilty if he still could.

"Sorry," she said.

I made myself busy smoothing the sheets on my bunk. She would not shut up.

"If you're innocent," she said, to my back, "you must be so pissed off, then. I mean, you must hate every single person here."

How wrong she was. She was new, so she didn't sense the connection. Didn't know the rhythm of our feet in the corridors, how it felt to be in tune with them, two feet among so many. To look like everyone else, to wear what they were wearing, to eat what they were eating, to stand up and be counted when they were counted, to sit down when they were allowed to sit. To fit in somewhere in the world, even if there were chains and gates and fences to keep us from running. And more—to have felt the magic of that night, that one night, when bungled technology failed our captors and winked instead in our direction. When the place was ours and the COs had vanished and we didn't know or care where, and the rain came down, and the song that played was made of our wails and our screams. We remembered it like a dream.

And she'd missed it.

She didn't know. She thought I was thinking of my innocence.

"How many years did you get?" she asked.

That was one question it was okay to answer. We all shared our time, and lamented over every last day.

But when I thought then of the time I had left, I didn't bristle. My blood didn't boil. My eyes didn't sting with the effort of not tearing up.

I didn't know how to say the words to her, or to anyone, but I wasn't enraged anymore about my sentence. In the beginning I was, choking on it in the night when my first cellmate was sleeping (Eva; breaking and entering; out in seven months). But I guess I'd softened. I'd gotten used to being here. I got used to the rules and having my jumpsuit buttons done all the way up and my shoes off inside the cell and my books off the bed and my eyes on the floor when a CO yelled in my face. The bad things, the very bad—like stripping down for the cough-and-squat we didn't like to speak of—I guess I got used to them. I settled, the way people do.

I've heard, or I read somewhere, that humans can find ways to adapt to most anything.

Now Ori paused, and made herself busy with her jumpsuits, folding them and neatening them, though we were issued only three and she was already wearing one. She was being shy now. Maybe I would show her the ropes, give her the what-to-always-do and the what-to-never-ever-do if you want to keep the nose unbroken on your God-given face. She had only me to show her. Look at how her hands were shaking, folding her oranges. I was all she had.

As she worked, she kept her eyes on the wall.

"Aren't you going to ask me if I did it?" she said. Maybe she wanted to pronounce herself innocent so we could be the same; that could be what this was.

I kept my mouth closed and did not ask. That was how to live around here, without asking too many questions. Better not to go around dangling your curiosities for everyone to view. That would be rude.

"No?" she said, wanting me to ask it.

"No. That's none of my business."

It was the most private thing we had left—held even closer than our bodies, because our bodies were searched, all holes and crevices and cavities in every horrible way that could be imagined. But no one could shake out the truth from inside us. They couldn't search us for that.

Our guilt and our innocence were only our own, and she should know to keep it that way.

"You can ask me . . . ," she started.

"No," I said. "I can't."

"Sorry." She apologized a lot.

I tried to remember how many she'd been said to kill—only two, or was it three?

I wondered what happened after she got her first taste. Would two dead be enough for her? Would three, four? Would any amount ever be enough? Would she always be chasing after more?

All questions I could not, and would not, ask her out loud. Least of all the question of whether or not she was guilty.

Then again, there were methods of wringing it out. The first way was easiest, and didn't even involve an improvised weapon, which was good, because all I had in the cell were two books and an extra bar of soap. There was a way of solving the question of her guilt without having to ask. There was always a way, and after enough time inside, we found our methods of digging without causing offense. I didn't even need words.

Guilt is in the eyes, for those of us who've been around long enough and know what to look for. And the first thing I saw of her were her two wide, brown eyes.

Hers didn't skitter or blink at odd moments. There was no shifting, no blank haze. When she looked at me—when I let her meet my gaze—I couldn't find the telltale signs, the way another one of us (Mirabel, Lola, Polly, Cherie, Little T., D'amour, I could go on) might have given away her true colors by a shrewd sideways glance or a distinct pupil jitter. This new girl only eyed me back. She wasn't trying to hide anything that I could make out. She wasn't trying to pull one over on me. I could sleep in the bunk below her with my bare neck exposed without any ounce of worry that night.

Mostly what I found in her eyes was a singular feeling, and it struck me. Past the sadness, I mean. Beyond that, and down deep in her sockets, what I found was surprise.

Part of her still didn't believe she was locked away in here. Only a skilled sociopath, a true mastermind, or a girl sentenced for a crime she did not commit when she thought the world would never do something like that to her, would reflect this back to me.

Life. We'd long known it was cruel. But she was new. I guess this was her first reckoning.

"Hey, so—," I started, until I heard it coming.

In the quiet it rang out. I heard the familiar glide and shuffle, shuffle and glide, the back wheel on the left spinning loose on its axle, off-track, and off-rhythm, from the others. The book cart came to a stop in front of our open doorway. There were a few minutes remaining of free time, and the cart had finally arrived on B-wing.

But I wasn't at the helm, and Ori wouldn't know me to

be. For her, from day one at Aurora Hills, the girl who ran the book cart and worked the library would be Peaches.

Peaches raised her chin to me. "What you want?"

I shook my head. I would not take a book, and I would not take one of her pills as an apology.

"Ah. Too soon."

I stared down the wall, which did not stare back at me. I wouldn't let her rattle me. The cart barely had any books on it, and the ones there were just tossed on, upside down, disorganized. It hurt to look.

"Got to check your window," Peaches said, shoving herself into our already cramped space to climb up on what was now Ori's top bunk. Ours was the only cell window that would open—everyone knew that. She plunged her arm out the barred window, searching against the stone wall outside, and came up empty. She tried again, and again empty. Then she climbed back down.

Ori watched without comment, confusion all over her face. I'd have to warn her about showing so much of herself so easily.

"There's this plant," Peaches explained to her. "Like this vine. I need it. But it looks like the last bitch who was in here smoked that shit all up." She shot a glance at me that I did not return.

"Need it?" Ori said. "For what?"

Peaches smirked and twisted her lips. She turned to me. "You sure you don't want nothing, Amber?"

"Nope," I said.

"Not a little story to read?"

"No, thanks."

Her attention shifted to my cellie. "You?"

Ori eyed the both of us. She must have sensed that something was up. Then, quietly, "I guess I don't feel much like reading. Maybe later?"

Peaches snorted, like she'd said something funny. "Okay, killa. Suit yourself." She wheeled the cart away, on to the next cell. The skip and slide of the wheels, the slide, the skip.

Ori's face was stricken. "Do you think she knows? Does everybody know?"

"What do you mean?"

"She called me . . ." She couldn't say it.

I shrugged.

She peeked out into the open space at the center of B-wing, where Peaches was wheeling away my cart. "You wanted a book, didn't you?"

I shrugged once more.

"I could tell." She waited for me to say more, but I wasn't going to—obviously I wasn't. But then I did.

"She took it from me," I said.

"What? A book? Like which one?"

I shook my head, wishing I hadn't uttered a word. "Not just one. All of them. Everything. She took everything."

She had this dense look on her face, as though she struggled with it, trying to understand. "Can't you just ask for them back? Explain it to her?"

I scoffed. "You don't understand this place at all."

"But—," she started. I waved her off.

"Don't talk about things you don't know," I said. "Chow

time soon. Don't ever eat the peas or the meat loaf. The days that suck are the days we have both peas and meat loaf, so those are the days you don't eat. Be sure to sit with me. Make sure to throw away your fork and spoon when you're done or they'll search you. Don't look at me like that. They're plastic. You'll learn."

It wasn't until the night, when we were alone again, and more alone than before because our door was sealed in the frame and its lock was turned and we couldn't get out this time, though once we had—it wasn't until this moment that she again chose to talk to me. She'd been quiet all through counts and dinner, all through after-dinner social and after-dinner counts. She'd been quiet as we undressed in front of each other. And when the locks turned, a momentous occasion for any girl's first night in Aurora Hills, I kept quiet myself, to let her have her moment.

We got into our beds. The lights went down, and B-wing hushed. I let my eyes close. I didn't think of her attacking me with a carved eye-gouger made from a plastic spoon, even though I hadn't seen for sure if she'd properly disposed of her plastic spoon, because I knew what I knew from before. I also knew other things, unremembered things, and it was only with my eyes closed and the blackness coming in to cover me that I sensed the tug and tickle that indicated they might come back.

What I was forgetting, I mean. What we all were.

I rolled over, away from it. I drifted. The walls held me close. I let my bare feet touch the bare wall, which was cold even in hot weather, eternally cold, the way I liked it. I found it comforting. I sank.

Then she woke me. "Um, Amber?"

I tossed over, my name a distant, bobbing thing I didn't need to pull from the water.

"Amber?"

I let an arm drop. I let a foot leave the wall.

"Amber, are you awake?"

I cocked one eye open. This, here, *this* was my angry face. "Now I am."

"You were humming."

I wiped the dribble of spit from my mouth, and the slick on my flat, rock-hard pillow made me have to turn the pillow over to try the other side, which felt even more flat and even more like a rock. I wouldn't be able to get back to sleep so easily now.

"Sorry. I thought you were awake."

"I wasn't." I looked up and could see her dangling, muscled leg.

"What's that song you were humming?"

"Don't know. I was asleep."

A long moment passed, and I let my eyes close again.

"Do you dream of it?" she said.

"What," I said, "what I did, you mean?"

"No," she rushed to say. "I'm not saying you did it. I'm not saying that. I mean of before. Home, I guess. Like, do you still dream of it even though you're here?"

Maybe she was trying to needle out the truth from me, still. "If we talk too loud, the CO will come, you know," I said.

"Oh. Sorry."

My mind flashed me a single picture in the dark of our

cell: It was an orange truck being licked by an orange ball of flames. And then my mind went orange and closed itself up.

It's not something I ever talked about. Other girls didn't ask. No one wanted to know how charred he was when they found him in the carcass of the truck, how passersby could only stand back and watch him barbecue. How no one could save him, because then they would have gotten barbecued, too.

None of the girls knew how I wished him dead. It wouldn't have been so memorable to confess that, anyway, seeing how many of them had also wished men in their lives dead. We could have put together a chorus.

They wouldn't have wanted to know about the lists in my diary, the collection I was building of all the ways he might die, in case.

Simple things, at first. Domestic things.

Slip on the ice while shoveling the driveway.

Fall off the roof while cleaning the gutters.

Get electrocuted by the blender while making a protein shake.

Then I started researching.

Spider bite. Snake bite. Wasp sting. Accelerated Lyme disease.

I sought out outlandish stories in newspapers.

Get hit by bathroom debris from a 747.

Fall in a manhole while crossing the street.

I had an idea, and I got on a roll.

Choke on a grape. On a peanut. On a Dorito. On a piece of hamburger meat in the parking lot of the McDonald's.

I got creative, and the ideas got more violent, more picturesque.

Mauled by a bear. Knifed in the gut by a masked robber. Run over by a Trailways bus. Decapitated by a Frisbee. Cut in half by a falling oak tree and then buried under its stump.

Suicide, with rope. Suicide, by exhaust pipe. Suicide, by oven. Suicide, old-fashioned, in a warm tub with a razor.

Pills, all kinds, in handfuls, swallowed until he foamed and choked.

So much was wishful thinking.

Shot to the head. Slice to the throat. Drano in the coffee. A two-by-four with nails in it smacked over his thick skull. Set the whole house on fire with him in it, and run.

(*Car wreck* was an early, obvious entry to the ongoing list. It hadn't occurred to me there'd be all those flames, so it was kind of like dying in a fire, too.)

If I told about my list, if I let that out, I'd have to let out the rest, like what he'd done to me or to my mom that would prompt me to make such a list, what he may have started doing to my little half sister, because I'd seen three purple blooms on her arm that looked like finger marks, even though she said she just fell off her bike. These were things that I couldn't find a way to talk about in the dark or in the sun. I couldn't put them to words in any kind of light. So I made my lists instead.

The thing was this: Writing something down on a piece of paper does not make it come true. It's like wishing on a set of birthday candles. Who ever woke up the next day to receive her pony?

Ori hadn't said a word in a long while. Maybe she was sleeping. But I wasn't. I was awake. I was remembering. I was alive, and he wasn't.

"Almost every night," I said. I didn't wait for her to ask me what I meant. I was falling back into it, as I'd been before she'd woken me. I was sinking, lowering, dropping, seeing the flashes. The orange truck. The hot burning hand on a windshield. The drifting, toxic scent of gasoline. The glorious black smoke.

I wasn't there to witness it, but how I wish I had been.

I WAS CURIOUS

I WAS CURIOUS about her, more and more curious. I watched her for the whole rest of the week. While she sat beside me in the cafeteria, where I told her to sit. While she stood for count outside our shared cell, where she was told to stand. Sometimes while she slept, which involved creeping up the ladder a ways to peer into her bunk, to see if she was really sleeping. (She was. She slept on her back, with her hands curled on her chest, as if she were squeezed into a coffin.) I turned away, though, in the night, whenever she got up to pee.

I noticed that she scribbled letters during class—at first, I didn't know who to. And there were times when she tried to see herself in the wedge of mirror on the wall of our cell, moving around in front of it as if a different angle would illuminate what she was hoping to find. Fear scrunched up her face sometimes when she did this. Other times, she looked the way she had when I first met her, which was sad, though not anymore so surprised.

I couldn't help but notice her feet, which had weird knobs up near her toes and rough, red spots. That was how I first learned that, on the outside, the way some of us were carjackers and gangbangers, and others of us were trouble-makers and bullies and mother-haters, she was something none of us were: a ballet dancer.

This sounded silly to us, like coming in saying you ride elephants, or you paint your face white and mime to strangers on the street for nickels.

But it was true: The news had flashed all those tutu'd pictures, bunheaded and serious, with what looked like deformed stilts molded to the ends of her pink feet. Lots of us had seen. And, once, I caught her leaning with her leg out, and then, before I could blink, she was practically halved and doing the splits with her cheek touching her knee. When she saw me looking, she crumpled up her legs again and slouched.

"Why don't you do that stuff?" I said. "Show us or something." She had to know we sought out entertainment anywhere we could find it. We always asked Natty to sing. And we had Cherie doing magic tricks when no one wanted to play gin rummy or spit, though about half the time she guessed wrong about which card we held in our hands.

Ori's face stilled. Her jaw turned to concrete.

"What?" she finally said between her teeth. "Do what?"

"Dance."

She shook her head.

"Not in here," I said, of our cell. Obviously there was no room. "Out there. Or where they make us do that yoga-stretching sometimes, maybe there."

"I don't." She went to the mirror, which was not a mirror, and tried to look in. Then she gave up and looked at the wall. "I don't dance."

"But—"

"Not anymore."

She spoke like she'd cast it off forever, the way Lian swore she'd never again touch a drop of booze. She acted like even hearing the word made her sick to her stomach, made some invisible part of her scream out in hurt.

Other than this, her first days in Aurora Hills made me think of my own. She moved through our halls under that same cloud of gummed numb I remembered being stuck inside. She didn't show fear. She knew she shouldn't. She couldn't. We'd feed on fear like we were wolves, and then there'd be nothing left to her but bones and the ugly, mis-shapen skin of her feet. We'd leave at least her feet alone.

She didn't fight with anyone, even when one of us got up in her face and tried to get a rise out of her. She didn't cry, not that I heard. Maybe she had that same buggy feeling I did, the one that crawled in her ears at night and scratched out the bad things. The one that said, *Now you're here, you'd better get used to it. You'll never leave.*

I didn't know, because, after that first night with all her questions, she'd gone quiet. I guess reality was setting in.

I watched her in class, for something more telling. Like I'd told her, classes were a nuisance. We had them mornings, five days a week. It was mandated by the state, but in each subject there was just one teacher for all girls age fifteen and older. When you read a lot, like me, what was there to learn in a class like that? Those of us beyond the material were given a seat in the back and a book to train our eyes on and told to study on our own. In this way, I taught myself algebra. I interpreted the symbolism in Shakespeare plays and made up my own answers. I considered the philosophies of Plato and Kant. I learned to knit, from a book, without needles and without yarn. I memorized the names of Egyptian pharaohs and European dictators. I did the same practice tests for the general-equivalency diploma over and over until I aced each one.

Ori ended up in a seat in the back of the room, too. She got the book of pharaohs, now that I was done with it, and she sat, eyes glazed, chin bobbing over the two-page spread of Cleopatra, just as I had, admiring the majestic gold crown. She got out a piece of paper. She asked for a pencil. I turned back to my *Foundations of Astronomy* textbook, mildewed and squishy in one corner, but a real find. When I looked up forty-three minutes later, she was still on Cleopatra. The book was upside down.

She wasn't absorbing everything she could about the Egyptian dynasties. Instead, she had her arms wrapped around the book to form a protective tent, and inside the tent she was writing a letter—furiously. The pencil made gashes in the paper, open wounds. At one point, a whole half of the page was torn away.

She saw the teacher glance up, and mistaking that gesture to mean the teacher cared, she hid the letter in a random page, near Xerxes the Great. I lagged on the way out of the classroom and pulled it out, speed-read it while in step for the door, and dropped it again in the nearest receptacle (a box of worn English textbooks from 1983) before entering the hallway. Loose paper without a reason to be carrying it was contraband.

What I remember from my brisk skim was this: The handwriting was practically illegible, so maybe Ori should have been in a desk up front, learning basics with the fourteen-year-olds. But I'd caught these words:

How do you sleep at night
that time we went to Great Adventure and we
It should be you.
~~*ROT. IN. HELL!!!!!*~~

This wasn't a love note. Ori wanted someone dead the way I'd wanted my stepfather dead. Who? And somehow, in my wildest dreams, the fiery, smoky ones that filled my head at night, there was a part of me that believed that writing did hold some kind of magic. I wrote it. *Car wreck. Car wreck. Car wreck.* And then it came true. Maybe Ori believed, too.

Getting a glimpse at her hidden letter made me watch her all the more. We were all of us hiding something. And since we knew that as well as we now knew our numbers, which took the place of our names, since we were escorted in here, trying to keep our secrets tucked in, we always had an eye out for someone else dropping one of hers.

The week went on, and I didn't take my eyes off her.

In Aurora Hills, infractions were picked up easily, as Ori would soon learn. She'd be more careful. There were many things that would get the COs riled up. Wearing shoes inside the cells. Being late for a meal. Showering at off-hours or not showering enough. Talking back or talking too much. Laughing (they thought we were laughing at them). Walking fast (they thought we were running). Sleeping at night with a blanket pulled up over our heads so they couldn't see us in our beds at all times.

Worse were scratch marks on our arms, legs, anywhere that could be self-inflicted, even if we had a monstrous itch that needed scratching. We shouldn't give in to temptation. No one wanted to be a Suicide, because then we didn't get to have the lights off when we slept, and no cover of blanket at night, only a thin sheet, and in the daytime, all day, in front of COs and everyone, anyone under Suicide Watch couldn't wear a bra. The straps could be used to strangle, we were told, thus giving us ideas.

I warned Ori about becoming a Suicide, but I couldn't warn her in time about every last thing.

It'd take a day or two, usually, before a new girl got on the wrong side of a CO. This meant a show of force. A power trip. The way we saw it, the guards jumped us and face-planted us and then, after all this, they told *us* to calm ourselves down. The way they saw it, it was discipline, and we deserved it.

Ori had wandered off from the line when it happened to her the first time. We were in formation, heading for lunch, when something out the window caught her eye. She drifted for the glass and put her hand on it, as best she could, what with the bars in the way. Out through that window was a bright summer's day, the blue sky with the sun shining, the green trees swaying in the breeze, a butterfly maybe—we saw them sometimes, flitting by. All of what was out there was proof of the world going on and forgetting us, and maybe that was what called her to stop. We didn't know, and it ended too fast for us to ask her.

A CO, Rafferty, had caught sight of her and shouted for her to keep moving. To return to the line. She was holding us all up, and if she did it for much longer, she'd keep us all from getting chow. Some of us whined, our bellies growling, but others of us didn't want the rubbery ham sandwich of the day, anyway, and looked on with faint smiles, knowing what was coming. It would be entertainment to watch her struggle, see her fly.

I wanted to speak up—warn her somehow—but I kept my mouth shut, because I didn't want it, next, to be me.

"Speerling!" Rafferty shouted to her.

She had her back to us, her face pressed between the bars protecting the window, the bright blue sky in her eyes.

"Back in line, Speerling!"

Her ears were plugged with memories, maybe. Her head pounding with regrets.

Rafferty left the head of our line and started charging. We oohed, we aahed, we backed away. One of us had a weak moment and covered her eyes.

Mississippi said she saw Ori grab ahold of those window bars and hold them tight. Mirabel said Ori didn't hold on at all; she only seemed shocked to be lifted off the ground, her mouth in a big, wide O, her hair a spill that clogged up the CO's eyes.

We all saw her go down, though. We saw Rafferty with his hands on her, and then she was flat on the floor, her arms awkwardly crooked behind her back and a man in uniform straddling her, and it was all some of us could do not to have flashbacks of our most heart-stopping arrests.

The "face-down restraint procedure" may have technically been illegal to use on juveniles in our state, but that didn't stop the COs from training in it, Olympic-style. The move involved them doing this thing with their arms hooked around our necks, coming at us from behind and scooping us into the air, and then sailing us forward on our stomachs until floor met face and arms bent behind backs and we could go nowhere.

They held us down, our nose and lips mashed to the ground, wriggling or still, struggling or writhing or trying to kick, crying or seething or playing dead. And, no matter what we did or felt or didn't do, we were theirs. We were their game.

Now Ori was truly one of us.

When she'd calmed enough for Rafferty to let her go, he allowed her to stand on her own. Her cheeks were tomatoes and tears dripped off the tip of her nose. She wiped her face with her sleeve. We smirked, or we tried to meet her eyes and give a smile to show we'd been there, or we looked down at our canvas shoes.

"Now get in line, Speerling," Rafferty commanded. "Chow time."

She took her space in line, which was directly behind me. She stood up straight, and with her posture and her height, she was tall and she was steady. I could have reached out my hand behind me and patted her on the arm, maybe, but being caught touching would lose me even more privileges,

and I'd already lost my cart. All I did was turn my neck, ever
so slightly, and give her a nod. Then we started walking for
the cafeteria as if nothing had happened. She didn't steal a
glance at the barred window and the blue sky beyond it as
we went past. None of us did. It had been wrecked for us
now, like by a bulldozer. It had been blown to bits by an
atom bomb.

By the second week of her stay, Ori had gotten used to
all the things we'd gotten used to: the face-downs and the
strip searches, the squat-and-coughs, the shame. Plus the
small things, and they added up. Being told our lives were
over. Being told the electric chair should be legal, even for
someone under eighteen. Being called "Inmate" instead of
our given names by some of the COs who liked to play this
was real prison. She got used to the sound of the lock turning on our cell door every night, that cold clunk.

All this she survived without complaint or many questions. It was odd, how easily she surrendered. It wasn't that
she'd gone soft. It was almost like she'd given up. Given in.

We were deep into August. We all had our life-skills as-
signments a couple afternoons a week. Ori's job was with
the groundskeeper, outside under the hot sun. She dug in
the dirt and pulled weeds in the garden. She learned how to
use a shovel properly, which could come in handy for bury-
ing things instead of planting them. She also had access to
whatever it was that girls like Peaches and D'amour were
after, but I don't think that had anything to do with her
enjoyment. Digging out there seemed to be the one thing
she wanted to do.

My life-skills assignment was in the kitchen then, and

I'd catch a glimpse of her out the windows, which were larger and gave more light than any other windows in the whole facility. I'd see Ori in the dirt, communing with the worms. I noticed how the groundskeeper kept his distance from her, but he must have heard the stories. He had to have been wondering about her.

Weren't we all, from girl to guard, from criminal to civilian? We wanted a glimpse at the monster inside. We thought we could catch a peek sometimes, a shiftiness in the eyes maybe. A rumble.

Each of us had our own monster, distinct to us. We were all different, one girl to the next, like snowflakes.

But Ori's monster wasn't showing. And I tried to see it. I tried very hard to make out what was wrong with her, to have been found guilty and shipped up here, no effort at an appeal. Because I couldn't figure it out. No way she actually was innocent, was there? The way the girls went around saying about me?

Her true self sparkled sometimes. Told me things in the way a premonition might have, if I'd seen the light. I knew there was something I was forgetting. My mind was dragging around a heavy part of itself. Like a phantom limb, it itched every once in a while; it prickled with electricity even though I couldn't lift it out.

All my attention was on Ori. I was judge and jury all rolled into one, and I was beginning to believe she shouldn't be here.

For instance, the cup. The way she saw that cup, when to us it was something entirely different.

We could never choose our dishes or utensils in the

cafeteria. We had to take the trays we were given, and the food we were given, though we could choose to chew and swallow and digest that food or starve, when the macaroni was extra rancid or the soup looked weird. But Ori had this one cup she liked to use, from the collection in the cafeteria.

Sometimes the red cup would be among those serviced in the dishwasher and offered at the meal that day. Any girl among us might find it on her tray. There was the luck of the draw to getting the red cup, instead of one of the many white cups or one of the grays. Before Ori arrived here, it was bad luck to find the bright object there on our trays, filled with the milk or the sour-tasting orange juice or the flat soda drink we were given. Most of us wouldn't dare take a sip. Whatever filled the red cup was cursed, and we'd rather be parched than drink it down.

Then came Ori. And, we realized, she always saw the good in something first, before any bad. Even after Rafferty caught her out of line, even when she tamped herself down and got quiet and went through all the motions without any outburst, any protest, even then. Her true self kept peeking out.

She saw what we couldn't. When it came to the inmates, she saw through our hard exteriors and the teardrops needled under our eyes and the bloodied scrapes on our knuckles from our wall-punching. It was like she saw that time one of us gave our only twenty-dollar bill to the man on the corner who slept in the box. Or she saw the time another one of us found the snail on the sidewalk and saved it from being smashed by walking feet, carrying its shell and slime over to the grass. She saw our outside goodness, those far-back memories in the rearview of our old lives, and she saw our inside goodness, too.

I had no idea how.

She saw us as we could be, if we weren't locked up in here. She saw what the judge couldn't see and what the public defender only pretended to see and what our own mothers, who refused to come on visiting day, should have seen.

Imagine a person who still looks at you the way your mother used to, when you were little and two-braided and good. That was Orianna Speerling, our new inmate, the closing of our circle, our forty-two.

So when the red cup landed on her tray for the first time, the second week of her endless sentenced weeks, Ori did something strange, something that caught us off guard. She looked down at the bright red spot on her tray, and she smiled. This smile lit up her face. We hadn't seen her face like this, hadn't seen that smile, ever, so a few of us in line stopped and took a moment just to behold it.

"You sick or something?" Natty asked her.

Cherie put a hand on her arm though there was to be no touching. "Hey. Are you okay?"

Ori only smiled, kept the light on, kept smiling. She turned to me. "Look what I got," she said. "Can you believe it!"

We each dropped our gaze in disbelief to her warped plastic tray, melted in on one side from the defectively hot corner of the dishwasher. In the cupped compartments on the tray there was a glop of potato, a slop of meat, a sludge of green beans, a rock-hard whole-wheat roll, and a slice of yellow cake with no icing. She didn't mean any of that, clearly. In the cup hole, there it was, the dreaded red cup. It contained a bluish dribble of what we had to assume was milk.

"The good cup's mine," she said, "for today." Almost like she wanted us to know that tomorrow the cup could belong to any one of us.

Ori and I went down the line, to grab our plastic utensils, and found a table to sit where we wouldn't be pounded for taking someone's preferred seat. She slid in across from me. We kept our heads down, as usual. I put my spoon in the gelatinous glop of potatoes and took a slithering bite.

When I glanced up, still, there on her face: the smile.

It made me lose hold of where we were for a moment. Confused me.

Happiness for no reason made a certain kind of light in here. Pulsing. Causing a blazing flare in the middle of the cafeteria. It hurt our eyes. It called attention.

"This will be a good day," she said, and everyone in the near vicinity turned to look. "That's what this means," she said. Some of the girls started whispering. One of the girls at our table—Mack—got up to move somewhere else.

"You shouldn't drink out of that," I told Ori. "We don't ever . . . we never—"

I should have warned her sooner. She held the red cup to her chapped lips and took a passionate swig of the maybe-probably milk.

We didn't understand. The other girls with nine months

left to their sentences, two years, two and a half months, two hundred twenty days, none of us understood. A "good" day? The last good moment for some of us was when we thought we'd get away with it. That the cop chasing us would stumble and fall. The alley we rushed into would have a detour, a way out. The getaway car would pull up, passenger door whipping open, and speed us into innocence. That was the last we knew of good.

For others, our good moments were few and far between. In the shower stall sometimes, two minutes left and the running water miraculously still hot on our sore shoulders. Sneaking a kiss with a girl whose eyes reminded us of a boyfriend's outside. Sneaking a kiss, period. Sneaking a moment to ourselves anywhere, anytime.

For me, it was being in the library, skimming a finger through a newly arrived book. That was always my good thing. Now, my last good thing.

But Ori saw good around every gray corner. She saw a brightly colored cup land on her tray of sad, terrible food in the detention center where she was to live out the last years of her teens, and she saw promise. She saw happiness. She saw a chance to drink the maybe-probably milk out of something nice-looking for a change, which would transform the watery, curdled taste into something rich and delicious.

She finished her red cup of milk, with a whole bunch of us staring. She set down the cup with a contented sigh. "That was good," she said.

After that, the red cup was coveted. Girls wanted to find

it sitting there, milk-filled or juice-filled or even tap-water-filled, on their trays. Sometimes a fight broke out over who got to drink out of it, and, twice that summer, girls were sent to the infirmary or the hole because someone said she had it first. Ori made it wanted. She acted like it was lucky. And forever after, it was.

WE REVEALED OURSELVES

WE REVEALED OURSELVES in art therapy, forcibly, in assigned groups once a week. Art therapy was run by an enthusiastic hippie, and mostly involved us drawing some abomination on a piece of cheap paper, then sitting in a circle to share it with the group after.

In her first session that August, my new cellmate didn't draw lumpy dragons like D'amour had, or cars like Mirabel did. No curvaceous porn-star silhouettes like Natty, who always spent most of the session coloring in the plump lips. She drew something important. She didn't know it then, but it was a message directed at me.

Ori drew a face. In her drawing—graphite pencil, all gray—the nose was a normal nose. The mouth was a normal mouth. The ears were normal ears. The eyebrows were thin and barely there, but normal enough. The neck was long, and no one knew where it ended because its lines swept off the page, so it could have been a giraffe neck, for all we knew.

The drawing was just a person's face. In pencil. That was it.

Even our group leader had few words for Ori in the sharing part of the session. This was her favorite time because she could interpret and read us the same way she liked to read star charts, digging through the murk and grime of our pasts.

But the hippie took a moment of silence, eyeing Ori's plain page. "A boy," she said—hopefully, I thought. She did seem to adore the idea of love affairs, so long as they didn't invade our circle of chairs.

Ori shook her head. "A girl."

"Oh!" the hippie said with an open mind, waiting for Ori to name the girl and their connection, but Ori didn't volunteer. All she was willing to say had already been said, on that piece of paper in the form of that penciled head.

"A very realistic portrait, Miss Speerling, thank you." Though, she suggested, next time perhaps, if she were so inclined, Ori might try letting go and giving her subconscious a big, fat *yes*. The hippie loved for us to tell our imaginations yes. She had no idea how dangerous that could be.

She was pleased with Cherie's contribution, which was a tree with the head of a man and the feet of a bird, possibly a chicken, and spiked eyelashes made of razor blades.

My own drawing was a house made of books, but where there should have been a door, there was a book, and where there should have been windows, there were books, and where the chimney should have been open to let the smoke out, a book was covering the hole, so if anyone was in the house, they couldn't get out. They'd suffocate, to be found years later, a desiccated corpse still marking its place in the book it had been reading with a knobby finger bone, head caved in by an avalanche of fallen books. As I said, I liked books.

Our hippie glowed with the miserable pride of a kindergarten teacher. She said I was finally getting somewhere. She urged me to dig even deeper next week, to push myself, to open up that book-door and let us see what I was concealing inside my book-walls. She wanted the walls to come crashing down. I was ready.

Natty rolled her eyes. Her drawing showed she was ready, too, she said. She was ready for some dick.

Our group leader flushed and mumbled a canned response about inappropriate behavior, which we'd just been talked to about last week.

I didn't let Natty distract me with her nonsense. I was struck by Ori's drawing. Something about that face.

It was giving me memories. And the room was spinning, and all of it (the face, somehow familiar, the room, somehow spinning, the hippie telling us to calm down or she'd call in a CO) made me unsteady in my chair. I tipped.

I recognized this face, you see. I remembered.

There was something I was supposed to remember.

I face-planted myself on the ground without a CO to help me.

The intruder. She'd broken through our walls and saw me, only me, and then she went running.

Ori had drawn our visitor, though Ori hadn't been locked up with us that night, so she couldn't have seen her. She couldn't have known. I'd told no one.

Now I remembered with perfect detail the face of the intruder—the exact same eyes, nose, lips as in this drawing. The intruder had called me not my own name but another girl's name, one that had tugged on me then but that I'd since pushed down and let sink to the bottom of the pool of names I kept track of, which now, right then, was forty-two.

Ori.

She was the one who helped me up off the floor, now, not our group leader, and not Mississippi, who'd been sitting in the chair closest to me. Ori lifted me up, though we weren't supposed to be touching; it was an infraction that could get us both sent to Solitary if the hippie wanted to be obnoxious about it and report us to a CO.

Ori had a question on her face, and I answered with a question right back from mine. I was standing now, and she stepped away and let go.

It was not that she was a brilliant artist; it was mostly the eyes, the frigid, deep blue eyes.

Then I blinked. Because she'd used only graphite pencil, which was gray, and I must have imagined the blue.

"Take your seats, girls," the hippie said. The bells around her neckline tinkled.

Ori folded her drawing carefully and didn't ask me there why I'd reacted so. We had all night to talk, she knew.

She took the drawing back to our cell after the session was over, after rec in the yard and dinner of gray cups and mashed carrots and patties of possible meat, after lining up to walk back to our wing, after waiting for what felt like forever to walk back, after walking, and standing for count in the corridor and removing our slip-on shoes before we stepped in.

When our wing made count, she turned to me, and the question from earlier was still hovering on her face. We were locked in, then, alone with our questions.

"What happened?" she said. "Why'd you freak out?"

I insinuated the drawing in her fisted hand. No need to say anything more, because the lights flashed. We had to change out of our jumpsuits into our pajamas now. We had to take turns at the sink and the toilet and make ready to get into our bed slabs for another night.

I was careful then, in those last moments between telling and not-telling. I changed with my back to her, aware of her body moving, breathing. Aware of what bodies were capable of, which was betrayal and lies. I'd learned that from having friends on the outside.

The friends I had back at home when I was thirteen were the very first people to talk to the police. They told what I'd confided at sleepovers, in buried chat messages, on the top of the bleachers when we climbed up there to try very hard to not have fun at pep rallies. These were the true friends I'd had in seventh grade, the ones who judged me guilty before any courtroom could do the same.

I couldn't recall the last time I'd had a true friend. A secret-keeper. A girl who would risk the hole to help me up when I fell off a chair.

I had begun to feel something for Ori, something I'd never felt for any of the other girls who'd been in here with me, even when I knew so much about them, from reading their notes slipped between the pages of books, and listening in on their secrets. I'd found the letter Ori had started and abandoned, but that was all I had on her. I'd heard her name at mail call and knew someone was communicating with her, but she kept those envelopes stowed away in her foot locker, careful not to let me see beyond the postmark noting they'd been mailed from Saratoga Springs. That was all I knew, and I wanted more. I wanted to know all.

But she was the one who got out the next question.

"Your drawing today . . . ," she started. "What did you used to draw before?"

"Regular houses."

She waited to see if I'd say more.

"Brick houses with windows and doors and chimneys with the puffs of smoke coming out. I guess normal houses, like the ones people live in."

She didn't ask if I'd lived in a house like that (I had) or if I ever peopled the houses I drew, showed the family out front on the green-crayoned grass under the yellow-crayoned sun, standing on their stick legs, holding stick hands maybe, wide-smiling mouths on stick necks.

I did not.

We were always careful with what we produced in art therapy—we caught on to this quickly—because indicating something on the page pointed an arrow not at it but at you.

"Aren't you angry?" Ori asked me then. "You don't seem angry. You should be more angry. Your life's ruined because no one believed you."

It was. They hadn't.

"Are you?" I asked.

"Angry?" she said. "No." Her scribbles while reading about Cleopatra had shown otherwise.

She saw my face, and I expected her to flat-out keep up the lie. She had no idea I'd seen it, even if she couldn't find it in the pharaohs book the next day.

Instead she added, "Maybe sometimes, okay? Sometimes I get so mad, I don't even feel like me. But I'm here. This isn't ending. I'm not gonna wake up tomorrow someplace else like this never even happened. So . . ."

"So?"

"So what's the point?"

I sat on my bottom bunk. She sounded so sensible. Her feet were bare, and her toes were long and hideous, and one of the nails was rot black and not from polish. She didn't try to hide them. I looked up at her face, and her eyes were honest. I couldn't help but wonder, if I'd met her on the outside, like at school, grade seven, if she'd been my friend, like up at the top of the bleachers with the others so we could ignore the pep rally, and if I'd said the things I'd said about my stepfather, who happened to meet his maker in a fiery accident not long after, what would she have done with that information? Would she have told her parents and gone to the police, like I discovered friends do? Or would she have been another kind of friend, the good and true kind of friend who'd have my back? Who'd stand up in a court of law and say I meant no harm. Who'd put her neck out. Lie for me.

I had to change the subject.

"Who's the boy?" I was testing her.

"My drawing, you mean? Why does everyone think that drawing's of a boy?"

"*Someone's* writing you letters." There were three already.

"That's Miles," she said so quietly, I could barely hear.

We needed to keep quiet anyway, because the CO would be making his rounds of the lower tier soon. The light would come shoving in through the window hole in our door, and we'd need to have our mouths shut at that point. We shouldn't risk talking, but I wanted to hear about this Miles, this three-letters-so-far Miles. This boy.

(The last time I touched a boy was maybe four years ago, on accident, at the town pool. He'd jumped off the diving board in the deep end and his hip connected with my bare shoulder, but it didn't hurt that much. Red swim trunks with the pockets sticking out like wings. Water up my nose. The sting of chlorine.)

Had Miles been the one she'd told to rot in hell, then crossed it out because she'd wanted to take it back? Was he the person who'd gone with her to Great Adventure?

She was doing it again, though. Like in the cafeteria, with the red cup. She was smiling.

"He was kind of like my boyfriend . . . We never named it officially, but I guess that's what he was."

"He sure writes you a lot. Three letters already."

"Five."

She'd hidden two.

"Five? He's got to be your boyfriend, then. Only boy-friends bother writing so much."

"He's trying to get on my visitor list, but I guess they

won't let him. I guess I don't have the clearance. Family only, so far."

"Mmm," I said. I'd been cleared for years, and no one—not family, not nonfamily, not anyone—had come to visit.

"The thing about Miles . . . ," she started.

We heard an approaching CO, and we got in place in bed, fast. The noise came and went, and I looked up into the darkness overtop me, and I asked her.

"What? What's the thing about him?"

"He's the only one who believed me."

The captivating idea of someone on the outside thinking *I* was innocent. Believing it so deeply as to write me stories about it, to go on record, on paper, where anyone could just pick it up and read it. I was glad that all I'd seen of her three (now five) letters from Miles were the Saratoga Springs postmarks and her name on the front. If I'd seen the insides, the naked parts where he confessed his belief in her, in her perfect innocence, in the idea that she was wrongly accused, it would have choked me up. It was choking me even to imagine it. Choked me like with tears.

She sensed that, maybe. She changed the subject. "But Miles isn't the person in the picture, you know."

I up and said it. "I've seen her before. The girl you drew."

Now she was the one who got quiet.

"I think it was her. Like in a dream. But it wasn't any dream. It was what happened before you got here. She visited, and she asked for you, but you weren't here yet."

I felt a shifting in the bed above me. Though the whole structure was bolted to the wall, I felt a jolt and a lurch as if it could come loose and drop us, one flat on top of the other, to the hard ground. But she was only climbing off her top bunk to come down to my level.

She wanted to see my eyes, I think. However much of them she could make out in our patch of darkness. She must have thought there'd be a way to tell if I was lying.

Here I was more afraid of this than at the idea of her long, graceful arm reaching out in the darkness and slicing my throat. I'd heard she killed those girls with knives. Everyone was saying that.

"Explain," she said.

I told her about our night. She wasn't there with us then, but she was a part of us now, and I told her. The locks, how they opened; the doors, how they let go. Our pounding feet in the darkness and the tide that took us and the great wide-open sea.

How we thought we lost D'amour. The flash of electricity, almost lightning, and then that girl, an exact replica of the gray face in art therapy.

I was describing her, all I remembered, every last thing. It was when I mentioned the one detail, only then, that I think Ori believed me.

"She had a gold bracelet with little people on it. These little—"

"Ballet dancers," she finished. She seemed as frightened as I was, suddenly. I made the connection. How, of all things on the girl's gold wrist, it would be the very thing Ori used to be. Like it was her, caught on the chain, for all eternity.

I nodded. "Her eyes," I added, "were very blue."

"Oh," she said. "Oh."

"What?"

"How'd she get up here?"

I didn't know.

"She was looking for me. She was saying my name."

I nodded, yes, I think she was. A dream, I said; it had to be. A hallucination. A slip of reality. A slip of memory. A slip.

But to see Ori's face in the moonlight through our narrow window slit, to see her eyes widen, the slack of shock in her open mouth. To see all that, none of us would think so.

"What did she say about me?" she said. "What did she say I did?"

A CO was coming, and Ori jumped back up into bed. We both kept still as he made his rounds past our door, shining the light in through our hole, blazing us up, and then leaving us alone, leaving us be.

Finally she leaned down.

"Her name is Violet Dumont," she said. "That's her name. She's why I'm in here."

Then she stopped talking, because she'd said too much.

Was Violet Dumont one of the girls she'd killed? I sat up, waiting for more, but Ori's head wasn't in view any longer. She'd gone quiet now. She wasn't telling. She was learning to keep her one true secret, and she'd learned that from me.

THEY CALLED

THEY CALLED ME in, first thing the next morning. A random Tuesday. There was no hearing I knew of, no counselor to meet with, no infraction to argue against. I couldn't think of any reason they'd call me in.

Santosusso was the CO who escorted me to the wood-paneled room in a part of the facility I'd never visited. He seemed oddly joyful about getting to take me, almost giddy. I could swear there was a spring in his step as he led me out of B-wing, a jaunty tilt to his blue-brimmed cap, a bounce to his gun. "This is going to make your day," he told me. "I don't want to get your hopes up, but this could be good."

Santosusso opened the door, and there they were, seated all to one side of a long table.

The state had sent three people. Two were women, one round and mean faced; one slim and sharp nailed and meaner. The third was a man, much larger than the two women combined, engulfing the chair he sat in. He wore a red beard, as if he'd been plucked from the great Norse myths of Thor. The Viking nodded at me; the two mean-faced women did not.

The walls of this room were made from wood panels like planks on the deck of a ship. It made the room seem darker, danker, even with the ceiling lights on. It gave an underwater feeling to the proceedings, as if I were drowning and they could reach out an arm across the table and choose to save me. Or not.

On the other side of the long table was one chair. That was to be for me. Santosusso led me to it and then sat me down. I placed my hands in full view on the table. My wrists were free.

"Good afternoon, Miss Smith," the round woman said. "Thank you for joining us today," she added, as if I'd had any choice in the matter.

Then they told Santosusso to leave us be. He'd be right outside the door, he said, reassuringly—and I didn't know if that was meant for me, or for the people employed by the state who were about to be alone in a room with me.

The door closed. My hands on the table stayed artfully still, like plastic mannequin hands that had all five fingers molded together.

Then they told me the news.

I wasn't clear on the details, and I didn't have the legal knowledge that Peaches did, from studying in case she ever got a new trial, seeing as she planned to stand up and go on defense for herself.

The gist was this: Something had happened on the outside, while I'd been serving my time. It was a "change of heart." This couldn't be a legal term, but the thin, mean-faced woman did say those words.

Whatever had happened on the outside had not been communicated to me until now. No letters or lawyers' visits, not a dime added to my canteen account so I could buy Reese's Cups. But that didn't mean my mother hadn't been fighting for me, the Viking said, leaning across the expanse of the table so he could almost pat my arm—almost. He didn't do it.

The gist was not that I was innocent. No. Never would they come here and admit to something like that, because that would be admitting to a miscarriage of justice, a terrible mistake made by those in charge. And we all knew they did not make mistakes.

Instead, I think they were saying that I'd been punished long enough for such a young person. There were questions lingering, about how much I'd understood at the time, about the almost-accidental nature of the impassioned crime that took place, as in, was it even an actual crime?

Such as, how was I to know that the fuel line I cut in my stepfather's truck engine would cause the gas leak that would cause the truck to explode like a box of firecrackers? I was only thirteen at the time, a child.

There was no evidence that I'd studied any of the engine manuals he kept on his neatly organized shelves in the garage. The garage was off-limits to everyone in the family but him, and no one had seen me enter his space, lights off, quietly letting the door slip shut one afternoon while he was still at work. That was a fantasy no one could outright prove.

There wasn't any evidence that either of the back tires had been punctured with the smallest of holes so the air wouldn't be felt leaking until he was driving on the road. No knowledge of any gasoline spillage on the floor mats, and no way to check anyway, what with the truck destroyed in a ball of fire and, when the fire was finally put out, so little remaining, they needed dental records to identify his remains.

This kind of crime wasn't as clear-cut as some others, such as a stabbing. At least then there was a murder weapon. Fingerprints. If they got lucky, a telltale trail of blood.

(Stabbing was an option I'd listed in my diary, though the three adults from the state did not bring up the diary the police had seized for evidence. And I did not remind them of the tiny book I had kept wedged in the wall beside my bed. The diary that contained my list, my proof of premeditation, my downfall.)

It was amazing, really, that I got put away for one man's driving accident. At the time of the incident, I was home sick from school.

But more amazing to me was the idea of my mother, back home, changing her mind.

This was the same woman who hadn't said a word to me in all these years. She hadn't come to visit. She wouldn't accept my collect calls, so I stopped calling. She never bothered to answer the letters I used to send her, so I stopped sending letters. The same woman. My mother.

"Do you understand, Miss Smith?" the round woman

asked me. "Your release papers are in progress. The final date is yet to be determined, but it will be in September."

No, I did not understand.

"Miss Smith," the thin woman said, "you can talk. You can say something."

"But does she know?" I choked out.

"She . . . who?" The thin woman shuffled her papers, and the round woman gazed, searching, at the shuffling words, which were every last thing they had on me. The Viking stared at me instead, searching my face.

"My little sister," I said. "My half sister. My . . . Pearl. She just turned ten, in June."

"We don't know anything about that," one of the women said.

I thought of Pearl, how she'd been seven the last time I saw her. She'd been carrying her Little Mermaid lunch box that morning, wearing her patent-leather shoes, black and mirror-shiny and with the taps built into the toes. Pearl, whose father burned alive in a car. Did anyone ever let her in on the details of that? Pearl, whose big sister got sent away soon after. Did she know why? Did anyone ever sit her down and tell her?

The morning of, little Pearl had tapped out of the kitchen, swinging her mermaid box. Then she'd spotted me in the next room, curled up on the couch. Wrapped in a green wool blanket, a cool washcloth draped over my forehead, I was feigning sick so I could skip school. I remember how she'd tapped across the hallway and into the den. How as soon as she entered the den, the plush carpet dampened her taps, swallowing them in silence. How she'd placed her lunch box on the floor and her small hand on my cheek. How she'd seemed so serious.

"You got a very bad fever," Pearl pronounced, like a miniature doctor, "but you'll be okay, Bambi." Bambi was her word for Amber, ever since she'd learned to talk, and since then, everyone in my family called me Bambi. "Everything will be okay tomorrow."

I don't remember what I said back to her, if anything.

Everything would be, if not "okay," then certainly settled, by tomorrow.

"Bye-bye, Bambi," Pearl had said. She was so little. So trusting and helpless. I didn't want him to ever hurt her.

"Bye, Pea," I'd said. "Have a good day at school."

She stepped onto the wooden floor of the hallway beyond the carpet and she tap-tap-tapped to the foyer and she tap-tap-tapped to the bottom of the stairs and she tap-tap-tapped a few last times, for good measure. Then she took off her tap shoes and put on her purple sneakers with the Velcro straps, like our mother always made her do before driving her to school.

I couldn't imagine that Pearl could still love me. Couldn't picture how she'd greet me, once I came home, looking like I did now, hardened up like I was now, after all these years inside.

"This news has surely startled you, Miss Smith. Do you have any questions for us?"

Smiles. Three.

I had only one question: "You're really letting me out?"

Three affirmatives. Details followed. Details about a transport bus I would take to a facility closer to my mother's house, because she wouldn't be able to come up to get me herself. Details on clothes they would provide for me, because I'd outgrown the ones I came in wearing. More details would come in September.

They wanted me to say thank you. That was what was expected of me here and now: gratitude, and lots of it. Possibly tears.

When I learned my stepfather had died on the road near our house, in his truck, I didn't cry. I didn't show much emotion at all at first. They left me alone, thinking I was in shock. I had a washcloth over my forehead, because it had been assumed I'd had a fever. Then they saw the couch was empty, the washcloth abandoned. They found me in the furnished basement, a part of the house he'd claimed as his own. I had my bare toes squished in his plush carpet, his drumsticks in my hands. I wasn't banging his snares, I wasn't hitting his bass, but I was on his stool, behind his kit, where I'd been told never to go. I was humming a song, and for days after, during the wake and during the funeral, after the hole was dug and the dirt dropped on the coffin, the headstone raised up with the BELOVED carved in gray stone, through the sobbing fits my mother would have whenever she passed the framed photo on the mantel that held her and him and my half sister and not me, through all these things I hummed it. The wrenching emotion that came out of her at losing the deep and passionate love of her life—not her children, but a man—told me what I already knew: There was no one my mother loved more than him.

All during these events and up until the police came for me, I was humming.

It was a song he used to play, a song I despised because it was a song from his youth that he adored. "Pour Some Sugar on Me," I'd hum. It turned my stomach, that song, sickened me with its sweet, raunchy whine. But in the name of hate, I'd hum it, the disgusting song he'd bang out on that drum kit no more.

When I made a plan, I kept to it. When poisoning his dinner didn't work (he thought he had a hangover and needed to sleep it off), and when causing him to slip and fall on the roof when he was fixing the shingles didn't work (he did slip; he only sprained an ankle), and when stabbing him with a steak knife didn't work (I picked up the knife, got freaked out, put the knife back in the drawer)—when all of the other options didn't work, I became resourceful. I listed the failures, and the dates of the attempts, in my diary. And I thought and thought. The prosecutor was right to call this premeditated. It was something I meditated on constantly, a soothing hum. I hoped on it. I prayed to it, as if it were a small gold god on a shelf.

Let me find a way.

Let me find *the* way.

Let me disappear him for good.

I heard how, when his truck blew out on the road, the whole cab went up in a blaze. I didn't know what I was doing, so I'd messed with the truck every way I could think of. At least one of my attempts must have worked.

A family passing in a car stopped but could do nothing. No one could get that close to the fire. They could only watch him clawing at the windows, howling in the melting red heat, and then it erupted in black smoke and they couldn't see him anymore. I heard it would have been terribly painful for him, in his last minutes. Agony, someone said. Excruciating—I remembered having to look up that word in the dictionary after I read it online.

I wasn't humming, then, in the wood-paneled room with the three visitors from the state across the table. I'd stopped humming for good at the trial. I didn't like to be reminded, so I squashed the habit. Turned out the only time I still hummed that song was when I was asleep.

The three visitors from the state studied my reactions. I couldn't figure out what they wanted from me.

I didn't make any sounds. I didn't laugh, hysterically, disbelievingly, though many of us would have, at sudden, sinking news like this. I could have held my head in my hands, trying to cover my face from view. I could have cried, and the cries could have been loud, louder than any sound I'd made since coming to this place. I could have done something else to show I'd fooled them all.

All I could do was go back to my first option. I thanked them for my freedom, the way a newly freed slave would thank her former master.

We all stood, four chairs scraping against the floor. My wrists were still loose and my head was still raised. We stood together in a room, like people do.

The door was open, and I was told I could go through it now, back to my cell, or wherever I was supposed to be this morning, and there'd be more news closer to September. Santosusso came back in to escort me, and the two women and the Viking went out first, leaving their best wishes. I didn't expect to ever see them again in my lifetime.

"See?" Santosusso said, smiling and flashing me his dimples. "What did I tell you? Good news, right?"

"Yes," I said. My mouth couldn't make a smile. "Thank you."

I could tell he wanted the best for me. Of course, he assumed that would be getting out. Everyone always thought that, not of what we had to go back to, at home. Maybe our parents had thrown away our mattresses. Maybe they'd told our siblings we'd been run over by trains, to make our absence fonder.

Not everyone had a parent. It could be that nothing was waiting for us. Our keys would no longer fit the locks. We'd resort to ringing the bell, saying we've come home, can't we come in?

The eye in the peephole would show itself, and that eye could belong to a stranger, as our family had moved halfway across the country and never informed us. Or that eye could belong to the woman who carried us for nine months, who labored for fourteen hours, who was sliced open with a C-section to give us life, and now wished she never did.

The juvenile correctional system could let us out into the world, but it could not control who would be out there, willing to claim us.

They'd said my mother had wanted me released, but until I saw her, until I heard that from her own mouth, I wouldn't be able to believe it.

Santosusso was walking me down the corridor, confused maybe as to why I wasn't leaping around for joy. He'd gone silent. We passed the window Ori had tried to see out of, and the blue sky flashed, and I turned my face away.

It was hard to take, knowing the release was mine and mine only. I would get out, and all the rest of us would stay here.

I thought of my new cellmate. Who would get her through her first winter? Not an ounce of me felt like celebrating.

Santosusso didn't escort me back to B-wing but to the academic wing, since it was morning and class was still in session. He let me go outside the classroom, and then there I was, with this piece of news so gigantic I didn't know how I'd ever put it into words.

That was when I heard the voices. Two girls were also out of class—and they were "congregating." We weren't allowed to "congregate" during class time; it was one of the rules.

I peered around the corner. There was Ori, still in orange (they'd issue her a few sets of gen-pop greens so she could match the majority of us in time; usually it took a few weeks). Her hair was loose and hung down to shield her face, but there was a diamond shine to her eyes. She couldn't hope to hide it.

Seeing her tugged at me, reminding me that I'd be leaving her behind. She was the last person I wanted to tell. How would I say it? Tell her she just got shoved in this cage, but they're opening the door for me, they're letting me fly free?

Ori was deep in conversation with Peaches, of all people. We all knew that Peaches couldn't be counted as a friend. The only time she showed interest in anyone other than herself was when we were buying what she was selling.

I strained to listen, but they hid their whispers with their hands. I caught only, "What can I do? Tell me." That was Ori. I didn't catch the answer.

Peaches had a way of keeping a stash of pills tucked firm between her big and second toes, hidden in her canvas slip-ons. She could walk by the guards' booth with her spine straight, without a telltale duck waddle, fully stocked and ready to distribute, and no CO could tell. But the summer had gone dry. Ever since the locks had come open, nothing new had been transported in. If Peaches had no pills to peddle, why was Ori huddled in the corner with her, having this intense conversation?

A door opened, and Ori went one way, Peaches the other. I crossed the hall and went to class. Ori followed, dropping off her bathroom pass at the teacher's desk.

Our eyes met, and whatever she was hiding sparkled there, bright and beaming.

The thought of leaving turned worse. Was she getting into drugs now? How long before she turned into D'amour?

Hours later Ori arrived, late from lunch, to B-wing. I heard her before I saw her. I heard the glide and shuffle of the wheels of the cart (I'd know that sound anywhere), as the back wheel kept getting stuck and someone struggled to right it. Ori came into view with the book cart and an elated grin.

Was she running the book cart now? Had she been transferred to the library? A bubble of mistrust and rage came up my throat first, but then it settled at the sight of her unwavering smile, at the diamonds in her eyes. I swallowed it, and my fists loosened.

"It's yours again," she said, stopping the cart in our doorway. "I talked to Peaches. I talked to a CO. It's yours."

How? I couldn't make sense of it, but it was in my hands

again, made of wood and piled with stories. There was *The Book Thief*. There was *The Giver*. Both *Flowers in the Attic* and its sequel, *Petals on the Wind*. There were the names on the spines, and though they weren't alphabetized, I told myself I'd fix that later: Woodson, Atwood, de la Peña, Christie, Allende, Gaiman, Myers, Zarr. There was that long-missing copy from the witch series lots of us got addicted to: *Sweep,* Volume 3.

This was the trill of happiness those three officials had been expecting when they told me I was about to be released early into the care of my family. I didn't feel it then, but I was filled up with it now. I was full to bursting.

I lifted my eyes to Ori's. "But," I said.

She only let her eyes sparkle.

"But how?"

She only shook her head.

I should have told her then. But I couldn't find a way, in that moment, to admit that it didn't much matter anymore. Come September, the cart would be free for the taking. And even as I thought this, I felt the creeping, crawling sense of something more I was forgetting make its way up my trembling legs. A foreknowledge that I kept pushing back. A blanking of my mind.

Something about seeing September.

Something about how none of us would.

Then it passed, and I was only leaning my weight on the cart.

She winked and took off, saying she'd be late for her life-skills job in the back garden and mumbling about some favor she had to do for Peaches.

I didn't think too much of it. The cart was mine again. And Ori did that for me.

That was the kind of person she was.

It wasn't only me. She made these gestures with so many of us that August. She had this way about her. She'd overhear that something was wrong, and she'd try her hand at making it right. She'd find a lost shoe before one of us got in trouble and had to ask to be issued another. She'd sacrifice her chocolate pudding to someone on dessert restriction. She'd wade in and correct a miscommunication between two warring girls, until the fists lowered and everyone went away laughing. She was one of us, sure, but she was more. She was better.

We began to talk about her when she wasn't around to hear. Since I was her cellie and knew her better than anyone else, I got asked to join in.

"Do you think she did it?" Mirabel asked. She, herself, always claimed innocence when it came to her own crime (reckless driving; running over a kid), though every last one of us knew she was guilty and knew she killed the kid.

"I don't know," Cherie said. "Do *you* think she did it?"

Mirabel shrugged and they all, every girl on B-wing, looked to me.

I opened my mouth, but someone interrupted.

"Judges don't see everything, you know," one girl said.

"Judges are blind and dumb," another said. "Mine was a certified idiot."

"They decide as soon as they meet you. Ten seconds in. If you're poor. If you're brown. If you're black. If you've got an accent. If your skirt's too short. If your nose is ugly—sorry, Cherie. If you're chewing gum. If you're breathing funny. If nobody from your family is there. If you're any of that? Or all of that? Have a nice life, because you're out of there."

We liked to exaggerate their biases—to us they were true. Besides, some of us had seen pictures of the pretty, gleaming victims on TV. We knew who mattered.

"But she was holding the knife," one of us said.

"It wasn't a knife. It was a box cutter."

Okay, that sounded serious. But still.

"But she was *holding* the box cutter. They *caught* her with it. I saw it on the news when I was talking to a CO."

"There's got to be a reason."

"Like maybe she was cutting up some boxes?"

"Like maybe she was hanging on to it. Like for a friend."

"My cousin got shipped upstate because of some gun in his glove compartment, but he didn't fire it. It wasn't his."

"My dad got picked up just for *looking* like some thug. Mistaken identity. That happens."

"My girl Nadia? From Peekskill? They said she was cooking in her kitchen, but it was just her mom's boyfriend used the place sometimes, and she's in Rikers now, looking at ten years."

We liked to talk of failed justice. To expose all the cracks in the system: How many times it had treated us and those close to us unfairly; how many times it had proven itself rigged. We were told that everyone faced equal treatment, but we knew the truth. We only had to look around and see who was here.

Then again, we also liked to make excuses.

"Okay, so what if she *did* do it? But it's not her fault. Like temporary insanity?"

"Totally possible. My brother goes temporarily insane all the time."

"Or she could've taken something . . ."

"Crank?"

"Dust?"

"Bath salts?"

"Ate a bad hamburger? Got indigestion? That'd make me want to kill someone."

They stopped chattering. They all looked to me. "What do *you* think? You think she did what they say?"

What I felt, and why I felt it, couldn't be said aloud, here, with so many of us listening. We kept the mushy stuff to ourselves. We held hands under tables, if we did even that.

But Orianna Speerling had changed me. I wanted everyone to see the good in her, far more than I'd ever want the same for myself.

"She's innocent," I announced. I knew it as if I had DNA evidence in a tagged bag in my foot locker. I felt so sure, as if I could stand up and prove it in a court of law.

Later that night, when she was on the bunk above me, I looked upward, at the ceiling of my bed, which was the bottom of hers. "Hey, Ori? You awake?"

"Now I am," she said, though not unkindly.

"Tell me what happened. With that girl in the picture. Violet. With the box cutter. With everything. Tell me the truth." We knew we weren't supposed to ask these things, but here I was, for the first time ever, asking.

She shifted in the bed slab above me. She breathed out

a long breath, but she didn't say no. Soon she'd start talking, and I'd know if she was the killer everyone on the outside said she was.

I already had my mind made up, before she started telling me.

You see, there were many things I knew, even though I was locked inside the walls of the Aurora Hills Secure Juvenile Detention Center and had been, since I turned fourteen.

I knew that just because people on the outside were free and clean, it didn't mean they were the good ones. They were the worst kind of liars. They were total assholes. They were traitors. They were bitches. They were snitches. They were cowards. They claimed they had your best interests at heart, but really they were in it for themselves. They said what they wanted about us. They threw us under buses, and then they walked away. Not everything said about us by those on the outside was the truth, not even close.

Even without Ori having to tell me, I knew.

PART V:
Vee and Ori

"How to Commit the Perfect Murder"
was an old game in heaven. I always chose
the icicle: the weapon melts away.

—Alice Sebold,
The Lovely Bones

Violet:

———

NOT SORRY

———

I END UP outside the prison, panting and bracing myself against a gray stone wall.

I ran from whatever I saw in there—all I know is I ran. I don't know anything else.

The wall, the whole side of the building really, is covered in climbing ivy, and I'm mashed against it, my lungs fisting up in my chest. Then I see the oily green leaves running through my fingers and snatch my hands away. Just watch—I'll get a nasty rash from this tomorrow.

I'm not going back in. No way am I going back inside. I don't know what's gone wrong with my mind that I thought I was face-to-face with a girl who's been dead three summers now, and then I found myself face-to-face with someone else. That maze of a place is playing tricks on me. Or someone else is.

Tommy, I think. Sarabeth, I think. Miles.

I pull open the heavy door and lean into the building. Darkness. Though not silence. There's tittering. There's some low murmuring, some rapid whispering. Then someone goes, "Shh!" and there's a sudden hush. I feel oddly like I'm hiding behind the velvet curtain and the audience caught me peeking.

"You guys!" I shout into the darkness. "Let's go. Come out, okay? Come out."

The quiet holds. It holds steady for the longest while, and in the distance, deep into the pooling blackness at the end of the corridor, I think I hear a rhythmic drip. Like someone's left a faucet on. It drips, and drips.

I pull out my phone and text Sarabeth. I text Tommy. A notice at the top of my texts says *Sending . . .*

No response.

The last text I got was from Sarabeth, from like two hours ago, which is weird, because I didn't realize we've been in here that long, and I never heard my phone ping when the message landed. It says:

Not funny. Where are u

That's it. No details about where *she* might be. No attempt to come after me, either. I mean, she could've hiked back down to the car by now. She could be curled up on Tommy's revolting green-and-white-striped hood, snacking on a protein bar and picking her nails, one of her bad habits. I call her, and it cuts to voice mail after the first ring.

A memory bubbles up. Three years ago, when I was fifteen and Sarabeth was fourteen and I called her Rooster, she wasn't exactly a friend of mine. She hasn't been holding that grudge for all this time, has she? Storing it up, acting dumb, waiting for the chance to bite?

I turn and look behind me, at what's out here. The light is falling, the afternoon turning to evening, which will pretty soon turn over into night. The forest in the distance looks thicker, wilder than I noticed before. It would be kind of beautiful if this weren't a prison where dozens of girls died. Between me and the forest at the edge of the property are three separate tall fences, barbed-wire walls, some that have been knocked down, some with holes wide enough for a large animal to charge through, but some still swaying in the wind, still standing.

I call out, one last time, through the dark doorway. "If you're in there, come out now."

The silence shifts. More whispers. Some scuffling. A cough. I let go of the heavy door and let it slam closed. Let them find another way out.

"Okay, then," I say aloud to myself. It feels better to be talking and making noise to cover up whatever else is out here, so I keep it up. "I'll just go around front."

Except, the thing is, I can't find the front. The gray stone building seems to go on for miles, and there's no sidewalk around it. The only patch of paved area heads out back, to this fenced-in square where there are two ancient basketball hoops, the netting hanging by a thread, and not much else. Chain-link surrounds it, making an outdoor cage.

Past it is another fenced-off area, and that's what catches my attention. My ears flood with noise. My eyes catch a spot of fire. Orange. Bright as neon. Practically blinding.

My phone pings, or I think it does, but what's that? What's that over there?

I find myself on a gravel pathway, narrow and winding. Over my shoulder, far away and behind me, I hear voices calling. Could be Sarabeth, or could be Tommy, but I don't answer. They took too long.

My body walks me forward. My muscles buzz, my skin warms, a pulse of blood sounds out in my ears like a bass drum. I let my body do the thinking, like I'm used to doing, my feet crunching gravel, step after step, like a dance memorized for the stage. My body steers me through the chain-link, knowing exactly how to solve the maze.

She's there in the weeds, you see. She's been there all along. And she's been digging.

I'm almost there, one last fence between us, when she looks up from the pit at her feet and rests her weight on her propped-up shovel and takes a drink of me.

Her eyes on me are shockingly cold.

The sun above—it's going down faster than I can understand, like time is moving at high speed.

She doesn't wave. She wears a bright orange puff suit, like she had on in the news. She picks up the shovel in both hands, grips it, plunges it back into the earth. The scent of fresh dirt. The wind tickling the hair at the back of my neck, exposed because I have it knotted up. The gravel under my feet, every sharp protruding stone through my sandals' soles. I'm hot. I'm cold. My ankle throbs. My shin aches. There's a crick in my knee. There's a pang in my neck, and I can't swallow. I'm dry mouthed. I'm dripping sweat. This is the impossible moment I've wanted and dreaded for three years.

She pauses in her digging again, to study me.

Do I look any different to her, in the time that's passed since she last saw me? I was fifteen. Now I'm eighteen. Can she tell? Have I lost my baby fat? Have I aged into my face? Are my ears as Dumbo-huge as they used to be? Can she tell I had my eyebrows done? Does she like the shape of my new eyebrows? She's never seen this shirt I'm wearing. Does she think it's my color? It's brighter than I used to wear. Does she notice? Would she have borrowed it from my closet? I'm taller now, I've grown two and a half inches. Can she see that? Would she want to stand right behind me, spine to spine, skull to skull, to see who's taller now? Would she get on her toes, or would she protest if I got on mine?

The fence feels so flimsy. I've got my hand on it.

I should say something. *Hello. It's good to see you again. You look nice*—even if she doesn't. *You look good, Ori*—even if she looks like crap.

But what words are there? Some actions remove words entirely from your vocabulary. Then all you've got left is your dry tongue.

Before I can find the right words, or any words, she lowers her gaze and goes back in with the shovel. It glints in the low light. Made of silver-gray steel. Wood-handled. Heavy-weighted. Curved. I let my own gaze lower down to where she's digging. There's so much soil to remove, if she wants the hole to fit a body. And I'm taller now, by two and a half inches, and now she's got to adjust for that.

Behind me, I hear voices. Boys' voices. A girl's. They *are* calling for me. They *have* come.

But they can't remember the things I remember. They

weren't there, they weren't close to her then the way I was. Those are the years that count, the memories that make us, the time before all the bad. She'll remember.

There we are. We're both eight years old, in our first pair of soft ballet slippers with the little strips of elastic sewn in, doing sloppy turns on the kitchen floor. Her dad is late picking her up again, so she's at my house. She falls, I fall, we help each other up, we go on, spotting our turns, skidding on the kitchen floor, fumbling, laughing.

Ten years old, we both are, running through the wings backstage, fake silk flowers perched with pins in our stiff-sprayed hair. One fake bloom pops out from behind her ear and drops, rolling behind the curtain. I dig my hand in until I find it. She's lost it, but I've got it back for her. I pin it back in.

Now we're twelve years old, or are we thirteen? We've advanced together to pointe class, finally. She's waited, and I've caught up. Here we are, standing one before the other, me in front, her behind, at the long, gleaming wooden barre. We relevé. We demi-plié. We relevé. We demi-plié. We tendu from fifth position. We tendu. We have a light touch at the barre, holding on but not giving it all our weight. We are one, all except her turnout is better. We're two of a kind, all except she picks up the steps faster than I do, her grand jeté is more grand than anyone else's in class, and then she's out front demonstrating, and I'm the one following her moving feet, I'm the one behind.

We are fifteen, both of us, just turned fifteen. Our last year together. She's caught me in the back rehearsal studio, having a little tantrum. I was kicking the floor and throwing my balled-up leg warmers. I was beating on the barre with my fists. She catches me with my mouth wide-open, silent-screaming. "Oh, Vee," she's saying. "It's a good role, really it is. You'll steal the show, really you will." She pats me, thump-thump-thump, like she'd burp an infant. She doesn't say I'm acting like one. She says, "Don't let them see you like this." And, "You can always show *me*. But don't show anybody else, okay?" I say okay. She retrieves my leg warmers. She fixes my face. She straightens the bobby pins in my hair. "Stand up," she says, and I stand. "Smile like you mean it," and I widen my mouth into the position of a smile.

There she was again, trying to make me feel better about what I didn't have, when she had it all.

Does she remember? She's the only one who could.

I've circled the last fence, and now I'm in. The plot of land is so pathetic, but now that my ankles are in it, my sandals sinking, I see it's been tended into rows. A long time ago this was a garden. Something's been planted here, but it hasn't been harvested off the vine in a long time. I bend down. I reach my hand into the mass of green, and there's mulch, wet and expanding, and there's muck, slick and sticking, and there's a rotting round thing stuck on a hairy vine that I twist a little, and then with a hard tug pluck off.

A small, shrunken tomato. When I squeeze, it bursts open like an animal that got run over in the road.

The hole she's digging is getting larger now. A girl could lie down in it and stretch out her arms, point her toes. She's a glare of orange. She's practically toxic.

"Aren't you," she says, stopping for a breath, "going to tell me you're sorry?"

Has she really said that to me? She has. Her ghost has. Her memory has. Ori, my Ori, has.

That's what she's been waiting here for, why she's come out, wanting me to find her. All along, all these years, she's been hoping for an apology.

But that's complicated. If I were sorry for what happened to her, I'd have to be sorry for all the other things that went along with it. And I'm not sorry about where I'm headed, or that I've gotten so good. I'm not sorry about New York City. That I'm happy. And alive. That I have everything now even though that means she has nothing, because I do wish she had *something,* like maybe I should've sent her a letter, one time, filled her in on all the things going on with me. I wish things were different, but I'm not going to give up everything so she can go dancing off into the sunset, even if I could.

She nods. She understands. I didn't have to say it.

Also, she knows the truth.

In the smoking tunnel, maybe she didn't tell me to get out of there. Maybe that's not how it happened at all.

Maybe she held the bloody weapon, waving it in the air, and I got scared, and I thought I might be next, and I took off, pushing through tree branches and stumbling over tree roots, and I almost rammed into the Dumpster, and I did run, but only to save my own skin.

Maybe that's how it happened, or maybe not.

She continues to dig. She knows I'm not going to say I'm sorry.

I'm in the fenced-in field, one of the rotten things in the rotting garden. I stand, spine straight, two and a half inches taller than when she last saw me, not willing to take it back and put up my hands and turn myself in. The hole gets bigger, and I'm not sorry.

FOOLS

NONE OF WHAT happened was my fault.

I mean, not at first. It started with a girl named Harmony. With Rachel and Harmony and all of what they did, so really this is on them, if you want to be pointing fingers.

They'd saunter into the studio in identical black leotards, caramel-colored hair up in same-shaped buns, the ribbons on their pointe shoes trailing. As they passed where Ori and I were stretching out on the floor, bending forward so our heads touched and our four hands made two, they'd always have a comment. Sometimes they called me ugly, or they'd point out my big stick-out ears. Other times I was fat for no reason, or a skeleton for no reason, it was one or it was the other. A few times they called me a lesbo, even though they, too, were best friends and shared leotards sometimes when one of them forgot a clean suit. Sometimes I was a pathetic virgin, and other times a vicious slut. It didn't matter. They never bothered Ori much, but maybe because she was so great, they had to pour it all out on me.

Some girls make enemies out of other girls, and you don't even know why. It's always been like that, like how every April the town floods with rain, and we have to set out a few buckets or bowls on the dance floor to catch the drops because the roof leaks.

Forever and always, Harmony and Rachel hated me. They'd slither by in the ballet studio, Harmony a whole stack of inches taller than tiny Rachel, but otherwise basically the same person, moving and sneering in unison, and they'd skank-cough at me, so if Miss Willow was nearby, it'd sound like they were regular-coughing, and then they'd take the best spots on the barre along the wall.

Outside, to the oblivious eye—adult eyes are always oblivious—they were the practically perfect ballerinas everyone expected them to be. Pretty and lithe and always able to control the frizzies in their buns. "Really nice," Miss Willow would compliment Harmony on her quick-moving assemblés. "Brilliant," Miss Willow would tell Rachel on her développé. "Girls," she'd say, to all four of us, like we were the same, "good energy today."

Our teacher saw only our steps on the dance floor. She didn't know who we were when we peeled off our pale pink tights and pulled up our skintight jeans and took down our hair.

It turned worse once boys got added in. We were fifteen when the boys invaded. They were what pushed everything over the edge. There were three of them, and at least thirty

of us, so they were outnumbered and easily outvoted during rehearsals, when we got to order pizza. Having boys
in our classes changed the whole dynamic. They saw us in
our skimpy leotards, adjusting our wedgies. They witnessed
just how much we could sweat after a floor routine. They
were on our turf, quiet mostly and clumsy and not worth
competing with, except for Jon, who never once dropped a
girl on the floor during partnering class, which couldn't be
said of the other two.

The other two weren't even dancers. They were football players. Which was ridiculous. Those two came to
class once a week and goofed off in their athletic socks at
the barre in the back. I think they were there because their
coach made them, and they got special treatment and didn't
even have to wear tights. Miss Willow let them keep their
sweatpants, even though you can't see the muscles in a pair
of legs covered by sweatpants, and the sight of them in their
floppy socks, snickering, eyeing our asses, made for a distraction I didn't enjoy.

Harmony preened whenever they came close, even wearing lipstick to class, though she'd sweat it off by the end.
Rachel tried looping them into conversation, asking inane
questions about games that involved balls, and when she did
her splits, she made sure to do them right where they were
watching, eyes cast downward, coy.

It was embarrassing. It was the way the boys looked at
us and, equally, the way we looked at them. The charge in
the air. Once, I was in the back hallway, wanting some focus,
and I was leaned forward, I guess, and there were my legs
wide-open and my chest flat on the floor. My leotard was

low cut, and if you were walking straight down the hallway toward me with your gaze pointed to the ground, you could see down my front. Stretched out like I was, thinking I had some privacy, I was more exposed than I thought.

Before the boys, I never would have given a second thought to stretching in the hallway.

But then there was Cody, and there was his sidekick, Shawn, and Cody goes to Shawn, "Hey, I guess she does have some." And Shawn goes to Cody, "Nah, not worth it, may as well feel up a nine-year-old. All nip and ribs and skin." And Cody goes, "That ass is still worth tapping, though, admit it." And Shawn says, "Nah, she's a two." And Cody defends me and says, "A six. For the ass." And all of this is said right in front of me, because voices do carry down that hall, and Cody has the nerve, as he's turning away and skating on dirty socks into the ballet studio, to lean back out and wink at me. Actually *wink*. Like we're in on this together, after he upped my rating to a six. Like now I owe him.

The saddest part is how I felt, standing at the front of the studio, at the demonstration barre with Harmony, knowing my back would be to him and that was his view. I did my pliés and my grand pliés, and all the while I was feeling his eyes. On my ass. As I moved through the warm-ups. His eyes. Moving over my thighs. I'd bend over, and he'd be watching me bend over, and I was aware of that. And I kind of felt electrified by it.

That's why it can't be explained, what happened next, and I know Ori wanted me to explain. I was in the back rehearsal studio, but I wasn't alone. I was in Cody's arms, on the bare floor. He was a senior, and I was still only a freshman, though it's not like I thought of him that way. We went to different schools, and here at the ballet studio I was so much better than he was, so it was like I was older. I only mean he was experienced. And his mouth on my neck and behind my ears, one ear at a time—it felt so good, I wasn't sure what to do apart from lie back and let it happen. At one point he told me to be quiet or someone would hear.

Then I was on my knees, crouched over him. Ori asked me later if he made me do it, if he talked me into it, if he shoved my head down there and pulled down those sweatpants I can't believe he was allowed to wear to class and told me to go to town. He didn't. It was just one of those things that happen without planning, a thing you've heard about, from other girls, or seen online, maybe. Something you think you're supposed to do, because everyone does, don't they? Didn't Ori?

I'm not even sure I knew what I was doing, what my mouth should be focusing on, what, if anything, I should do with my hand. There was a point when I got all fumbled up, lost my rhythm, and he shifted, and something happened with my teeth getting snagged, and he cursed.

I heard laughter coming from one of the mirrored walls. I was confused, and suddenly on high alert. My leotard top was rolled down, stuck somehow, and I couldn't get it back up. The laughter was bright and tinkling. Girl laughter.

The second wall of mirrors was not only a wall—it was a sliding panel behind which was a crawl space, a storage area for old costumes and props, large enough for someone to be hiding.

Even knowing that, I don't think I understood what was happening until I saw the flash. Bright and swallowing us in the dark rehearsal room, glaring with judgment and peppered with mocking laughter.

"Who's there?" The top of my leotard still wouldn't come up, but Cody had his pants back up, fast. He was sauntering over to the mirrored wall. He was saying hey.

Everything else fell away and time focused in on itself. The mirrors, darkening. The floor raising me up. And Harmony, and at her tail Rachel, cell phones in their hands, wormy smiles on their faces. Cody didn't even matter anymore. What mattered was what they'd seen, and captured, and would hold over me now, forever.

"Later," Cody threw back at me, like we'd meet up later. The two girls followed. The door shut, and I was alone then, in the center of the wooden dance floor, on my knees like I'd just collapsed after a grand jeté.

To this day, I'm not sure what had been planned before Cody and I went in there, and what had been an accident of bad luck, and what had just happened because things happen.

When Cody had said, "Later," I thought he meant it. Like I took it literally. I waited for him after class, but he grabbed his bag and took off with Shawn, like always. I thought he might call or text, but he didn't have my number. We weren't friends online. I didn't follow him, and he didn't follow me. I saw him the next week, at the basics class the boys attended and that I did demonstrations for, and at the partnering class that followed, in which twelve or fifteen girls took turns with the three boys, letting their bumbling hands lift us up by our armpits. He hung by Harmony's side. Once, with sweat darkening her hair, Harmony looked right at me, her mirror-eyes on my mirror-eyes. Now she was the one who winked.

Maybe I should've been embarrassed, ashamed. Buried it and never let myself dwell on it ever again.

But any embarrassment had gone away. I didn't feel dirty, and I didn't feel ashamed.

I felt enraged.

I knew I had a temper. But then it started affecting my dancing.

When roles were announced for the next showcase, Miss Willow gathered us together to say which pieces we would each be dancing. I caught the pride in her eyes when she came to Ori, who would dance the role of the Firebird, and even Harmony, who would play the thirteenth enchanted princess, the one who gets her happy ending with the prince.

I would be princess six or seven. Even Rachel was the first princess, first row. I would dance around with a yellow Hacky Sack that was supposed to be a golden apple from the enchanted golden-apple tree. I'd watch the proceedings like a nobody. There'd be no standing ovation for any of the background dancers at curtain call. No one would re-member me.

When I asked Miss Willow why, she said she felt like something had been off with me lately. She couldn't quite put her finger on it. Something that was distracting me and showed whenever I stepped out onto the floor.

I knew who it was. It wasn't just one distraction—it was two.

"I want to kill them," I told Ori late one night, and I'm sure I would've been crying if my eyes leaked tears like normal people's eyes did. When I was sputtering out those words to Ori, I did have emotions. They were in there, even if I have a hard time finding them now. I think back and I'm all raw. I'm filled with frustration, and it's mostly at myself, for letting it happen, for getting caught, for having hormones, for being stupid, for thinking I liked some boy, or if it wasn't that, for wanting some boy to like me the way Ori had a boy who liked her, and thinking that was the way to do it. I kept seeing the flash of light. How it bounced off all the mirrors and seemed like many flashes of light. How maybe it had been, how I couldn't be sure. I kept expecting to get a forwarded message from an anonymous number and I'd open it and there'd be an attached picture—worse, a video, with sound—and it would be me, and everyone would know it was me, and my parents would see it, and the kids at my school would see it, and Miss Willow would see it, and whoever I was as a ballerina, the person I'd been for years and years, would vanish because of that thing I did one day, in the rehearsal room, just the one time.

Ori and I were upstairs in my bedroom. If my parents heard the shouting, the spat-out froth of hate I was spewing as Ori and I took turns sipping from a borrowed bottle of their Bacardi, they didn't climb to the landing of the stairs, as far as they'd ever climb, and peek up through the banister to ask if we were okay. They didn't even call up on the intercom, or try my phone. I could have been chopping up a body up there and they'd never have known until the smell drifted down.

"I want them to die," I was saying, "horribly."

"Who?" she asked. "All of them? Harmony and Rachel . . . Cody, too?" She seemed truly concerned, and I wasn't sure if she was worried more for me or for *them*.

"I don't care about Cody. He's just a boy, and he plays football. I mean them. I mean Harmony. I mean Rachel."

She nodded. She'd been hearing me complain up a storm about them for years. She'd long stopped trying to analyze them, to come up with long-lost traumas to explain away their wicked behavior or at least make them into something halfway human. Usually she'd just listen while I insulted them. But that night she had questions.

I remember the pink of the bedspread and the pink curtains. I remember how, at one point, I toppled off my bed and spread myself out like a starfish on the pink plush carpet and felt like I had in the rehearsal room after Cody had left with Harmony and Rachel and they closed the door and kept the lights off. Heavy. Dancers were not supposed to feel like lead.

Ori joined me on the carpet, sitting cross-legged beside where I was lying on my back. She rubbed my arm.

"But what'd they do this time?" she asked.

"I don't know for sure, but something!" I may have shrieked it. She may have covered her ears.

"But why'd you go off with Cody, anyway? I didn't even know you liked him."

"You have Miles," I said, as if the two were connected.

"So? So what?"

"So I don't know," I said, losing patience.

My fists were balled. My sight was clouded. I really only wanted to talk about Harmony and Rachel. "I want to flay them alive with their straightening iron. I want to cut off their ears and mail them to their mothers. I want to shoot them in both feet and make them dance all night. I want to hang them by a rope and watch them turn purple and suffocate, and I'll take pictures."

"Okay, but you're just kidding," Ori said. "You drank too much rum."

She wasn't getting it. They never teased *her*. They never followed her around with their phones, trying to catch her in a compromising position. They never called her a ho-bag or a troll or said she danced like an elephant on crank. They never, not once, dribbled pee in her ballet bag or stuck shaved pubes in her ChapStick. They never told her she wouldn't ever be good enough to make the New York City Ballet, and that they'd wave to her from the stage, maybe, one day, if they remembered who she was when they were famous.

"I want to take this"—I lifted the box cutter from my ballet bag, where I kept it for making adjustments to our old pointe shoes, deshanking them to use them for practice, as we were going through a pair every few weeks—"and"—I waved the box cutter, but it was kind of sharp and the plastic cover on it was loose, so I just put it back in my bag. And forgot what I was going to say.

Ori was the quietest I'd ever seen her, her brown eyes wide.

"And what?" she said. "Why don't you put that in a drawer or something?"

"And I'll . . . slice up her face," I said halfheartedly. I was kind of scaring myself, too.

The night went on. We didn't do much more than say hateful things on my plush pink carpet—I said them, she listened—and we didn't bother hiding the rest of the Bacardi, because it wasn't like my parents would come all the way up the stairs and find it.

At one point there was a tapping on my window, pebbles from the rock garden plunking one at a time on the glass. I rolled my eyes, but my stomach was sloshing too much to tell him to go away.

"I'll deal with him," Ori said. "I'll tell him to go home." She checked her rum breath against her hand and then slid open the window. Miles was down below in my backyard, dodging lawn ornaments, aching to climb the lattice.

I heard her hissing at him, and him whisper-shouting back, but I tuned out what they were saying. It was all the lovey-dovey stuff that turned my stomach. He hadn't said, "Later," and closed the door on her and left her on the floor of a dark room with her top bunched around her waist and her mouth kind of sore and her body kind of warm all over even though she didn't want it to be. Miles and Ori had been together for six months. They'd had sex, and he didn't dump her after. He'd even dropped the L-word on her, though she told me she hadn't yet said it back.

I was thinking about the showcase, about what happened. I wasn't sure what wounded me more—that Miss Willow thought I was so insignificant, or that Harmony and Rachel and definitely Cody did. Maybe it was all hammered together, and one couldn't be pulled apart from the other.

I wanted to be important to someone. To matter. To have
the spotlight on me and have no one able to pull their gaze
away from the gorgeous shape of me under the bright-hot,
mesmerizing beam of light.

The way Miles looked at Ori, actually.

I closed my eyes and let the room spin. Even with the
spins, my mind was bloody and sharp. The pictures were
vivid and spotlit on the stage of my deepest fantasies, where,
like usual, I was a prima ballerina for the New York City
Ballet and won the heart of every director and choreogra-
pher. But then the stage showed other things.

Bad things. Murderous things.

Things I would never really do. And things I would
forget about in the morning, because I'd wake up feeling a
whole lot better. I knew right from wrong, Ori and I both
did. We were not terrible people. We were not fools.

RED FEATHERS EVERYWHERE

THE FIREBIRD IS only a fairy tale.

The story of the ballet goes like this: In an enchanted garden, a bird is kept captive. An evil magician holds sway over this garden and won't release the beautiful, red-feathered bird, who glows like the moon in a patch of darkness. But one day when a lonely prince is passing through, he catches sight of that stunning red bird over the garden wall and decides he must have her.

Soon the prince has scaled the wall and gone after the bird, chasing her through the enchanted trees, determined to steal her. She begs him to leave her be—she wants to stay in her garden, where she's been her whole life—but he won't stop, so she has to come up with a plan to make him go away.

She gives him this feather, from her own body, bright red like her skin. Says, if he ever needs her help for any reason, he should take out the feather and call on her. Then, fast, she flies away.

The rest of the ballet is all about the prince finding love and defeating the evil magician, with the help of the Firebird, who does come when he holds out her feather, and the show ends on a happy note of celebration. But I keep thinking about the bird.

All focus—plus the stage spotlight—is on the prince and his beautiful dancing bride, their happily ever after. Everyone forgets the bird who made it possible. Does she fly off into the great blue sky, or does she stay put in the garden now that the enchanted walls have come down? Does she die, alone, because she's given away too many of her feathers and everyone's always wanting something from her and plucking them off her and she doesn't know how to put herself first and say get away from me, you greedy bastards, say no?

It's just a story, a fairy tale fit for the stage.

Because if it were a real thing, with real people, she would have said anything to save herself. She would have lied. And then, when she was called on, when the guy stood up with the drooping feather in his hand and said he needed her, she would have ignored his call.

You can't ever blame someone for putting herself first.

In the ballet world, the role of the Firebird is an intimidating one. You have to be powerful on your feet and with your turns. You need real stamina. You've got to be worthy.

We weren't doing the whole ballet in our spring showcase, just a few variations, but Ori, at only fifteen, got the starring role.

Miss Willow was having her try on the Firebird costume for fittings, and a hush came over the whole studio when Ori stepped out from the changing room with it on. It was bloodred with sequins over the sheer sections, like the skin of her chest, and her arms and back were rouge hued and naturally gleaming. The tutu was stiff and red feathered. The toe shoes were dyed as red as a vodka cherry, the ribbons making slash marks across her arches and her ankles.

My own costume for that showcase was plain. Pale, cloudy blue. Flat, droopy skirt without any tulle. I was watching Ori in the mirror like anyone else. I was kind of coveting the red, the sharp shape of her tutu. Kind of imagining myself in her costume, *as* her, blazing so vivid bright, no one would ever leave me behind in a dark room.

"She looks scary," Ivana, one of the other dancing princesses, was saying, eyeing the red reflection in the mirror. "Is the Firebird supposed to look so scary?"

"You mean *nasty,*" Harmony said. "And slutty, too, don't you think?"

Ivana agreed, as girls tended to do when Harmony or Rachel asked anyone an opinion. Ori looked like a nasty, dirty slut in her beautiful red costume, and now no one would be able to see the Firebird of our show any differently.

I don't think Ori heard, but then again it wasn't even meant for her—Harmony was looking right at my reflection in the mirror when she said it. Mirror-Harmony was doing something with her mouth and her tongue, something pornographic. She wanted me to know she hadn't forgotten and she'd make use of what she had (pictures? videos?) later. *When?* I wanted to ask her. *When?* She grinned and licked her pink lips. She'd never say when.

Rachel sashayed over then, all done up in her princess costume, but somehow she made it look better than I did. Her delicate frame was graceful and refined in the simple costume, and she'd been given a small gold crown to wear in her hair, and no one had asked if I wanted a small gold crown for my hair.

Ori didn't get a crown, either—but she didn't need one, because she had the headpiece. The costume designer had created this contraption that seemed made entirely of red feathers, like plumage on a tropical bird, with a masked wire frame making the feathers burst out of the back of Ori's skull and trail down her spine. The feathers moved as she moved. When she breathed, they seemed to tremble with breath, too. It was how I would always remember her—in red. And it wasn't just because that was the color of her costume.

The costume designer wanted to see how the contraption would move. Ori did a halfhearted spin. She shrugged and said the headpiece felt good, moved fine, and then went to get back into her plain leotard. When she walked out, our eyes met in the mirror, and I could tell that the attention embarrassed her. She knew I was upset. She knew I cared so much more than she did, and it made her feel guilty. She'd rather I be in the bright sequins and she the one who had to dress like a milkmaid. I think she would've quit ballet years ago if it weren't the one main thing we had in common.

Still, no matter how effortlessly good she was, the most flexible in class, with splits we all envied and arches we stretched and deformed our feet for hours to match, I don't think there was anyone at the studio who hated Ori. You couldn't hate her. She once helped Chelsea P. search for a lost set of keys for a whole hour after class one night. The senior girls that year treated her like a pet, when she overheard in a bathroom stall how one of them was getting an abortion, and she wouldn't tell even me who it was because she didn't want to reveal someone else's secret. Her loyalty said something about her character.

But she was far more loyal to me.

The plan was to swipe their phones and delete the pictures, if there even were any pictures. We weren't positive there were pictures. We needed their pass codes, though, to get into their photo albums, and it wasn't like we could ask. We'd have to trick them somehow. Or do some threatening. There was thinking that needed to go into this, and I hadn't gone through all my thinking by the time dress rehearsals started.

That was when Ori came up to me backstage, between numbers, to warn me. "I heard them talking, being kind of weird, and they got quiet when I walked by."

A bolt of panic seized me. I thought of a picture of me in a compromising position. I imagined it enlarged and projected onto the stage during the performance. I saw myself doing a pirouette in front of it, having no idea. Lifting my arms, pointing my toes, having no idea. And every last person in the audience gasping. And my mother getting sick in her pocketbook and my father too shocked to cover his eyes.

Dress rehearsals always introduce something unexpected. Some new problem the director has to iron out before the show. Choreography that proves itself too complicated with the stage scenery and has to be changed. The final show never ends up being what you thought it would be, not exactly. Ballet is this living, breathing thing. It's not prerecorded and set in stone or celluloid. It's in the moment. It's live.

Sometimes I forgot that life was, too.

Harmony and Rachel were acting as if nothing at all was going on. We were onstage. The number was blocked and working fine, and in the V formation of dancing princesses, Miss Willow had given me center spot.

Anything could've happened onstage during rehearsal. Rachel could have beaned me in the head with one of the golden apples we tossed to each other during the enchanted garden scene. She had good aim. Or Harmony—the thirteenth princess, the one who captures the prince's heart like he tries to capture the Firebird, played by Ori—she could have tilted her arabesque just a few ticks to the left, and the hard-packed box of her pointe shoe could have caught me square in the eye.

But we rehearsed it in costume once, twice, and nothing. They were on their best behavior while Miss Willow sat out in the auditorium, calling out adjustments, nodding her head, a few times smiling.

Ori did her solo, and she couldn't remember half the steps. Sometimes she'd just make up some of her own, and other times she'd fudge through to get to what she did remember, the next sequence where she got to do some spins.

Out in the empty audience, Miss Willow had lost her smile, but even she had to give up and simply watch when Ori found her stride and the music grew to encompass the thrilling shape of her movement and the magic descended.

I was watching, and then I was fiddling in my ballet bag, looking for some cheese or something to eat. I let my guard down, I guess.

The note was inside one of my pointe shoes. It was scrawled on the back of an old program. Cody wanted to meet me out back, behind the theater, during my break. The note didn't say more than that.

I left without telling Ori. She was still onstage. She had other things to do. She was out there, effortlessly being brilliant, and I was in the wings, trying so hard at being me.

I knew where to go. I took my ballet bag with me. The smoking tunnel behind the Dumpster was where girls could go and sneak a smoke, then spray themselves with garden-scented Febreze and saunter back in, saying they'd only needed some fresh air from all the dancing.

The entrance to the tunnel was covered over, some leafy branches carefully arranged to be in the way. When I parted the branches and stepped inside, I found them there in the leotards they'd had on under their princess costumes. Waiting for me.

"Hey there, Vee," Rachel said, lifting and extending her leg to stretch out the muscles, multitasking. "Looking for someone?"

"Not really." The lie must have showed on my face.

"She hasn't heard," Harmony said. She always did have

this way of speaking to others about me when I was standing right there and could easily be spoken to directly.

"She thought he really left her that little note," Rachel said.

"She doesn't know he quit the show."

"Cody quit?" I said. "Why?"

"Oh, *you* know . . . ," Rachel said, which probably meant she didn't know, either.

Harmony had an idea. "He's probably too embarrassed to wear the tights. What he should've been embarrassed about is hooking up with *that*."

I was pointed at, like one of the trees.

They both shuddered theatrically. Harmony played at gagging with a finger down her throat. Then they went back to talking as if I weren't standing inches from them in a space the size of a prison cell. It was all so boring, so tired, so unnecessary. And would it keep on going through the rest of rehearsals? Were they saving the big finale for the Saturday night show, when they'd whip out the photo and I'd be mortified within an inch of my life?

I should have turned around and walked away, but something kept me rooted to that spot. Some solid part of me did not want to leave and let them get the chance to win.

In the dim afternoon light, shielded by the thicket of branches in the tunnel, we looked like we were putting on a show of our own. But this one would not have any dancing.

"Harmony," I said. She didn't answer, and kept chattering, hand shielding her mouth.

"Rachel," I said. She didn't answer, and kept nodding,

eyebrows raised, little ooh sounds coming from her mouth, as Harmony whispered into her ear.

"You guys," I said.

In the distance, faintly, coming from inside, I could hear the lilting sounds of the music. It was the very last piece before the death of the evil magician. Before the Firebird reveals the secret way to kill him. Before everyone onstage gets to dance around gleefully, celebrating their freedom and his downfall. Ori danced in that piece, too. Ori wasn't here, and this was all on me.

"What do you guys want from me?" I said. There was this desperate edge to my voice, and it sounded like someone else's voice. Someone whining. And I guess that's the last thing I remember clearly, from inside that tunnel, before it happened.

They might have answered my question, made it really clear what it was they wanted and why it was so much fun to poke at me, like with sticks. But this is where my memory skips. We're talking—I'm saying something, and then they're saying something, and I'm standing there being talked about—and we're in our costumes, with socks pulled over our ballet slippers to keep the pink satin from getting stained and jackets over our leotards to keep out the crisp spring chill. Harmony has a cap perched up like a trucker's over her bun, and Rachel has her neat little bun and the gold crown ringing her head. It's like that—and then it shatters.

Gone.

When a dancer finds herself onstage, before an audience, and comes upon that dreaded moment that can happen even to the best of us, when her mind empties of her choreography in a flood of panic, there are three different reactions she can have. In each one, she's like a wild animal in the headlights, but the question is, which animal will she be tonight? She could be a rabbit, squeaking with fear and jetting off into the safe and darkened wings. She could be a deer, frozen in place, arms raised up like two antlers. Or she could be something with teeth, like a mountain lion. She'll charge forward with a set of steps, any steps, even if they aren't the ones belonging to this song or this routine. She could dance anything, anything at all, because at least she'd have the chance of fooling them, the audience. In most cases, they are too stupid to know the difference.

I would have thought my first instinct in the smoking tunnel would be to squeak away like a rabbit. That was pretty much how I'd been handling the two of them for years.

But my body had other instincts I didn't know about, and those instincts took me over. Truth is, and this is not bragging, I have never once been out onstage in front of an audience and forgotten my choreography. I know exactly what I'm doing at all times. At least my body does. It's muscle memory. There's always a part of you that's left aware when your mind goes dark. Your hands do the work for you, just like a dancer's highly trained feet.

I blink out and when I come to, it's everywhere. On the trees, on the ground, on my arms, in my eyes.

Blood.

All the blood.

Blood on my pale blue costume, and then dirt on my

costume and in my hair and in my mouth as we were rolling in it, Harmony and I, slicked wet with the blood and scrabbling in the hard dirt. Rachel was on me next, and then she was off me. She was so easy to push off. The tunnel kept us close—the three of us—and it also shielded our fight from the back door of the theater, if someone happened to wander outside and look behind the Dumpster. But there was so little room that there was nowhere for anyone to run, if anyone was thinking of being the rabbit and going running. There were three of us on the ground and I was all muscle memory, all instinct, bile-hot and vicious.

Then there were four.

There were eight arms, there were forty scratching fingers, there were four buns and then no buns as all hair came loose. There was one trucker hat and one crown. There were four mouths and eight legs and eight feet. There were sharp sticks. There were bobby pins everywhere. There were rocks. There were birds up in the trees, chirping.

Ori pulled me off Harmony's body, shaking me. "What did you do, Vee? What did you do?"

Rachel was crumpled in the dirt, so tiny she could have been a child. The red marks were on her throat and neck.

Harmony was on her back, eyeholes gazing upward at the dark ceiling of the tunnel, mouth open, nose mashed to a flattened lump of pus and blood. The center of her stomach was full of feathers, red feathers, but also blood, which to my eyes looked like feathers, and above us the birds still sang, though it was growing dark in our tunnel and we couldn't see them.

Rachel sat up then, like a zombie come back to sudden

life, and grabbed onto Ori's leg—cast in red tights, and the red hid all the blood—and then she dropped back down like it hadn't happened and her hand opened and in the center of her palm was one red feather. I almost laughed. I almost laughed at all the red feathers covering the stage we were on and how Rachel was forgetting our choreography. Then Ori was turning to me, all blank faced like Harmony's staring eyes were blank, and saying she was going to take it from me now.

"Take what?" I said.

"The knife," she said.

She reached out and unclasped my fingers from around it and took it from me. From out of my hand, she took the box cutter. I never had put it away.

I'm thinking back. This is what I've done, over the years, thought and thought on it. Sometimes I tell the story to myself a different way, to see how it feels.

But the story is what it is. The killer was always me.

Ori must have known we'd be out in the tunnel. She might have seen us leave the wings, first the two of them, then me.

She had to finish her rehearsal first—Miss Willow would have wanted to run it all the way through—and then she would have excused herself. She would have left the building in her costume, red feathers still pinned in her hair.

That spring was the last time anyone used the tunnel for its first, more innocent purpose. I don't know where people went to smoke anymore, but it wasn't there. When the crime-scene tape finally got taken down, tattered and stretched out and barely hanging on, and the morbidly curious stopped coming around, all that was left was the tunnel itself: a passage from civilization into the woods behind the community theater.

The bodies—there'd been two, in leotards and once-pink tights—had lain on the forest floor, with the leaves and dirt and pine needles. Now, to those who go searching and sneak out the back door, circle the Dumpster, and push through the hanging branches to stand in the spot where all of this happened, there are no signs. There are birds, still, like there are always birds. But they don't sing any stories, because the only three witnesses to what went on in the tunnel are dead.

The memory is blacked out from this place almost like it is in my own head. And when you can't remember something, you grasp onto whatever you can. You turn things around and get them twisted.

When I woke to Ori taking the box cutter from me, I immediately began the twisting.

She had me in her arms, and if I had been flailing and fighting, I wasn't anymore. I had gone frozen, deerlike. I was looking up, right at her.

I guess what I was feeling could be described as shock. And people who are in shock are often confused. And there was blood. There was the color red, the color I coveted, and it may have been on me, but it was also on her.

I opened my mouth. Then I said it.

"What did you do, Ori? What did you do?"

She let go of me. "Wait," she said. "What?"

"Ori," my mouth said. Horror then, the twisting complete. "Ori, no."

The bloody weapon was in her hand. In those moments when I came back to myself, I saw the box cutter, and whose hand it was in, and I thought I knew what happened. I thought I saw the arc of her arm in the air and the guts of Harmony splayed open and the stab and the stab and the stab of the stabbing blade and birds singing and the tunnel squeezing out all light.

"No," I was saying. "No, Ori. No. No. No."

I looked down at the dirt. There was a lot of blood, and in the blood were all these red feathers from her costume. There were red feathers on the bodies, red feathers on the ground and in the tree branches, red feathers on me and on her, blood-soaked red feathers everywhere.

CLEAN HANDS

I DIDN'T HAVE to spend the night in jail.

I was questioned, released, as within moments, it felt like, my parents had secured me a very capable attorney. Ori was to make do with the public defender. She would have to stay overnight. The showcase was postponed, indefinitely. What remained of her glorious costume had been seized for evidence.

Sometimes I don't want to think about it, but there's truth to it. Money—my parents' having it—goes a long way. I was home the same night, peeling off my tights in my room. Washing my face in my sink. Washing my face a second time, a third time. Washing up, though I couldn't get myself to feel remotely clean.

It took me years to face this, but money *can* buy you freedom, because look at me—I'm free.

Soon there was my mother, standing on the landing of my staircase, high enough that she could call up to me and I'd hear her, but too low to see me washing off the blood in my sink. I could see the crown of her blond head through the bars of the banister.

"Darling," she called up from the landing, "you need to eat something."

"I'm fine, Mom," I called down to her. "I'm not hungry."

My head, really, it was spinning. The blood had spattered my cheeks, and my white hand towel was pink now, my favorite color. And it had soaked through my tights, so it was all over my legs. The explanation was that I'd been there—I'd seen it. Surely I must have tried to stop it, the travesty, the killing of such young, talented girls with their whole lives ahead of them. Surely. My attorney advised saying nothing at all to this question, as for now it was assumed.

"Darling," my mom said, "I think you should come down and have dinner with us tonight."

This was a constant theme with her. Had I eaten yet? Would I eat now? Did I want to join them at the dining room table for more eating?

Usually when she came up to the landing of my staircase to tell me I needed to eat something, it involved the same question she asked most nights. She'd say, "Is your friend joining us for dinner tonight?" Even though, most evenings, that would be a given, as Ori would have dinner at my house most nights, or we'd skip dinner and share a bag of M&M's. Come to think of it, I didn't even know if there was food at her dad's. But my mom was always asking. She never did like my friend from the wrong side of town, did she? She never did approve of my being so close with the girl with no mother, the girl who lived only with her dad who did who knew what, the girl who went to public school and probably had sexual relations with her boyfriend and tracked mud into the house whenever she came over. I guess my mother was longing for the night when I said no, Ori wasn't joining us for dinner, it'd be just the three of us tonight, like it used to be. That was this night.

"Okay," I said. "I'll come down. Just let me wash up some more."

My mother clapped her hands, once, sharp, like she was delighted. She didn't ask the questions maybe other parents would've asked. Maybe our attorney told her not to. She didn't ask the questions, and by not asking, she was saying she believed me.

I pulled a stray red feather from my arm and left it on the dresser.

"Come down when you're ready," she called up. Then she left my landing.

I had quite the appetite, which was very unlike me. There were three of us at the table that night. We had mashed potatoes, a roast, and pearl onions mixed with peas. I had a tall glass of juice, and in the glass I had cubes of ice. I cleaned my plate.

As I ate, I considered. I'd give it a week or so, I told my-self, and then I'd talk to Miss Willow about the showcase. I knew Ori's role so well, I was practically her understudy. Other girls could step up to be the dancing princesses. Why not go on with the show, if here I was alive, and I could dance it?

My parents, who were generous with their funding projects, helped do the convincing, but when we did perform the variations from *The Firebird*—the spring showcase postponed so long, it was no longer in the right season—I had a new costume. Fewer feathers. Only a couple sequins. Not so much fluff. Still, I was all in red that weekend, when I danced the starring role in the showcase. I couldn't be missed, not from all the way in the nosebleeds, and the very last row.

I was stunning, they told me. They were heavy on the praise, after she was gone, and after Harmony and Rachel were gone. Maybe because I was the only good one left. I was dazzling, they told me. I was transcendent, even, they said. I swear I read that in the local paper the next day.

Even now, three years forward, my mind keeps whirring. Time gets confused. Was I dancing it that night, the night those two girls got themselves dead? Was I always dancing it? Was I always the star?

Memories come up, and I keep needing to shove them down in the dirt where they belong. I keep seeing faces. At first it's only Ori's with her long, dark hair down from the bun, her hair that's longer now, that almost reaches her knees now, since she's been gone. Then I shake that away, and what comes are the others, their honey-colored hair shining and pinned up neatly, the sharp ends of their barrettes glimmering like we're under stage lights. Their painted lashes batting at me in the mirror while I perform a step perfectly, and I know they're hoping I'll fumble and fall, and it kills them when I don't. Their honey-haired heads swishing close together while they talked about me in the tunnel, and then what? The skip in my memory, and some time is lost. Their bloody, honeyed heads squashed on the ground. Another skip in my memory, and more time is lost. The back of the police car. The questions in the mirrored room. The strange, practically weightless feeling when, with my parents flanking me, my parents who've donated to the police department for the past fifteen years, the officer undoes the cuffs and says, "Thank you, Miss Dumont. You can go."

Time skips once more, and I'm looking at them during the car ride home, in the backseat, spreading them out on my lap and looking at them. My hands that they let me wash in the sink after.

My clean hands. My mistake.

I turn my body in the backseat, and my palms on the back windshield, pressed to glass, and the police station retreating, and the car moving, and my parents' saying it's over now, it's over, and the mistake, getting smaller and smaller the farther down the road we get from the station, until it's irreversible, it's a speck, it's gone away, it's gone.

Her word against my word.

My hands against her hands.

The worst thing I've ever done, and then some. I'm always looking down at them. Like when I'm lacing my ribbons on my pointe shoes. When I'm putting toothpaste on my toothbrush. When I'm pushing Tommy away and saying, "Not now." When I'm scrolling through photos on my cell phone, thinking how maybe Harmony and Rachel didn't have any pictures after all, since they never showed up anywhere in all these years. When I'm painting my toenails purple, alone. When I'm holding the barre, practicing alone in my room. When I'm folding my leotards to take with me down to the city. When I'm putting my makeup on. When I'm buttoning a button on my new turquoise shirt. When I'm closing the clasp of my charm bracelet and letting it drift down to the base of my wrist. When I'm eating a piece of cheese. When I'm alone in my room, doing nothing.

I'm looking at them. Studying them. My hands that no one ever accused of doing anything so awful as to kill a girl. Two girls. Let's count Ori and say three. My clean hands.

TRAITOR

"THERE YOU ARE," he says from behind my back.

He's found me in this pit of green weeds and dirt out behind the prison, in this cage, with the body-size hole at my feet. Except now I'm all alone. The sun is setting behind the trees, and there's the moon, somewhere up there, wanting to come out.

"Hello, Miles," I say. She's gone now, and he's probably the reason she took off. She never said "I love you" back, did she, Miles? I bet that's crushed him.

He's standing at the edge of the overgrown garden, saying nothing.

"Time to go?" I ask.

"Didn't you hear us calling you?"

I shake my head.

"We looked everywhere. Sarabeth's bawling in the car. She couldn't find you, and she freaked out. She's been begging us to call the cops."

I guess I've been out here a good long while. All I can remember is Ori in orange, digging this hole, and the rest of what I remember is how she looked at me, so betrayed. She knows the real story, even if neither of us will say it aloud.

"Sarabeth went back to the car?" I check my phone and see an endless scroll of her missed texts.

> Not funny. Where are u
>
> Omg this place is crrrrreepy
>
> But srsly where are you hiding? Can we lv soon?
>
> Tommy wants to go to Denny's ok?
>
> Swear to god a ghost just tried to eat my hair haha not kidding omg
>
> I'm so out of here
>
> Ur scaring me! Are u coming out or what?

And more even than that. I stop reading. There are no texts from my boyfriend, not even one, all afternoon, and I don't know how long I've been missing.

"So where's Tommy?"

Miles ignores the question.

"Is Tommy down at the car, too? We should go. Sounds like Sarabeth really wants to get out of here." I make for the exit in the fencing, but my sandal's stuck in the loose dirt and I falter, rolling my ankle again, the same ankle as before, and if this turns into something serious before Juilliard, an injury that'll keep me from dancing for even so much as a week, I'll have a conniption. I pluck out my bare foot from the ground and brush it off. The sandal won't come up so easily.

"What's that in your hand?" Miles says.

For a moment there, for a gap in time that's like holding your breath and trying to stay upright on one pointed toe, I forget where we are and think we're in another place. Caged in, with green all around, the sky a dark ceiling back then because it was covered by tree branches, and the sky a dark ceiling now because it's just growing dark. I think he's caught me. I think, wildly, furiously, desperately, that I've been caught and can I get away with it a second time? Who will grab the blade from my hand now? Who's going to take the blame?

That's not what he means, though. It's the same color, yes, when I lift my hand and open my palm. Yes. It's blood-red and pulsing even redder in what's left of the light, and at first I think I've gashed open my hand and I wonder why it doesn't hurt, why nothing hurts, why I haven't felt a hurt in years. Then I focus. It's only that feather from her costume, dirty with old gore, three years hidden in my bedroom, still smelling of murder and shame and, I admit it, relief. I've had the feather balled up in my hand this whole time.

"Nothing," I say. Now it drops into the dirt. The hole is deep. The shovel she was holding leans against the tall fence. It's rusted and crusted over with dried mud. It's not as shiny-steel new as I remember.

Miles watches the feather fall. It takes forever. It holds in the air like a ghost is puppeting it, making it dance, and then it's at the bottom of the ditch.

Miles knows what it is. Miles knows everything that Ori's told him. And he's blocking my way out of the chain-link plot of dirt. He's blocking my way. And he knows too much.

Ori never did talk much about Miles. I knew he was obsessed with her—that was plain—and I knew he liked to stay at the edges of rooms and watch her—that was creepy—but that was all I knew. He went to her school, so I didn't know him from mine. I couldn't read the guy at all. He could be drunk right now. He could be psychotic. He could be hiding a weapon behind his back, about to hack me to pieces.

Who's closer to the shovel? Who can get to it first? That's what I'm thinking.

"So where did you say Tommy was?" I ask, going for distraction. "Over there?" I scope out a bunch of nothing in the distance. "Is that him over there?"

Miles doesn't even turn to look.

"He's done with you," he says.

"Tommy's done with *me*? Ha," I say. "Ha. Ha."

"So if you call him, he's not coming after you."

Now I *am* searching the property for Tommy, or for Sarabeth. Are they really down at the car? Both of them? Now I'm checking the long, gray wall that runs along the back of the prison. I scan the fenced-in area with the basketball hoops.

"Oh yeah. I wanted to ask," Miles says. The shift in his voice is hard not to notice. It's almost like he's performing for an audience gathered at the fence. "How'd you like the flowers?"

The flowers. That bouquet, rigged to make me scream.

Of course that was him. That's all he is, just some dolt of a boy still enraged over the loss of his girlfriend. He doesn't know where to fling his energy, so he's flinging it at me.

I need to be sensitive, here, I tell myself. Besides, he's blocking the way out.

"Thanks for the flowers," I say. "So very nice of you. I hope you enjoyed the performance. So . . . are we going or what?"

I keep my voice in that place between hard and soft, the air of not caring, the eye roll and whatever. But my head's hammering. I'm hearing things. I can't say the things are in Ori's voice exactly, but it's not *not* her voice. *He knows. You know he knows. You think he's just going to let you go off to New York, since he knows?*

I cock my head at him and study the kid. His eyes lidded, unfeeling. His mouth held tight. He's let that scruffy chin beard grow in since Ori knew him. I bet she'd hate it, and if she didn't, I would've taunted her about it, so in no time she probably would.

Right now, though, I just want to rip it off his face, and if skin comes off with it, so what.

I take a step forward, even without my sandal. The shovel's a few feet behind me now. All I have to do is make a swift turn, clockwise, not even a full circle, and grab the handle. I can do a turn that fast in my sleep. It's barely the effort of a single pirouette and I'm balanced here, on ground, on both feet. He's got no idea what's coming.

What I hear next is strange, out of place, and I whirl around to see where it's coming from. It's a whispering, a tittering. A sucked-in gasp of breath. A few coughs. A hushed mob of voices coming from over my shoulder, just behind me.

Then the sound cuts out.

I feel it then. It feels like I've been knocked in the head. There are sequins in my eyes now, there are stars. I'm down in the dirt, and the last thing my open eyes see before they lose focus is my sandal. One of the straps is broken, and I need to get it fixed.

Then I sense Miles above me, hovering. I sense others, too, circling. My feet point for no reason. A spotlight brightens all around me and I bask in it, my face raised up to let it light me, and it's everything I ever hoped it would be. But then the spotlight dims. It darkens without warning and leaves me all alone down here, turning away from me like a traitor.

PART VI:
The Innocent

No live organism can continue for long
to exist sanely under conditions of absolute reality;
even larks and katydids are supposed,
by some, to dream.

—Shirley Jackson,
The Haunting of Hill House

Amber:

WE REGRET

WE REGRET SO much. We regretted what we did on the outside. We regretted taunting someone or egging someone on or being the one to do nothing. We regretted our cowardice. Our loyalties. Our hot tempers. How naive we were, how childish, how slow, how reckless, how senseless, how dumb.

Most of us regretted our crimes, of course.

We regretted the blades in our hands and the guns in our waistbands and the lies that dripped from our mouths. We regretted things like hitting our grandmother. Like lifting that baseball bat. Like breaking that window. We regretted a cold winter's day in the parking lot of a 7-Eleven when we made a decision that would lead to a whole new world of regrets.

But that's us.

I couldn't know for sure if our newest inmate, Orianna Speerling, regretted going outside after her friend that day, if she wished she had taken one look at the bloody scene and had turned tail in her heavy, red costume and run and run.

She should have—if she asked us. She should regret the day she met Violet Dumont.

Sometimes it could be the smallest thing that could topple over a whole life and, in the end, destroy it. When we looked back on our own lives—the thirteen, fourteen years we had; the fifteen, sixteen, seventeen—it was from a great distance, as if we were in the clouds above ourselves picking out our existence from among a swarm of ants. Hard to see.

We gazed down on what we were and tried to find that first mistake buried in our heap of mistakes, like how Mack focused in on when she stole the pink bike with the tassels, her first true regret. Each of us should have had one. D'amour's involved a boy, and so did Cherie's. Natty said she had no regrets, but we knew she was only confused by how many there were to shuffle through. Annemarie's warped brain didn't know the word *regret,* but she did miss her sister, sometimes, which was kind of the same thing. And I could have closed my diary before I wrote a word in it. I could have thrown away the tiny silver key. I did regret that.

These were the gateway mistakes that opened the door to the next mistake, and the one after. If only Ori hadn't gone to investigate the noise behind the theater—though that was one of her last regrets; others came before.

Retreating back in time even further, back and back, with Ori shrinking shorter and shorter, and the light in her eyes growing brighter, brighter, brightest, we have to think that if only she hadn't scuffled into that dance class at the age of seven and taken the spot next to the skinny girl with too many pins in her hair, then everything would have been different.

She could have chosen another spot, sure. But why make her go to dance class at all? She could have fought her mom and said she'd rather play soccer instead. That was what she really wanted—to kick a ball around a grassy field with a bunch of boys—before she met Violet.

That was the last year her mother was around, Ori told me. Her mother had been the one to sign her up for ballet; her dad, a long-haul trucker who had to change his route once it was only the two of them, wouldn't have thought of it.

Her mom left without warning on Ori's half birthday, when she was tied between seven and eight years old. She has a memory she can't escape, as we all do. The kind we want to shake from our skulls, or step back into and shout warnings. But what could she have done, at seven and a half, to stop this? It was an empty regret. What we call an inevitability.

Her memory involves a woman with long hair—insanely long, in her memory, and dark, in her memory, it was darker than damp dirt. The remembered woman has bad teeth that jut out from her jaw, but her closed-mouth smile works to hide them. She approaches the creaky kitchen table. One table leg is shorter than the others, so it constantly tips. She serves a slice of freezer-burned ice-cream cake from the supermarket, the kind with the chalky flower garnishes that turn tongues blue. No candles, not seven and not eight.

"Go on," says the woman. "Eat."

The spoon fills. The woman watches the spoonfuls go down. A yellow, sagging suitcase in the doorway. The spoonfuls slowing. The sense of being sleepy. Saratoga Taxi honking in the driveway. A quick-closed door. The click of the lock. Eyelids so heavy. Then the quiet of an empty house and the darkness of two closed eyes.

Her father found her hours later, asleep at the creaky kitchen table. The remaining ice cream on the plate had made soup.

This was why, to Ori, the halfway mark of anything felt like it was begging for disaster. It was also why she couldn't eat ice cream, which may have been lucky, since we never got ice cream in here.

Many of us had lost our mothers (and some of us would have kicked them out ourselves as soon as we could walk, had we been able to pay the electric and drive the car). There was no new level of sympathy for being motherless—it was a common kind of hurt quite a few of us shared. But to have a mother there one moment and gone the next, no explanation, no cancer, no knife to the gut, no new boyfriend who says he'll take her to the Bahamas just without the kids, not even a note on the table saying why. We understand how that might make a girl crumble.

When the bad came for her, as it came charging for all of us here at Aurora Hills, Ori didn't duck out of the way, like so many of us tried to. She didn't deny, though she could have and should have. She hung her head. She let go of the weapon that had somehow ended up in her hand, and she watched it catch the light as it fell.

It all made a sick and perfect kind of sense to her. Violet was pointing at her. Violet was crying and screaming and pointing. Then Violet was rescued from the scene and pulled away, and she couldn't see Violet anymore.

Ori was alone, but for the bodies. A police officer yelled for her to come out with her hands up, but she didn't understand, and she was too slow, too slow to make sense of this, and then the police officer was on her, forcing her to her knees, making her understand. She didn't struggle, the way Jody might have. She didn't kick, like Polly surely would have. She didn't keep her head raised, defiant, like any one of us would wish we had. She lay down like a log. Her costume was so heavy, and her body inside it was even heavier. The heaviest part of her was her head.

She let them lift her and carry her to the police car. The backseat was the first cage she'd ever entered, but it felt familiar somehow, to be caged. Her hands felt freezer-burned. Her tongue felt heavy in her dry mouth, blue. She wondered if she should text Miles, and then she realized she didn't have her phone.

Besides, what could she have said in a text message? Soon this would be all over the news.

Deep down, she believed everything good in her life was something she'd never deserved to have in the first place, and that included Miles. The deep-down feelings were the ones that came up first. The anger at Violet would come later. In those first minutes she had a random thought, slow like a drifting feather that takes forever to reach the ground. It took the shape of a yellow suitcase. It tasted like sweet cream mixed with codeine cough syrup, and made her eyes heavy with remembering. Her mother had been right to leave. Her mother now lived in Florida, of all places, and had a new family, two sun-bleached little girls (she knew because she'd looked her up on Facebook). Orianna Speerling closed her eyes and kept them closed until the police car reached the station. What was happening to her life was the first thing that made sense in seven and a half years.

What do you deserve, if you don't deserve a mother? I wouldn't know. When I was halfway between seven and eight years old, my mother still loved me.

I knew the truth about my new cellmate's crime now, and knowing that was like knowing all. But there was something I was keeping from her.

I couldn't make my mouth say it, not to her, and not to any of the girls.

It had been days since I'd been given the news of my approaching release. The woman who'd made it happen—my mother—did not write, and the idea of being let go, from out of nowhere, wrenched tighter around my neck like a noose. I wasn't entirely sure what I deserved. I'd gotten so used to what I had in here.

On the next visiting day, I approached the queue, to ask.

Blitt was guarding the door, white-knuckling her list of approved names.

"Nope," she said, with a sharp shake of her head. "Not you."

"But maybe she's here. Maybe I—"

"Not on the list," she said, which closed off all further communication. Of course my mother wouldn't have driven all the way up here. Our first words after three years, one month, and however many days would take place in person and not inside these walls. And if she wouldn't come here to face me, I wouldn't collect-call her to try to gauge how much hate she had left for me from only the sound of her voice.

Visitors could be heard on the other side of the green wall—I knew they were visitors from the way they talked too loud, too fast. Laughed when no one was laughing. Tried too hard. They also spoke of outside things, alien experiences, like visits to movie theaters and concert halls and items of clothing they'd walked into a store and bought. Through the reinforced window, laced with scratches from girls left waiting for their visitors, I could see in.

I saw Lola shove through into the visiting area. Mack, crying at the first sight of her family, who came every week and called her Mackenzie, was swift on Lola's heels. Even Kennedy had a visitor, a woman with shorn hair, so she must have known of Kennedy's habit and didn't want to come in tempting her. I heard the shorn woman—Kennedy's mother? Big sister? Former parole officer? Lover? Pastor? Aunt?—ask after Kennedy's faint echo of a black eye, and I heard Kennedy use an excuse my mother once used, which was that she'd been in the shower and accidentally knocked a bar of soap into her own eye. I saw Lola, at a nearby table with her own visitor, release a small, smug smile.

Then I spotted Ori.

A teenage boy was at her table, slouching and with hair in his eyes. Her hand and his hand were under the table, clasped together and stowed out of sight of the CO on duty nearby. So this was Miles.

It made me want to shove a fist through the glass, if that glass was even breakable. She hadn't mentioned a visit. She avoided talking to me about him—like she had to keep us in separate rooms. I wanted to get close enough to make him sit up straight and force his hair out of his eyes. I wanted to see how much he knew about her, and whether it was as much as I now knew. But Blitt was guarding the doorway.

Though their hands touched in secret, and I can't know how tightly their fingers were laced, how sweaty their palms, their faces showed me so much. His was rigid, and red with frustration. Hers was drawn, opaque as a swirling storm. He was trying to convince her of something. She was shaking her head no. I liked that.

An adult hovered nearby—his parent or guardian?— and held out a bag of potato chips from the vending machine. Ori reached out to take a chip, but the adult shifted the bag across the table, to Miles. He grabbed a handful and gave them to Ori. She crunched. No one had ever shared anything from the vending machine with me, in all my years here.

This wasn't necessarily what love looked like, but it was close enough to cause the other girls, at separate tables with their own visitors, to turn and stare.

After, I asked her what she and Miles were talking about.

She shook off any surprise at how I found out but wouldn't meet my eyes. "I told him there isn't going to be any appeal," she said. "And he should stop pushing me and pushing me. He should move on with his life."

"But . . . ," I started. In fact, I agreed with him.

We were in our cell, the steel door open because it wasn't

yet time to be locked in. It was here that the sound of an approaching CO quieted us. Santosusso came into view. He was smiling, and I wished he weren't.

"Amber," he called to me. "Guess what? You've got a date on the books."

I approached the doorway, my feet bare and my shoes in the tub on the floor, my number on the wall above my head. Others from B-wing leaned in, listening. I saw Mississippi. She had ninety-three days left to serve on her sentence and was doing crunches against the wall. The crunches stopped. I watched Jody (more than two hundred days remaining) drop her hand of cards.

They knew.

Ori didn't know. I sensed her behind me, brimming with questions.

Santosusso told me the day of my coming release. It was in September, as had been promised. None of the other girls said a word.

"Get ready," Santosusso said, waving his arm at the tiered cell block, the barred doors, the green walls, the bolted-down tables and rock-hard, immovable chairs. "Soon you'll be leaving all this."

I couldn't imagine it.

With Santosusso gone, the others came up to say their piece. I was offered congratulations, mumbled bits of luck. I was told to write letters, though they knew I wouldn't. I was asked if I'd pass along messages to ex-boyfriends and current boyfriends and old friends. I was told to eat a good meal at the closest White Castle and think of them.

She didn't speak until they'd all left me be.

"You're getting out?" Ori said.

One of my shoulders made a shruglike twitch.

"Next week?"

"Ten days," I said, "yeah. I guess that is next week," and how soon that seemed, ten days and only ten, ten out of how many hundred that had come before. My stomach heaved, and I almost made a break for our shared toilet, to throw my lunch up.

"How long have you known?" she asked.

"A while," I admitted. "I was going to tell you."

"You deserve it," she said, and how wrong she was. "They're acting funny because they're jealous. Everyone knows you should never have been here." Wrong, again.

I looked down at her hideous feet. All dancers have them, she'd told me. I wondered what those feet used to look like when they were moving, whipping around in the air, her body making pretty shapes for an audience. It seemed so absurd, but something about Ori made me believe it. Now I'd never get to see.

"You know you'll do fine out there, Amber," she said, sensing my fear. "It'll be good. Really. You'll get to go back to school, and graduate. And see your sister, who misses you so much. And you'll meet someone, I bet. Some guy, and you'll have to write me and tell me all about him."

I wanted to say no. No, to all of it. Especially to meeting someone, because why. Because who.

"What about you?" I said instead.

"What about me?" She sat with her legs crossed on the bottom bunk. All the surrounding gray brought out her eyes. "I'm basically never getting out," she said. "Not until I'm like forty-five. You know that."

I did. At least, it was what the court had determined for her. Once her juvenile sentence was over, she'd be transferred to serve out the rest of her time with the most violent adult female offenders the state could serve up. That was what happened to us when our days at Aurora Hills were over and our time was longer than could fit in here. She would become an adult in prison—like I'd thought I would. She'd be nothing like the person she was now. In thirty years, I wouldn't even recognize her.

I wasn't sure if she looked ahead at her life inside and wanted what I'd told myself I'd wanted, which was a place to call my own within these cold stone walls.

ALL SHE KNEW

ALL SHE KNEW was that she was trying to help. Ori had returned the library cart to me—or so she thought, as my transfer from the kitchen still hadn't made it through all official channels. With my release date on the books, I wasn't sure it would in time.

Nothing in Aurora Hills was ever so easy. Some efforts felt endless, and others turned around whip-fast so we kept looking over our shoulders, checking to be sure it was true. All actions here had consequences. It was only a matter of when.

Ori started returning from afternoon yard duty with the plants she must have promised Peaches in exchange for my cart. Day after day, she managed to transport bits and pieces of the vines inside to hand over, and not one of the guards heard the rustling inside her jumpsuit when she walked past their stations or noticed the petals she'd sometimes shed on the stone floor, pinkened with pigment and gummy enough to stick.

She'd meet Peaches, do the handover, and then Peaches would come swinging by, lingering at the doorways to our cells or in the hallway outside the woodshop, and those of us who wanted what she was selling would offer up items from our canteen accounts, or make promises we wouldn't have the time to keep. There were many ways to come up with payment.

Some of us were seeking escape, even more so after the night the locks malfunctioned and let us loose, and then took it all back and said never mind. But I didn't want to be numbed up with any drug, the way Peaches and her crew wanted us all to be, the way D'amour used to long for, probably still does. I wanted my mind clear.

I thought it was.

But the memory was there. It was hanging around the corner, waiting.

I saw the haze that enveloped so many of the girls around me, and a certain saccharine scent that lingered after one of us had succumbed. The drug made us forget. I wondered what would happen if one of us took too much—would we remember? And remember what?

Peaches accepted what was owed, but that didn't keep her from holding it against one person, and that person was me. It was midweek, a handful of days away from my release, when she shoved into the cafeteria line in front of me and grabbed the top tray and the closest cup, which was the red cup. She took her time in the line for slop, chatting, sucking her bottom lip, stretching out her back and scratching a roaming itch.

I couldn't push, and I couldn't tell her to keep moving. These were rules so well-known among us that they didn't need to be written. Power was taken here, and once it was solidly in hand, those of us who didn't make a grab for it, or who did and missed, were bowled over, mown down. She may as well have been standing on my prone body, a foot jammed in the back of my neck, her arms raised in a victory V.

I stood in line behind her and waited for her to move on.

"What?" Peaches said to me, about-facing to shove her jaw in my direction.

"Nothing," I said under my breath. There was no other response to make in this situation. If I said another word now, anything at all, even something silly to make a joke of it, I'd risk losing one or more of my front teeth. I'd been here for years and still had all my original teeth. I was hoping to keep them.

"No, what?" Peaches said. "What were you going to say, what?"

"Did she say something?" Jody joined in, many heads taller than both of us and casting us in shadow. "What'd she say?"

"I didn't."

They stared me down.

"I didn't say anything."

I'd gone around their backs. That was what Peaches and Jody were communicating to me. I had my precious book cart, didn't I? So was I happy now? How happy? Because if

I was too happy, they'd go ahead and make me miserable, as only the happiest among us deserved to be.

I left my unfilled tray like I wasn't even hungry and headed for the table where I usually sat with girls from B-wing. When I approached, it emptied, leaving only my cell-mate, Ori, who looked to me in question. She tried to share her food, but I shook her off. It was coming. Retaliation.

More and more of them had turned against me. I was used to them letting me be, ignoring me so I could sidle in and listen to what they said, catalogue, mull over, keep for later. But a line had been drawn, and Peaches and Jody were on one side of it. I found myself on the other.

I was in the library during free time, sorting the books, dusting their spines and jackets, wiping clean their glossy faces, and straightening their bent corners. It wasn't offi-cially my life-skills job anymore, but I couldn't help wanting to keep things nice.

The stomping sound of their approach startled me. I set down a stack of books.

"Hey there," Jody said. Peaches grinned. I knew then to cover my head.

It was Jody who delivered the first blow. She didn't use her fists—she had her fingers gripped in a white sock, and weighted down in the hanging toe of the sock was some-thing heavy. It could have been a bar of soap. A hunk of brick. It could have been the smallest book on our shelves, one of the pocket classics. All I knew was that it hurt on impact and gave a good pounding.

Peaches came next, and the socks in her hands were two. I curled into the smallest shape I could make myself, which wasn't so small. Tucked my head in, wanting to keep my teeth. There was the feeling of everything—and the feeling of nothing, which I guess comes when the pain is too much and you pass out.

Maybe that was when I decided to do something, hovering in that state halfway between waking to consciousness and being blacked out. Because even then, even after this, I knew where I belonged in the sea of all the earth's strangers.

Where we all belonged.

What justice might look like, if I were the one to wield it, inside these walls, where no one used to look at me or pay me much attention, but now for sure they would.

How inevitable it felt, how perfectly timed and carved out to fit the pieces together without any gaps between. It was as if I had the key to every last lock.

I stood, wavering. I gathered up the rest of the breaths sifting around in my lungs and made a rhythm of them. I braced myself against a bookshelf, and then I let go.

I stopped in our cell in B-wing on the way, and maybe I knew what I was doing and where I was going because I'd done it before, and maybe I knew nothing. We all wished we could plead "not guilty."

I made it, somehow, to the kitchen. It was a Thursday afternoon, or a Tuesday, but surely afternoon, and I was due for my life-skills assignment in the kitchen. I found myself in the back near the burners, as I knew I would. I found myself stirring the peas. The pot of peas. The peas were supposed to be green, but they looked more gray. The swirl of gray-green in the pot. The spoon gripped in my hand. The spoon making circles. The circles of the spoon.

Maybe that was what got my memory circling, then clearing and starting to show something visible there, down at the bottom, crusted like the burned base of the pot and not coming loose from the spoon. Something I forgot. Something I'd been trying to remember, all this time.

The pot itself was enormous, large enough to cook a human stew. The spoon was as long as a hunting spear. My arm ached, and parts of my face pulsed, and one of my eyes wouldn't open all the way. Somehow, nobody in the kitchen noticed. They saw what they wanted to see. Outside, in the world beyond Aurora Hills, I'd heard it's even worse.

The noise and activity of the kitchen roared all around me. There was Kennedy, doing dishes, her hands too deep in the suds to yank off some of her hair for eating. I still didn't know her crime, but I felt for sure she must have been guilty. There was D'amour. Had she gotten out of the infirmary and assigned a new cellie? Or did she have special permission to return her own meal trays? She sloped past, a loose bandage trailing the floor. No question she was guilty. Natty dumped a tray of cups in the vat, nodded, moved on. One of the cups was the red one, the one I still hadn't found on my tray, though I looked for it every day. It floated to the top, shifting the others aside. Natty was guilty.

A group of girls could be heard passing in the corridor— every last one of them was guilty. Out the window in the kitchen, I could see the barred windows of D-wing, filled with Suicides and anyone on restriction. Guilty.

And myself? Guilty then, and still guilty today.

I stirred the peas, gazing into the pot. There was nothing to see at first. Only the green peas and the gray.

Then there was more and more gray. A different kind of gray. Gray like the stones that stacked to make our walls were solid and gray. Gray like white paint after so many years of being allowed to stay dirty. Gray like a girl's heart when she's been forced to reckon with what she's done and no one believes she really is guilty. That kind of gray.

Then I realized why. It was how my head was turned, toward the ceiling. How I was looking up instead of looking down, at all of us.

There was something below me, something wanting my attention. My eyes drifted and flickered, seeking focus. One wouldn't stay open, but the other saw fine.

My nose took a whiff of the abominable smell.

When I turned my neck, slowly, the tendons creaking as if I hadn't used this part of my body in years, I could see the feet first. Our feet. Our canvas slip-on shoes—they were white, but white never stayed white for long in this place, so really they were gray. Some of them were splayed on the tiled floor, some had been lost in the shuffle, and some were there, wedged on. The feet of so many girls I recognized—from C-wing and A-wing and B-wing—all dropped to the floor as if we were playing a game and that game was pretending to be dead.

Where was I among them?

I sifted through the crowd, looking down on all of them, far enough away to not get the mess on me, but not far enough to escape the stench. It was rotten, and it was also sickly sweet. It was terrible, rising up to choke all my senses.

These girls weren't playing. This was the cafeteria, where we gathered three times a day to eat our meals, those of us who weren't on lockdown in Solitary. There were the tables and the trays, but there was none of the usual din. There was no noise. I could see Little T. in a seat at the end of the table. She was slumped over the side of her stool, head to her knees so her face was hidden. Her arms were slack and hanging, but her fingers were still clasped tight around the handle of a plastic spoon.

Peaches had fallen face-first onto the green floor, her hair flung up over her head to reveal the tattoo on the back of her neck that she'd always kept hidden. It was a braided series of flowers, feathery and delicate, really quite beautiful. The spittle coming from her mouth was green, too, and all that green brought to mind the forest that surrounded our compound, the climbing vines from the garden and grounds where Ori worked, the drug so many of us ingested that summer, giving us green-hued dreams and green crusty eyes in the morning, all the green in this gray place that hid us from the law-abiding world.

We were a part of this place even more now. We were as essential to its continuing existence as the moss and the grass and the trees.

There was Cherie. She'd fallen backward off her stool, and in the drop, which must have been sudden, and which landed her on another sharp-edged stool behind her, she'd broken open her skull. So the green goo spewed from her mouth, but pooling around her neck, coming out of her ears, was red. And green and red make brown.

All this I took in without emotion, as if petty things such as feelings had been carved out of me the way melons get scooped of their seeds.

If I could only remember where I was sitting and eating dinner that day, I'd be able to find where I fell.

I drifted over the aisles, plugging up my nose as I went. The fallen trays scattered the little things everywhere, and they were round, so they rolled. Some had been mashed into paste, but many were still intact and kept rolling across the tile, all the way to the outer ends of the room and back again, like more than my memory was sloshing.

Once-green, but gray because they came out of cans. Peas.

But mixed with what? With the mashed-up pulp of that plant we'd never found a name for because it wasn't in any of our books? Shouldn't that just give us hallucinations, like before, trips to the sky and back and faint heart murmurs, fits of giggles? Did anyone know it could do so much more if too much of the stuff was mashed in? Didn't anyone notice how sweet the peas tasted that day, how sugary and almost delicious, like gumdrops mixed with dirt?

And then I remembered who'd been at the pot, stirring. I remembered my own arm, my own hand. Shouldn't I have known there was something wrong with the peas? Or had I known all along?

Someone was approaching, and joined me by the trash pails. The scorch marks on her face hadn't fully faded, so she hovered there, lavender in hue.

"You've gone and done it now," D'amour said, though without surprise, like she'd known all along this was coming. "Now we can't ever leave."

We couldn't ever leave. I hadn't been able to face that

D'amour was seeing our future before, but she must have seen this. So had I. I'd just forgotten.

The doors were open now, the locks were undone, and we couldn't go.

I looked around once more. I was mistaken about the gray, because when I blinked, it was gone.

Where there had been gray walls, there were green-growing vines, and where there had been partitions and cordoned-off sections to keep inmates from roaming too far out of sight of the COs, there were open, shaggy spaces of field. There were gaps in the fence that would let a whole herd of us escape into the forest. There were graffiti tags on what was left of the cinder-block walls, showing all the strangers who had snuck in here. This place had come falling down, and all that was left was us now. We girls poisoned to death during dinner by one of our own, we'd be here longer than these walls would be left standing.

"Who did this?" I was asking D'amour. "Did you do this? Did I?"

She shook her head. She was caught up in it, staring as if we were fresh off the blue-painted bus, here to observe one of the Great Wonders of the World.

I shouldn't be here. I'd been released—in days, I was supposed to be taken out front and let go. I was going to be issued street clothes. They'd have to give me real shoes, and I'd walk out onto the sidewalk in those shoes. They were going to let me out, in the care of my mother. I was supposed to see September.

They might as well have backed me up against the rear

of the building and had me shot in the head by a firing squad. The last time I was out there, in the world, I was thirteen. The last time I saw my mother, she'd turned her back on me like I was the bullet.

I didn't want to go. I didn't want any of us to go, ever. Was that why I'd done it?

That was when I saw the body by the far table. It wasn't my own. The two long legs were clad in orange. One of the feet had lost a shoe, and the foot was bare and blistered with a bulbous, purple-callused toe.

Hadn't I told her never to eat the peas? Wasn't that advice I'd given, her very first day?

D'amour wouldn't say it, and the others, about to be awakened and risen to join us, none of them would say it, and my one good eye started tearing up so neither eye could see the cafeteria without blurs.

Only one of us didn't deserve to be here, not even for a night. Orianna Speerling was the only one who was truly innocent.

It was all too much for me. My mistake. Facing my fate, which was all of our fates entwined as one, even hers. Seeing it plain. Seeing myself, even if I didn't yet find my body.

I was back at the pot again, stirring what would be our poison, and I couldn't make myself stop.

Because it had already happened.

Because it is happening now, as I stand here. I'm watching myself stir the peas as we speak.

And my skin goes electric. My entire body does. The kitchen, from end to end, lights up with the blaze of blue light that fried D'amour, boiling my memory, getting time confused, and my brain blackens into a wall without windows, and my body drops like one last bag of useless meat to the floor.

This is what happens when I let myself remember what I did. It happens every time.

WE'LL FOREVER BE

WE'LL FOREVER BE pointing fingers. Playing detective, to see who might be caught red-handed, overheard in telling a bald-faced lie.

Peaches says it has to be Kennedy. Peaches found a hair on her tray, she says, a curly Kennedy-colored hair in her peas. Half of us want to point the finger at Kennedy, and if we had keys to our jail cells, we'd have locked her in Solitary long ago and shaved off all her hair. A couple of us say it was Annemarie, though with her kept in D-wing it's impossible to say how she would have done it. Lots of us say it was Peaches, and many more say D'amour. None of us think it was Ori. If she helped someone else get to the vines, if she smuggled them inside one afternoon after her work in the garden, it was only for my benefit; she had no idea what anyone would do.

None of us knows for sure it has always been me.

Here we are, pointing fingers and devolving into arguments, and those arguments can last all night, now that we have eternity. Because, when we think of it that way, what's a night or two?

We don't know what they say about us on the outside. They don't deliver newspapers up here.

We were the juvenile delinquents of Aurora Hills, and while a good number of us were sent up for some of the worst crimes anyone could imagine, more often the crimes that sealed our fates started off teaspoon-size. The virgin infractions for a few of us were laughable: Writing our name on an already written-on wall. Jumping a train turnstile. Pocketing a tube of lipstick.

We were infamous only after. Before our names were drawn in crayon by Sunday school children onto construction paper angels left on the fence down at the bottom of the hill, these were names not many people would remember.

The scene when the ambulances climbed the hill and the gates opened and the police found us was one that couldn't be hidden from the public. Word of a tragedy travels. People delight in demise. So it was chaos in the cafeteria—and that was after we were all dead. Officials were brought in to make a count of all of us, just as we were used to being counted multiple times a day.

The bodies were numbered at forty-one, including those who'd been served their dinner in their Solitary cells on D-wing, and the one still bedded in the infirmary. Forty-one.

Which could not be, Aurora Hills corrections officers said, as there were no escapees left unaccounted for, every girl locked in her rightful place, and so the count should be forty-two.

Those counting went back to the head of the line of bodies, clipboards at the ready. One, two, three. Four, five, six. Enough of us to build a small army, had we still been fightworthy. Enough of us to make a true mark on the world, good or bad, had we lived. Ten, twenty, thirty. Thirty-seven, thirty-eight, thirty-nine.

Forty.

Forty-one.

They'd counted. Then they had to count again.

As they neared the end of one more count, there was a pause—had they lost a girl in the shuffle? Had one been released to the morgue without the right people being notified; who is to answer for this; will we have to try doing the count over, *again*? Oh, sorry.

They must have miscounted before, because suddenly the outcome was right. They reached the final body and it was as expected: forty-two.

There was so much activity after we died that we must have made it worse, with all our confusion. Some of us were still clinging to our throats, wanting to spit the bad bits out. Others of us drifted. We didn't need our legs to walk, but we needed some sense of direction to propel us through the crowd, and it was a challenge to get control at first. We headed for the kitchen, but none of us could find the obvious culprit. There was a frenzy around the spilled plates and cooking pots, causing a haze that made the living humans—those in uniform trying to perform the forensic investigation—start gagging even with their protective masks on and have to leave the room.

Immediately after death, emotions are so raw. We were powder white and livid, but it was too late to stop what had already happened. The bodies we left under the sheets out in the cafeteria had choked and turned green.

The frenzy of discovery lasted a long time, and when we'd finally calmed, there was no one else left in the kitchen with us. The living had gone. They'd left, and they'd carted out our bodies with them. There was no one guarding our doors. There was no one working our gates.

There was quiet.

Outside these walls, time marched forward without us. We died early one evening in late August, but the world didn't stay put in that humid state. We were so preoccupied howling and crying and being wounded and wronged and upset, I guess it took us a while to see it.

A rainstorm broke through and then dried up. The wind swept up the hill, and the air chilled. The leaves fell and the snow covered them. The ice decorated our windows and then melted clean away. The tree in our rec field bloomed in pale flowers, and the ivy that climbed our gray stone walls flowered in bright colors and grew thorns. The heat came, and by the next August, the world outside our walls had grown wilder, but beyond that it hadn't much changed. The only difference out there, if we took it down to the nitpicky details we could see through our chicken-wired windows, was that no one from groundskeeping had kept up with the gardening or the mowing of the lawns.

As time moved forward and the seasons changed, the Aurora Hills Secure Juvenile Detention Center in the far northern reaches of our already northern state was closed. No new girls came in, and there were no newly freed girls to be let out. The second August came around. A third August came, and a third August went.

Now it's another August, marking the day we overdosed on the poison plant mixed in with our green peas, and we can no longer tell just which August we're living in. We forget what day it is. We forget there's a reason we wanted to skip dinner. We forget what's coming, and that it's already come, again and again.

The outside world hasn't forgotten us entirely, but the people don't think of us often anymore. We are names above a rotting mound of teddy bears on an iron gate. We are hated, and occasionally, by those who can see it in their hearts to forgive, we are mourned. We are proclaimed, by believers who, if only they'd spent time with us before our end, think we could have been saved.

Saved from what?

From living these weeks over and over, we guess. From forgetting—and then remembering, so much worse each time, because we tried so very hard the last time not to forget.

We have some ideas about the afterlife, about why we're still here. The thing about a life being cut short, when it's not by choice and not with any rhyme or reason or hinted at by diagnosis or threat, is that sometimes, some of you will want to hang on.

We do. We can't seem to find a way to leave.

WHEN SHE RETURNS

WHEN SHE RETURNS, we gather by the window slits, charting her progress through our yard behind the facility. We move from window to window, from wall to wall, watching as she weaves through our fence lines, as she wanders our grounds in the shadow of our barbed wire without seeming to sense any of us eyeing her from above.

The intruder never once looks up at our barred windows, though we will her to do so. A few of us shout down at her, but all she seems to hear is the wind.

Some of us get shaken at the sight of her, so clearly is she from another world. We critique her clothes. Make fun of her tightly slicked hair, her shiny barrettes. We brag about what we'll do to humble her, if she comes up here and gets close. But there's a sadness beneath our mocking, a shred of jealousy. We won't say it, but we know she's still alive. Everything about the way she walks and holds herself tells us she is free.

"Has anyone seen her before?" some of us ask the others. "Who is she, anyway, and where'd she come from?" None of us offer up any answers, especially me. I'm waiting for Ori to come to the window and recognize her. Then I'll help explain.

Ori rushes then into B-wing, and by her face I know she's seen Violet, the girl who's come again to haunt us. The ghost from her past who now all of us can see.

Dirt covers Ori's arms and crusts her knees—she must have been working out in the garden again. She's come running inside to find me, as if there's something I can do.

"She's back," she says, panic rising in her eyes. "I don't know why she's here. She's not sorry."

The question is why. I'm beginning to sense the answer rising.

I've turned from the others, so I don't realize at first where they're going or what they have in mind, though I should have. They get down there faster than I expect—the gathering noise outside tells me.

Ori, though, isn't moving. "I don't want to see her ever again," she says, and a prickle of electricity inside me says she won't have to. We've got other plans.

Ori has no idea what we're about to do. She doesn't go down to watch, but I can't help it.

There they are—there *we* are—outside in the rec area behind the facility. I emerge from the back door, and find myself drawn closer. We're all hanging back, watching.

The intruder is no longer on her own. A boy has joined

her. I recognize Miles straightaway, and I'm delighted to see what might happen with the two of them facing off, but I know this is not something most of the rest of us will understand. They don't know who he is, who they both are, how they got in here, why the boy is so angry at the girl, why the girl might seem so familiar, why she becomes as bright as a beacon and the boy turns faceless and forgettable, and they don't much care about him.

Still, we step closer. The light in the sky flickers. We feel it in our bones. That's all we are now—bones. We sense that something is about to happen, and more, that we will be the ones to make it happen.

We hope Ori is watching from the windows, because this is for her.

Jody steps up. Natty gets a distinct smile on her face as she cracks her knuckles. But it's little Annemarie, emerged from D-wing as if she traveled like vapor through the flimsiest of our walls, who is quick-thinking, and so resourceful. She's got a shovel in hand, and she whips it fast. Barrettes go flying. For a lovely moment, the intruder seems to coast through the air, dancing for us, and some of us have never seen that kind of dancing, but then she drops into the dirt with a hard thump. A leg goes crooked. A foot bends funny. Her mouth opens, and red drips out. She's stopped moving, even when Jody gives her a kick.

A piece of jewelry has fallen, and before anyone can say the word, we know it's too shiny to stay here. It may be gold, but among us it's worth nothing. Polly, who has the best pitching arm, throws it over our heads to get rid of it. We don't know where it lands, except that it's far away.

We've forgotten about the boy entirely. We can't even see a trace of him anymore. Our hunger is for the guilty one. The girl. Only the guilty can truly see us, just as our shadowed eyes want to focus in on the guilty right back. We recognize the light she carries—blinking, beckoning, telling us what she's done—like a long-lost sister will recognize you as family after years apart because you share the same nose.

The body rolls into the hole and makes so much noise. To look at the body—so compact, with the long legs and the long arms—we assume she would have weighed a few ounces, her bones made of cotton puffs and air. But it's like a box of dishes pitched off the side. She makes such a clatter. And we've always heard ballerinas were full of grace.

This girl down in the hole is the brightest light I've ever seen. She belongs with us.

I climb down into the ditch. Mississippi puts out an arm to help me.

I place the fallen girl's head in my lap and stroke her hair, now that it's lost its pins and decorations. The back of her skull has a giant gash from the shovel, and I cover the soft, gooey spot with my hand. She is showing up so clear that I can feel the strands now, come loose from her bun. We are both hurting. It's the first time that I let myself feel that I am. My hands move along, to trace the planes of her face. My hands are red from her, and on her face I get some smears. I am getting to know her, the way I've gotten to know Orianna Speerling before her, and D'amour Wyatt before that.

The others drift away. They're letting me have her.

She comes to, but only to convulse, choking on what's

left of her breath. It won't be long. There can't be much air remaining in her lungs now, and the seeping gash in the back of her head will end it all soon, since she's losing so much blood.

"Ori?" she sputters, the very last living word she lets out. She still thinks I'm her friend. I'm not her friend; I never will be. But I guess now we're family.

"No," I say. "Not Ori. But you'll meet me soon enough."

We hear the sirens in the far-off distance like they've come calling for someone else. It's only as the sirens get closer that we realize, yes, this is happening again. This is our last day again, and this sound belongs to us.

Again.

The swarm of people in the cafeteria makes it hard to keep track of one another. We call out over the din, but what we're doing is creating the din, howling and crying and bleating our panic, the way we always do. Each time we reach this day, we go through it at this heightened state, and then we forget. We want to forget. We forget that, too. We forget it's what we wanted.

We are lined up for count again; that's eternal. The warden has a long list of all our names. I'm on it and checked off quickly. Ori is on it, but she's not so easily found. I don't know where she is.

We hear them counting. We watch from the ceiling, look down from above. They have reached thirty. They have reached thirty-one, thirty-two, thirty-three.

They have reached forty now—and how long does it take to walk down a row and count all of our bodies? We're so impatient—they have reached forty-one.

Here they pause. They don't see her yet, but I do. I know it's her by the funny bend in her foot. They can't hear me point her out; they're not so attuned.

Forty-two. She is right there—just look. Forty-two.

Finally a head swivels. One of the COs, but they've all gone as gray and blurry as distant spirits and I can't tell which one. There. They see her. A small crowd gathers. She's not wearing a jumpsuit like the others are. She's covered in dirt, as if she'd been buried and dug out of the ground to join us here. It makes sense they're so confused.

"Which one is this?" one of the COs says.

The other rattles off names from his list of different inmates. There are a lot of us, but none of the names he gives belongs to the girl on the ground.

They haven't noticed her twisted leg, the way it bends backward at an angle that defies medical science. They haven't turned her over to view the gash in her head.

All we know is she is now one of us. We lost one of our number and no one noticed, but how quickly our number has been restored. It seems we are meant to stay at full capacity, which for this facility is forty-two girls.

They use the blue-painted bus to cart all the bodies away. It takes three trips. We watch the front landing area from our window slits, crowded around the openings as we used to on the days new inmates were due to arrive.

We watch them take us out in body bags, and from this distance we can't tell whose body is whose inside the opaque plastic. We can only guess at what belongs to us, whose hanging arm or whose dangling foot, whose hair is caught in the zipper.

Our bodies are piled in the back. There we are, so still, so docile, we no longer need chains. The doors are closed on us, and the bus leaves the curb for the last time and heads for the gate.

Violet Dumont (cold-blooded murderer of two fifteen-year-old girls, traitor, and unrepentant liar; never caught, never sentenced, never jailed, not until she visited us and we made it right) is new among us and not yet sure of our ways or our rules. She refuses to look out the window with the rest of us.

She's having a hard time settling in, which so many of us can relate to. We wonder how she'll break on her first night, and we offer up a few suggestions and catcalls and bets to pass the time. I abstain, as she now has top bunk in our shared cell, and I don't want my eyes clawed out while I'm sleeping.

We figure she might rave and kick and fight the first night the locks slam closed, but she'll get used to it, in time. She'll have to, now she's finally being punished for what she did.

All we can tell her of eternity is what we have right here.

IF WE'D KNOWN

IF WE'D KNOWN, we might not have been so angry, so fused solid with rage, so willing to kick a girl when she was down and walk away.

This is night. And we've finally located the one we called Ori.

The late-August heat hovers over her as she descends the hill and gets on her knees to crawl through the hole in the fence.

If she could see a mirror in the night—a mirror better than the tinfoil hung for vanity in our cells—she would be struck by the changes. When she was sent upstate, after sentencing, she had round cheeks and dark, endlessly long hair. The detention center made her cut her hair, and the stress and shock and fear of being accused and then found guilty for a crime she did not commit took away the apples in her cheeks and most of the shine from her eyes. If she saw who she would turn into, outside our walls, upon exiting the hole in our fence, she would have been startled.

Three years have passed on the outside. Outside our walls, she is eighteen.

We watch her down there, now. We see how she's just emerged through the hole in the fence.

There is a hand, a boy's hand, and it's reaching out to help her up. The night sounds keep in time with her breathing— a bleating of insects, a rustling in the woods, but no birds beyond a lone owl. If she looks up, she could have seen stars. *Look up,* we want to tell her. *For us. Look up.*

"Hey," the boy says. "You okay?"

Miles is just as she remembered him, but more wild-eyed maybe. Longer hair, scruffy chin beard and stubble. He seems dazed, but he's only out of breath from running down the hill. Did he see what she saw? We can't know. But we can assure her it's him, absolutely and inexplicably him, though she doesn't need us to tell her.

She would know for sure it is really Miles when she took his hand and felt his palm, which would be warm and dry and strong in grip, as strong as she remembered. She could trace his lines. She could reach up and map his face, draw the whorls in his ears, stick her fingers inside, though he used to hate when she did that and he'd squirm and say stop. She could lean in close and breathe in the particular smell of his neck, which would be just as she remembered, as he still used the same soap. She could put her mouth to his and make like she was going to kiss him, only she'd suck his bottom lip, taking it inside her mouth like she wouldn't let go and holding it there, a piece of him. She hasn't been able to do so many things to him in so long.

But she hasn't been let out for a boy. She knows that, as we do. There is a whole life out there, waiting for her. Even the shoes fit.

Miles tries to help her stand up, but it's all too much for her, too much. For a moment, she has no breath in her lungs. Her knees bend back down to the ground, and her legs, still muscled, still strong, have turned to jelly. She's in the grass, on the damp ground outside the fence. And the ground here is littered with stuffed bears and headless dolls and doll heads, and candles burned down to the nub so no match could ever hope to light them. There are ragged, crumpled pieces of colored paper that give best wishes to the dead for an eternity in heaven (or in hell), though what exists beyond this iron gate is neither.

Miles crouches down at her side. "C'mon. They want to get going."

He points to a green sports car she's never seen before in her life.

He's still trying to pull her up. "You said good-bye like you wanted. But we've got to drive back. Juilliard is waiting. I thought you said you had to pack."

Remember? We are pushing her to remember.

In increments, particle by particle and piece by piece, she begins to recall it. Then, as she stands back up again, she sees it. The glint like a spark in the darkest patch of night. She bends down to pick up the delicate gold strand from where it must have fallen. She recognizes it right away as Violet's.

Miniature sculpted ballerinas hang from the strand, tin-kling. How tiny their toes are, how spindle-thin their raised arms, too minuscule to contain fingers. But there is a knot in the chain she can't get out, a clump of dried mud or fungus or something in the clasp. It's blood, but she doesn't catch that.

The bracelet fits around her wrist as if it had been made for her. Violet had never let her even try the bracelet on before, since it was expensive, she said, and all those charms were special, bought for her by her dad, and her parents wouldn't like it.

"Let's go," says Miles.

Someone is leaning out the open window of the green car, someone she recognizes, vaguely, from a long time be-fore. Violet used to be cruel and call this girl Rooster.

"We waited forever!" the girl says. "We were so worried. We were going to call the police!"

And another boy, in the driver's seat, is waving her over impatiently now. He's hungry, he says. He wants to stop and get something to eat.

And Miles again. Miles. "It's over now," he says low, near her ear.

And he's pulling her by her arm. And he has her weight and she lets him help her, and then she doesn't need his help and she wants to walk on her own two feet and she lets go.

And she is lighter than air. And she walks on air to the car. And does he not know where she's been? And does any-one know where she's been? And for how long?

She has no idea we're still watching. She's split off, be-come separate from us, so she doesn't feel our gaze hovering over her as she takes one last look at our iron gate and then goes back, to prop up a few teddy bears that have fallen and to take a peek at the cards and signs that say our names, looking for her own name.

She'll never find it, because when she exited the gate, her name was sponged off in an instant and replaced with another.

We will always be an even forty-two.

She gets in the car. She wears her seat belt, as she believes in safety first. Tommy starts the engine, and Sarabeth gives her a hug. Miles holds on, firm, to her hand. Once inside the car, she does not look back again.

She got her justice, thanks to us—and, thanks to her, we will always be watching the road, to see who might climb the hill and take the place of one of us. To see who might claim our guilt, so we could be innocent, too.

For us, it is perpetually August. We come awake in our cells, sweating. We wear our green sleeping clothes because it's night and our green jumpsuits are hung up for tomorrow on our hooks. We hear the rain and the wind. We don't hear the locks coming open, for reasons we don't think we'll ever know, but we do hear Lola scream. We hear Jody ram her thick skull against the door, and we hear the door come open and her roar of delight as she shares the news.

We step out of our cages. We are free, like we sense we've been before. We're alive, or are we? At least we know she is.

We lose sight of her when the car makes the turn. We can see the green sports car with the stripes for as long as it keeps straight on our road, but when the car heads for the highway, that takes her out of our line of sight. We can't follow now. Our world stops where the gate stops. Our feet can't run that road.

We wish we could see her down in the city some of us had been born in and some of us had committed our crimes in and some of us had never gotten to visit, and wished we could have at least climbed the Statue of Liberty once, before. Violet will tell us all about it, in time. She got so close.

But Violet's not the one anymore. It's Ori we're wishing we could see.

She'll be wearing black, for us. That's how we picture it when she steps out onstage and stuns the crowd. She will be everything we couldn't be, and more.

In our heads we will give her a standing ovation. From down the hill and down the state and hours away, hours and years and memories, we hope she can hear us. Our applause. How proud of her, how thrilled for her, how envious we'll be. We'll clap our hands for her. We'll stand in our seats. We'll shout, we'll wolf whistle, we'll scream. We'll make thunder for her. We'll make thunder for ourselves.

In the sky above the ruins of what was once the Aurora Hills Secure Juvenile Detention Center, there will be a flash of lightning, a clap of thunder, and then we'll be washed in rain.

Acknowledgments

My agent, Michael Bourret, believed in me and in this strangely woven idea and helped me be brave. My editor, Elise Howard, gave me a beautiful new home and saw the heart of the story I wanted to tell, guiding the book into everything I hoped it could be. I am honored and grateful to work with them both.

Thank you to my wonderful publisher Algonquin: Eileen Lawrence, Emma Boyer, Krestyna Lypen, Kelly Bowen, Elisabeth Scharlatt, Emily Parliman, Connie Gabbert, Donna Holstein, Jay Lyon, Shayna Gunn, Sarah Alpert, Craig Popelars, Lauren Mosely, Brooke Csuka, Debra Linn, Brunson Hoole, Jane Steele, and everyone who worked on this book.

Special thanks to these amazing women: Libba Bray, Camille DeAngelis, Gayle Forman, Michelle Hodkin, Kim Liggett, Micol Ostow, Julie Strauss-Gabel, and Courtney Summers.

Thank you to my Brooklyn workshop, in which some key scenes were written: Aaron Zimmerman, Libba Bray, Ben Jones, and Susanna Schrobsdorff. To the KGB Fantastic Fiction reading series organizers Ellen Datlow and Matthew

Kressel, and everyone who came to hear me read these words for the first time. To Lauren Abramo at Dystel & Goderich, Asale Angel-Ajani, Cat Clarke and Caroline Clarke, Lavonne Cooper, Rachel Fershleiser at Tumblr Books, Barry Goldblatt, Margot Knight at the Djerassi Resident Artists Program (and everyone on staff!), Kelly Jensen, David Levithan, Martha Mihalick, Molly O'Neill, Cristin Stickles, April Tucholke, Sara Zarr, the Binders, and my Djerassi writers, who've been cheering me on during the writing and publishing of this book. Finally, thank you, especially, to my readers who continue to support my weird stories. I appreciate every one of you.

This book was written thanks to fellowships from the Hambidge Center, the Millay Colony, and a miraculous emergency residency at the MacDowell Colony, where I wrote more than forty-three thousand words of the first draft in a whirlwind two weeks and would never have made my deadline otherwise. (Grateful thanks to Karen Keenan!) Thanks also to my local writing spots: the Writers Room, Housing Works, and Think Coffee, home of the best baristas in New York City.

The epigraphs are from authors and books that influenced me as a young person and as a writer finding her voice. Special thanks to Margaret Atwood, Heather O'Neill, and Alice Sebold, and to the estates and publishers of Edna St. Vincent Millay, Shirley Jackson, and Jean Rhys for allowing me to use these quotes from works that meant so much to me.

Love and thanks to my beloved mom, Arlene Seymour;

my brother, Joshua Suma; and my little sister, Laurel Rose Eng.

And to Erik Ryerson, my partner-in-crime and my partner in this life: Thank you for the late nights spent reading this manuscript, the eternal support and belief in me, the plot genius, the website, the patience with my mess, and the title.

ERIK RYERSON

Nova Ren Suma has an MFA in fiction from Columbia University and a BA in writing and photography from Antioch College, and has been award a fiction fellowship from the New York Foundation for the Arts. She is from various small towns around the Hudson Valley and now lives in New York City. Her previous novels include *Imaginary Girls* and *17 & Gone*. Visit Nova online at NovaRen.com and find her on Twitter: @novaren.